About the Author

Tanya Rose, a graphic designer and photographer, was born in Victoria, Australia. Residing in the leafy outer suburbs of Melbourne with her family, she recently fulfilled a lifelong dream with the release of her first novel, *The Wave*. Despite the challenges presented by pandemic lockdowns, Tanya embraced the opportunity to slow down and tackle her long-awaited projects. Supported by her family and friends, who provided the encouragement she needed, she transformed her dream into a reality. Join Tanya on this exciting journey as she brings her imagined world to life.
www.tanyarose.com.au

The Wave

Tanya Rose

The Wave

Vanguard Press

VANGUARD PAPERBACK

© Copyright 2024
Tanya Rose

The right of Tanya Rose to be identified as author of this work has been asserted by her in accordance with the Copyright, Designs and Patents Act 1988.

All Rights Reserved

No reproduction, copy or transmission of this publication may be made without written permission.
No paragraph of this publication may be reproduced, copied or transmitted save with the written permission of the publisher, or in accordance with the provisions of the Copyright Act 1956 (as amended).

Any person who commits any unauthorised act in relation to this publication may be liable to criminal prosecution and civil claims for damages.

A CIP catalogue record for this title is available from the British Library.

ISBN 978 1 80016 985 2

This is a work of fiction. Names, characters, businesses, places, events and incidents are either the product of the author's imagination or are used in a fictitious manner. Any resemblance to actual persons, living or dead, or actual events is purely coincidental.

Vanguard Press is an imprint of
Pegasus Elliot Mackenzie Publishers Ltd.
www.pegasuspublishers.com

First Published in 2024

Vanguard Press
Sheraton House Castle Park
Cambridge England

Printed & Bound in Great Britain

"Music, once admitted to the soul, becomes a sort of spirit, and never dies."
— Edward Bulwer-Lytton

I would like to acknowledge my family members and close friends; you know who you are. From great trauma comes strength and resilience, and we all have that inside of us. To Lou, Tristan and Liam, you are my life, and to Valmai, you may not be here in person, but I know you gave me a helping hand along the way. I hope the coffee is hot, and the conversation long.

To the readers: The romance lovers, the bookish girls who love to escape in the pages of a book, this is for you.

FYI: I'm not embarrassed to admit I write sex scenes. My boys are, horribly embarrassed, but I'm not. Enjoy.

Tanya Rose

Chapter One

THE OFFER

My head is thumping to the tune of Baha Men's 'Who Let the Dogs Out?'... Hangovers, hurt. I know who is calling me at this ungodly hour... my manager. I move over to the bedside table with a groan. "This better be life or death or you're fired," I mumble into the phone.

"Hello, Little Bee, GOOD MORNING, BEAUTIFUL," she shouts in my ear.

"Ahhh... Really? You just had to make it worse, didn't you?" I should have turned my phone off last night. I sigh and rub the sleep from my eyes.

"I'm sorry for calling you so early — well, early for you, that is; the rest of us have been up for hours working, you know."

"Hhhmmm."

"Don't go back to sleep, Bee. Listen, I have some important things to talk about and I need your full concentration."

I flop onto my back, "OK, let me get caffeinated first; you know I can't think without my hit. I'll call you back in five." I answer.

"Make it two; it's time-sensitive."

I let out another sigh… it's the best I can do on five hours' sleep. I click the end call button and look at the time: it is ten-fifteen a.m. My manager Mel knows never to call me before noon; that is my first rule in our work/friendship relationship. I am not a morning person; besides, I work nights, and my day starts later and ends in the early hours. That's the way it's always been, I guess. At the ripe old age of twenty-five, I am not going to change my ways any time soon. I like my nocturnal lifestyle. I do my best work at night.

I drag myself out of bed, looking in the vanity mirror on the way to the door: my golden hair is a disaster, fluffed all around my face, hanging past my shoulders in long layers; I still have last night's make-up smudged everywhere; charcoal eye shadow rims my green and amber eyes. I was told I have unusual eyes: very little melanin, a burst of lipochrome, and the Rayleigh scattering of light that reflects off the yellow stroma makes for various shades of green… My eyes change depending on the light, sometimes a deep green, and other times a pale emerald with amber highlights. Like a crystal held up to the sun.

Only two percent of the world's population have this eye colour combination. I don't feel any different, or special. I know they are unusual and interesting because people so often comment, but I'm not so amazed by them; they are just the eyes I was born with.

I don't bother with trousers. I wear black underwear and a faded Coldplay concert T-shirt. I barely remember taking my dress off last night, falling into bed somewhere around five a.m. I can't function with any manual activity until I have had at least half a mug of steaming hot coffee down my throat.

I pad over to the kitchen island, the warm light streaming in from the large Victorian-style windows. Cringing slightly from the brightness in the room, I pull out my favourite coffee mug from the dishwasher and turn on the coffee machine. It holds my cherished coffee beans, blended and roasted by the little Italian deli down the road. I'm not addicted to many things, but my morning coffee is a given; no, more like a ritual. It has to happen when I wake up or I am not human for the day. I only allow myself one caffeine hit a day, because the rest of the time I drink herbal tea with honey: I need to keep the vocal cords in good order.

Once the machine is primed, I put my mug underneath and press the button for a long black. The machine lets out a little noise, a bit of steam, and the dark, golden liquid starts to flow. I relax: I am getting my hit, I am going to feel alive again soon.

I call Mel back, just as I take my first sip of hot steaming goodness. "Are you human yet?" she laughs.

"Just… Now, what is so important that you had to drag my hungover arse out of bed after such a huge night last night?"

"I'm sorry I couldn't be there, Bee. I wanted to see your last show and celebrate with you, but Simon had to work late and Kate was unwell with a tummy bug. I think she caught something from crèche again," she huffs out.

Mel is my whole life, a mother figure, a sister, my manager, my rock, my everything. I can't stay mad at her for long. She is married to Simon, a successful finance investor. They have Kate: she is eighteen months old and the light of their lives. After putting off having children to look after me for six years, they deserve this time as a new family together. I have been independent, living on my own since the age of twenty-one. I wanted to give them some space after all they had done for me; to move into my own home and carve out my place in the world. It's been four years now, and I finally feel like I have my life on track. It was a tumultuous youth for me; I need control, I need to make decisions for myself. I would never be owned again.

"It's alright, I know Katie comes first, I wouldn't want it any other way. How is she feeling now?"

"Good, much better. She is napping now, so that's why I wanted to talk."

"OK, shoot… I'm ready, lay it on me," I say, as I take a sip of hot coffee. "Mmmm, this is so good. I wish you could smell my kitchen; it's like walking into an espresso bar in Rome." I shut my eyes for a second.

"I bet it does, knowing how strong you like that stuff; awful, really," she says, laughing. She is your typical tea-drinking English lady on the outside, yet sweary army drill sergeant on the inside.

"I know you just finished your three-month contract at the Cavendish last night; well done by the way. I have been receiving amazing reviews all week; they were stoked, and the foot traffic was up forty-five percent on the nights you sang. Social media has tags all over the place. I can't keep up with the messages, comments, photos; it's all crazy. They didn't want you to leave, and I would normally suggest you stay a little longer, and build up more of a following, but I have been hounded all week by a new venue; they haven't left me alone. Knowing you were finishing your contract, they want you desperately! I didn't want to bother you and talk about it until you were finished and had time to think." She is talking a mile a minute, her voice excited.

"Alright, tell me about it. I need some time off, though, to recharge the batteries; my voice is a little rough, a good two weeks' rest before another job starts."

"Got it. Take all the time you need. Once you give me a final decision, I can negotiate the terms. The Cavendish wants you back for another three-month contract; you have a great following there, regulars, and the venue is perfect. However, I've been almost hunted down personally by the manager of The Wave; he wants you, a six-month contract, double what the Cavendish paid, including a hefty couture allowance for dresses, shoes, hair and make-up."

"Wow... six months? You know I don't usually take on such a long contract, just in case the place goes stale. I don't want to be stuck singing to a half-empty bar with old men eye-balling me all night". I make a sound of annoyance. "Besides, what is The Wave? I have never heard of it," I ask.

"It's an exclusive cocktail lounge in the Houston Hotel, mostly high-rollers, upper class, no riff-raff, so to speak. They have great security there, beautiful lush styling by some famous TV interior designer; it's known to have a young and fresh vibe. You can check out the Houston website and see the images for yourself."

I hear her tapping away at the keyboard; she must be in her home office.

"I just sent you the link; check your email later and let me know what you think."

"The Houston, hmmm, I haven't been there myself"

"It's a whole entertainment complex with restaurants, bars, private functions, five-star hotel — it's the full package. Look, Brooklyn, it's owned by one family, The Houston Corporation; they are known for luxury entertainment venues worldwide, no bad reports so far, and they have big-name acts that perform regularly. This would look fantastic on your website bio; just being asked to sing for one night is a huge accomplishment, let alone being stalked for a six-month contract. They want you, you can set the terms, whatever you want. Just think about it," she says excitedly.

I take a few breaths... It is a big decision, one I need to think about. "OK, give me a couple of days. I need to rest for now, then I have to do some investigating, look at their socials, their website and such. If I'm happy, I will call Will and see what he thinks. I know I have the final say, but he is my one-man band, and I need him with me or it won't work."

"Sure, I understand. Get back to me by Sunday afternoon. Talk to Will; whatever you decide, I can have the new contract ready to sign on Monday. I will hold off Daniel till then — he is the manager of The Wave, you will be liaising with him if you go ahead."

I can tell she wants me to take it just by the tone of her voice: it is excitement mixed with a little bit of something else, pride maybe. Mel has known me since I was fourteen when she took over as my manager, a fireball of fury, a protective mother, a lioness. Mel is not a woman to mess with: as little as she is in stature, she is mighty in personality; she can make grown men cry.

"Super. I will get back to you soon. Have a good day. Kiss Katie for me, I miss her."

"I will, as soon as she wakes up; and Bee... it's just the start, your life is beginning now. I'm so proud of you." I can hear the tears in her voice, the slight watery low tone she uses when she gets emotional; but being such a hard arse, she tries to cover it with a cough.

"Thank you... I couldn't have done anything without you, you know that, don't you? You, Simon, Kate and Will are my family." I breathe in deeply. "Now, I'm hanging up before your pathetic emotions infect me through the phone."

I hear her mutter "bitch", laughing before she hangs up.

Mel is ten years older than me; at thirty-five she is mature, strong, foul-mouthed and absolutely the best person in my life. She is pretty with straight modern-cut, shoulder-length auburn hair, a tiny frame, more like a lithe gymnast than the female tornado she is in reality. She came into my life when I needed her most.

I was a child with enormous talent; I don't know where it came from, but I was gifted with natural vocal and musical skills.

I was born Brooklyn Grace Barrett, to a poor single mother called Samantha Barrett. My birth mother had Nordic heritage; that's probably where I got my naturally fair complexion and eyes from. Samantha was a drug user, she left home at thirteen, got pregnant at fifteen with me, and somehow expected that it was my duty to take care of her.

I was supposed to save her from the life she had, use my talents — rather, I should say 'exploit' my talents — to gain her money and fame. She groomed me to be what she couldn't be. She wanted a talented, beautiful, star… To make her money. She had no qualms about using a child for her benefit.

Sick really; what kind of mother does that? But Sam was never a mother; she was a user, a person in my life who gave me a rough start, who let me be handed out to men and exploited, all the while making me sing, perform like a damn circus monkey. I was her golden egg.

I had a recording contract at the age of thirteen. Sam acted as my manager in those days. I was a fresh face on the 'teen scene', prized not only for my voice but my beauty; apparently, I was the full package... To her, I was a cash machine, nothing more, nothing less. When Mel found me, I was a shell of the person I am now. I have worked for ten years to change my life, not be the victim any more, and not let Sam or any men in the recording industry control me any longer. I was my own person. I wanted nothing to do with that life.

Makes me think of singer Mariah Carey and her marriage to the Columbia Records boss back in the day. It happened before I was born, but I read the press articles a few years ago, claiming she was abused and controlled, a toxic relationship she thankfully got away from. The industry hasn't changed since I was initiated at the age of thirteen. No wonder so many child stars go down the drug and alcohol road. Mel got me out.

No more sleazy music execs trying to get into my pants, promising me everything if I just put out, no more society parties, drugs, alcohol, exploitation; I was done with that life, and I would never go back. Not for anyone. Mel was the catalyst in helping me be emancipated at the age of fifteen. I disengaged from my mother's claws. Liberated, I left that life behind with a 'fuck you!' and a two-finger salute.

Mel and Simon had taken me in, a scared teenager, recently legally separated from her birth mother, with much less money accounted for after platinum record sales and live shows; but I didn't care about that, I just wanted a life of my own. Mel invested what money I had left, she bought me the flat I live in now, renting it out until I was old enough to move in, and paid for me to go back and finish my education, eventually studying at the Royal Academy of Music in London, majoring in Vocal Studies.

I have been singing again professionally for three years now. I have no interest in recording contracts or making albums any more; I just want to perform, I want my voice to affect people, real people, I want to give them goosebumps and take away their worries, if only for a night. I make a decent living, I have no mortgage or rent, I own outright the flat I live in, I make enough to cover my food, and expenses and indulge in loading my wardrobe up with must-have pieces. Shopping is a second love for me, that and having a nice holiday once a year. That was all I wanted: just me, the music, my friends, to be self-sufficient, and most importantly... my freedom.

Getting my body to move is an effort. Last night was my last show at the Cavendish Hotel; the vibe was amazing, I had a great time over the last three months. I sang in their main lounge, the patrons were lovely, I was really getting a good turn-out each night I sang, but last night was an absolute crush.

I stayed after my show and had drinks with the Cavendish staff and Will, my bandmate, my long-time guitarist, pianist, and disgustingly talented professional musician, whom I love. Will and I have been playing together for ten years; he was one of the studio musicians who played on my first album. It sold five million copies and went platinum twice; I was a child star... until I couldn't do it any longer.

It is too painful to think about what happened to me back then, how the industry changed me from a vibrant young girl who loved ice-cream and singing old songs, to a broken, dismal reflection of that girl. The light left my eyes, I was a zombie, my singing lacked any effort, and the more I diminished, the more Samantha pushed me into the hell that was my life.

Will stayed with me, and protected me when Samantha tried to come after me; he helped to save me, too. I owe him my life. Will is not only my one-man band and backup singer, he is like a big brother to me. I know I can count on him to look after me, support me, let me make my own choices, and like last night, when I decided that I could not drink another gin and tonic with fresh lime for fear of losing my guts all over the beautiful hardwood bar at the Cavendish, he called me a taxi and escorted me to my door, making sure I got inside, locking up before he left.

Last night was a blast. It has been a while since I let loose. I knew he was there, like my big personal security officer, scaring the men away from approaching me, fending off drunk women wanting a night with him. If I was around, he didn't drop his guard. I didn't want to keep him from having fun, and I told him numerous times to let it go, but he wouldn't. I guess he knows my past, he knows how much it affected me to be treated like a piece of meat, nothing other than a pretty thing to use, to fuck; he knows I need control, and when I let that go on occasion, like last night, drinking a little too much, he is there to catch me. I appreciate him, we are a team.

My coffee has all gone by the time I finally make my way to the couch. I think a day of nothing is due, I muse to myself.

I have worked hard, I need a rest day. I have washing to catch up on, cleaning my flat, and grocery shopping to do; but fuck it, sometimes a girl needs a Netflix and ice-cream day. That day is today. I am even too tired to shower right now. So I get back off the couch, open the freezer, and find a tub of my favourite salted caramel ice-cream. I reach over for the thick wool throw, cover myself, and settle in for a day of romance movies, starting with the love story of all love stories... *Pride and Prejudice.*

Chapter Two

HONEY BEE

The Sunday sun is filtering through the sheer blinds, creating a diffused soft light across my bed. I have enjoyed a few days off, catching up on cleaning my flat, doing my laundry, dusting, and all the regular stuff we mere mortals have to do weekly. A person is never truly humbled until they have to bend down and scrub a bathroom... which is now gleaming with perfectly white subway tiles and black accent taps. I am not one of those obsessively tidy people; I usually have half my wardrobe strewn all over the bed, but I do like clean-scented bathrooms and kitchens. I grew up in some filthy places,
shared houses, I still recall the smells.

My flat has amazing light. I am so grateful to Mel and Simon for locking in the purchase so many years ago because if I had to buy this now, I certainly would not be able to afford it. The location is a dream; flats like mine go for a million or more. It was built in the Victorian era, located in an idyllic tree-lined street of Victorian townhouses, enviably located just off Kensington Church Street and a short stroll from the iconic Hyde Park.

It was once an elegant mansion before it was sold and divided into six stunning flats. Three storeys high, my flat is on the top floor, refurbished before I moved in four years ago. It has a clean modern marble kitchen, French oak floors throughout, three bedrooms, one I use as a studio/music room, and an airy open-plan living space.

The ten-foot ceilings with architectural details have been kept, thankfully, giving my home the character it deserves. I picture the grand Victorian days with women dressed in corsets and silk dresses, and men with top hats and walking canes.

This old girl has had a modern facelift; she is still just as beautiful, but now more fitting for the twenty-first century. I'm in the perfect spot, great considering I never learned to drive — well, who would want to in the city anyway? I mean, just stepping out onto the street on a weekday was dangerous. Taxis are a dime a dozen, so easy to find, and the drivers know the routes around London by memory. They never use navigation: they pride themselves on knowing the fastest and most direct route possible. Boutique shopping is nearby, and amenities and transport links abound in the area, with Kensington High Street and Notting Hill Gate tube stations both within easy reach, not that I catch the tube much; I'm a taxi girl.

I left a message yesterday for Will, asking him to call me today for a chat. He, of course, knows to call me later — that is my hard rule… no early morning conversation. I need to gently wake up; no alarm clock, just a natural slow coming to awareness. Sometimes I love to stay in bed and just read a little before I get up.

No nine-to-five life for me.

I hear the coffee machine calling to my subconscious, "Turn me on... I'm waiting." Yes, I smile, I need my morning hit, I have decisions to make.

After having a nice steaming cup of coffee and toast with honey, I'm ready to start my day.

I switch on my laptop at the kitchen island and check my email messages. I open the one Mel sent — with a link to the Houston Hotel website. I click on the link and it opens onto the main home page, with a picture of the exterior of the Houston Hotel, located not far away, at the crossroads of Park Lane and Oxford Street. It is a gorgeous building. I know it well, although I have never actually been inside. It is located just opposite Marble Arch, and it looks very posh and stylish. It was built in 1919 and fully renovated again a few years ago with five floors, a boutique hotel and an entertainment venue with five-star restaurants. Wow, I breathe. This is next level... a little intimidating, to be honest.

I find the drop-down menu with the amenities and click on the listing for The Wave Cocktail Lounge. "Holy cow!" I breathe. It is stunning... and I haven't even gone past the home page yet.

The screen shows me an enormous bar area with pale blue walls, architectural moulding, plush azure blue velvet seating, art deco style, that are ribbed and plump; they look mind-blowingly comfortable and elegant at the same time, like you want to lie down and sleep on a cloud — utterly delectable.

The gold accent touches — tables, wall mirrors, lamps — just scream 'Affluence', 'Extravagance', 'Old Money'. It has hardwood herringbone, wide plank timber floors, and a massive central bar, with a rounded marble surround that is exquisite. I can see just from the home page the venue has won numerous awards for its style, food and cocktails — three years in a row, no less. How have I never heard of this place? I guess it was not something you could just walk into off the street; this bar would most likely be a members' only place. It certainly looked very exclusive to me.

I recall Mel mentioning the offer included an allowance for couture clothing; no wonder, this place is *Gatsby*-level opulence. The large windows will have a heart-stopping view of London at night, no doubt. I am intrigued. I have a poke around the site: during the day it looks to be available for professionals and hotel guests, light lunches, high tea — of course with an award-winning chef on hand.

It has a very modern English menu, mixed with French fusion flair. During the evening it is a cocktail bar.

I click on the cocktail menu. "Holy shit," I breathe, "£32 for a cocktail? It better be one amazing orgasm-inducing beverage for that price," I peruse the menu and find one that sounds interesting called the 'I'm Perfect Martini', with discarded grape-skin vodka, grass amazake,

Fierfield Birch and over-ripe nectarine. "Mmmm, that sounds nice."

I am interrupted by my phone grooving to the sound of Bruno Mars' 'Count On Me'… I always know who is calling me; I assign a song for each person in my life, unless it's an unknown caller, which is not often, as my manager handles all my work-related calls; plus, I have a private number — I like it that way.

I pick up the phone. "Hello, you."

"Hello, my favourite Bug," a masculine voice chuckles on the other end.

"A bee is not a bug, silly, it's an insect!" I fire back at Will, my friend and bandmate.

"Well… Bug, insect, whatever, you are still my beautiful Honey Bee. How are you enjoying your rest time?" he asks. I picture him smiling, I can hear it in his voice.

"Well, actually. I'm heading out to do some grocery shopping soon; stocking up on my favourite ice-cream is a priority you know, but it's been nice to just chill out for a few days. The hangover has vanished, thankfully."

"I bet. Wish I could say the same. I'm working today, just calling you during my break. I'm laying guitar tracks for a pop rock album in Soho. What did you want to chat about?"

"That sounds cool; let me know when the recording is finished, I'd love to have a listen." I say, "So, Mel called me a few days ago with another offer. It's a place called The Wave, in the Houston Hotel on Park Lane, some exclusive cocktail lounge, VIPs and such. They asked for me specifically. Will, they want a six-month commitment, double the pay we got at the Cavendish, actually…"

Will lets out a long whistle. "Congrats, Bee, that sounds fantastic. I haven't heard of it, but if it's part of the Houston, then it would be pretty amazing; the hotel is five star. How do you feel about the six months? You've never taken on such a long contract."

"I know. I don't like to over-sing my welcome, so to speak. I don't want to risk the patrons getting sick of me." I hear him smother a laugh… "Mel said I can decide the terms; that's how keen they are on having me sing. I'm thinking of committing to four months and see how it goes?" I ask like it's a question, I want his opinion.

"That sounds reasonable. Well, I'm happy to go along with whatever you choose; you are the main act, honey, whatever you want, it's up to you. I will be there for you either way. Listen, I have to go back in now. Get Mel to send me the details by email if you take the job."

I knew Will would be cool; he lets me make the decisions, even though we are a duo — he respects me.

"Sure, I will. And thank you again for getting me home the other night. At least I didn't embarrass myself and vomit my guts up. I'd like to play the Cavendish another time in the future," I laugh. "And Will, I'd say break a leg or good luck, but I know you already know how good you are, and honestly, I just don't want to make your head any larger than it already is!" I snicker into the phone.

"Oh, that one will cost you, Honey Bee, big time." He tries for a serious tone, but I know him too well.

"See you later, Mr I'm-too-talented-for-myself music virtuoso."

"Shut up, Bee. You're the real talent, and everybody knows it. See you soon."

I am still laughing when I click the end call button. Seriously, I don't think he realises how talented a musician he is; he makes me look good, that's for sure. Will Stanton is thirty-two, seriously good looking, around six foot tall, with long wavy brown hair that he either leaves loose almost to his shoulders, or ties back in a low messy bun. He has that hair that girls would love, and girls do love it, as I've witnessed many, many times at gigs, but the kind women would love to have themselves: effortless loose waves, kind of a mix of grunge and surfer hair. He never does anything to it, but somehow it just looks perfect. Makes me sick — does he understand what we women have to do to accomplish that style of nonchalant hair perfection?

His forearms are bare, but his shoulders are covered in tattoos, very rock star-esque — it suits him. With caramel coloured eyes, a straight elegant nose, and firm but full lips, Will has grown into an attractive man, larger now than when I met him in his twenties; I guess working out has helped him put on some bulk.

Not overly muscled, but just enough that you can tell he looks after himself. His arms hug his guitar effortlessly.

He has no trouble in the romance department, but he is very professional when we play: he never accepts an offer when we sing together. Of course, I tease him about it mercilessly. I'm not sure why he is still single: he is such a great catch. Honest, hard-working, funny, and gentle. Not to mention a total rock star who sings and plays multiple instruments.

Will was a young musician when I met him years ago, and is now a solid performer on the London scene, playing live with me, and hired out as a recording session guitarist and pianist. He grew up in a musical family outside the city; his mother is a classically trained pianist and his dad is a music teacher. With those genes, how could you not learn to be an exceptional musician?

He is asked repeatedly to tour with many famous bands, yet always turns them down, only offering to lay tracks on the albums and stay in London. I questioned him about it, but he always replied he just didn't want to travel for months on end. I guess he is a homebody, I still think he gave up too many incredible offers for staying here and mostly playing with me. I hope in the future that he will take on a worldwide tour — I'd be so proud of him.

I decide to send Mel an email, before heading out to do my weekly grocery shopping.

Hello, my lovely crazy manager,

I spoke to Will regarding the Houston Hotel offer; he said he was good with my decision either way. So I have decided to go ahead and sign. I just want to make a change to the time duration. I feel six months is a little long-winded, and would like to negotiate for four months with a possible-continuation clause.

Honestly, the place looks to-die-for amazing; I mean right out of The Great Gatsby *novel amazing, and YES it does appear to be everything a girl like me could want: stylish, great location, award-winning venue, blah blah, you get it. I was seriously taken aback by the place just seeing the photos online. I also want to know more about the clothing allowance, because fuck...! Mel, it looks so grand, royalty could turn up any day. What if I married one of the King's sons? I could be the next Princess of Wales!*

Seriously, I have nice outfits and dresses for my gigs, you know that, but I would need something more for this contract. So, let me know the specifics and I think the rest is perfect.

You can handle my usual requests: dinner break for both of us, water, tea. Let me know how you get on. I'm happy if you book a meeting with the manager before we sign, just so we can see the place in person, and get a feel for it.

I'm heading out; email me any information you need me to view, and I will look at it when I get back. Send Will the details when you are ready. Love your guts, you pathetically amazing woman,

Bee xx

I press send, and walk to my bedroom to get dressed. I have ice-cream to buy.

I arrive home two hours later, my arms filled with shopping bags, trying to manage my front door key, when big hands settle on my shoulders and I am graced with a smacking kiss on my cheek.

"Honey Bee, I haven't seen you in ages... Here, let me help," he says in that velvety smooth accent. My heart does a little dance at the sound of his voice. My neighbour and best friend Anton is home.

Anton leases the flat opposite mine. He is of African-Caribbean background, but came to London when he was a teenager to study ballet and dance. He is enormously talented, and graceful in every movement, just as you would expect from a professional dancer.

With him taking the shopping bags from my hands, I manage to put the key in the lock and open my door.

"Thank you," I breathe. I don't know why, but I always go to the shops with a list, and for some reason beyond me, I come home with twice what I need.

"I haven't seen you in two weeks, Honey; how have you been?" he asks me, as he strides elegantly into my kitchen and places the bags on the island bench. He is wearing baggy ripped jeans and a white T-shirt, still managing to look perfect in such a plain outfit. His dark skin is glowing with some magical product, or it just could be him. He tells me those green juices are magic, but I just can't bring myself to swallow enough down without gagging.

"I know, we have both been so busy, I just finished my run at the Cavendish last week and I'm taking a couple of weeks off before I start a new contract," I say, as I rummage through the bags, grabbing items to put away.

"Oh, how perfect. I finish my show at the National Theatre next week; it's been great, but eight months of daily shows have my body wilted. I need a break, too. I have a few auditions for the London Ballet coming up, but otherwise, I am available to hang out, and this time I should get a night off and come to see you sing," He smiles at me with perfect white teeth. Gah, he is so genetically blessed.

Anton and I have similar lifestyles: both performers on stage. He is mostly contracted to longer-running shows, musicals, ballet, and modern artistic dance performances. He is just finishing a run of *Wicked* — which I watched him perform three times, loving each show just as much as the first.

He is a dream to see on stage: his body is long and lean, with short-cropped dark hair, dark brown eyes, perfectly sculptured eyebrows, and chiselled features that should be on the cover of a magazine. He has been dancing all his life, and it shows.

I don't think I have ever seen him eat any junk food at all in the past few years. He is as healthy on the inside as he looks on the outside. And much to my annoyance, he makes sure I make it to the gym to give my own body a workout more frequently than I'd like. I'm not a natural gym junkie, but I have to keep my body in decent shape, seeing as I work on stage with hundreds of eyes scrutinising me during every performance.

It can be a little unsettling, to be honest, but it's part of the game: people want a hauntingly beautiful voice — and a face and body to match. So I keep it real. Enjoy my ice-cream on weekends and let Anton bust my arse during the week to eat healthy and attend at least four gym sessions.

"I have to run, dinner date with Trey. Are we on for Monday Margarita's tomorrow night?" he asks me.

"Give that hot boyfriend of yours a kiss for me; you know he loves it when I smother his face with kisses," I squeak, as he smacks my butt, laughing. "And YES, my god yes, I am in for Monday Margaritas."

Anton pirouettes out my front door with perfectly pointed toes, even when his feet are wearing boots. I roll my eyes with a smile.

"I love you, Honey Bee," he yells while blowing me a kiss, shutting the door on his way out.

After I have made myself a quick healthy dinner — warm chicken pasta with avocado and pine nuts — I get my weekend fix of ice-cream — strawberries and cream this time — and sit at the kitchen island to check my emails.

I shove the spoon in my mouth and moan... "Oh my god, so good. I could die happy with this in my mouth." I scour through the junk mail, deleting as I go, and see Mel has responded to my earlier email:

Hello back, Little Bee,

And YES, I am pathetically amazing, if I do say so myself, but keep reminding me in case I forget. You can also send me a nice bottle of bubbly when you are the toast of the town, and the entertainment pages of London when you take this gig at the Houston Hotel. Bee, I know it will be sensational for you. I'm so happy you said yes! And the royals would no doubt love you for a daughter-in-law. I can see you now: golden tiara covered in emeralds on your head, your hand doing that stupid fucking wave thing the royals do... [She adds in hand wave and laughing emojis.]

I practice the stupid little hand wave myself. I have always wondered why they do it like that. She continues:

I have set up a meeting with Daniel, manager at The Wave; he is very eager to meet you in person. Please be at the Houston Hotel tomorrow at two-thirty p.m.; someone will escort you up from the lower level — just let them know at the front reception desk. I will meet you there. I have a teleconference call that I can't miss. Don't be late!

Love you to bits, my annoying Little Bee, Mel xx

I shut my laptop and happy-dance to my bedroom. Shit... what am I going to wear?

Chapter Three

THE MEETING

Monday rolls around, and after my morning coffee ritual, I'm answering a few emails, then checking the photos and comments on social media regarding my performances at the Cavendish, and I'm impressed. No nasty comments as you would assume — some trolls just can't help themselves — but I do skim over the dirty comments: some men just can't help themselves either... Comments like: "I want to fuck that mouth" and "Are those tits real, I'd love to find out". Grrr.... I hope the Cavendish has someone in marketing that works fast on the platform to delete and block! Sickos. Mel would cringe reading that dribble.

Putting me back in a good mood, I see some nice remarks: "She sings like an angel" and "Her voice is better than Adele", and my personal favourite, "This is a perfect example of pure harmony; her singing, and the dude on guitar, I'd pay to see them perform in concert, just magical". Ahhh... so many beautiful reviews have been left on the page, and I'm so glad I had such a wonderful experience there.

I must remember to send the manager Monica a thank-you gift; however, Mel has probably already done that. I check the time, and I have to get ready for my afternoon meeting at the Houston Hotel.

I head to my wardrobe and take out the outfit I settled on last night — high-waisted, long black wide-leg trousers with gold button detail, and a pale blue silk sleeveless blouse that gets tucked into the trousers. I'm trying to complement their blue and gold theme, a subtle nod to the elegance of The Wave. I top it off with peep-toe black pumps, giving me a little extra height; as I'm five foot seven inches, my average height can handle the high heels.

I leave my long hair out, and style it with some heat tongs, just to kick in a little natural-looking wave around my face, then I add some orange blossom hair oil to make sure the heat didn't damage it too much. I rub it in, scrunching my hair as I go; it smells so good, and I rub a little on the tops of my shoulders for a nice glow.

It looks great, I think, sexy but not too 'I just got out of bed' sexy. Next, I sit down at the vanity and apply some light foundation. I am naturally pale, I don't really tan much, and the sun can burn me so fast. I use setting powder and start on the eyes. I think a vintage make-up look will go with this outfit, something old Hollywood glam. I do black-winged liquid eyeliner, no eye shadow, and use my thick mascara for extra-long lashes.

My eyes do the rest of the work; the black brings out the crystal-like gems. Hmm, I'm considering a red lip, but I think nude will go better today: lets my eyes stand out more. I add a little dusty pink cream blush to my cheeks and lips with my fingertips, then I inspect my handiwork. Yes, I'm happy: I look good, I feel good, and I'm ready.

I pick up my work folder; it has my music notes, venue notes, song choices, whatever I need — it's my bible of songs. I grab my phone, throw it in my black handbag and head out the front door.

As I'm locking the front door, I hear a wolf-whistle. I turn around and Anton is standing at his door in just athletic shorts and trainers, no shirt, wet with sweat; he probably just came back from a run. Looking all ripped and fit.

He gives me a little spin motion with his hand, and I dutifully do a slow twirl, not near as good as he can do, of course, but I try.

"Well, Honey Bee, whoever you are meeting today, I wish them luck, because you are going to make them forget their words." His eyes are laughing at me. "If I was straight, you know I'd hit that."

I can't help but laugh at his comment. We have been friends for years, nothing he says can offend me, and I feel safe knowing he doesn't actually want to rip my clothes off and use me like some one-night stand.

"Well, let's hope they see me in person and realise the money they are spending to secure me is well worth it," I shoot back with a cheeky grin.

"Worth it and then some, Honey Bee. See you later for margaritas and you can tell me all about it."

He blows me a kiss and goes inside, probably to shower; the manly sweaty stink was beginning to permeate the hallway, I think as I take a sniff, scrunching up my nose.

On the street, I wave for a taxi and I'm on my way.

I arrive right on time at the front of the Houston Hotel. The taxi drops me just around the corner, the traffic making it hard to stop any closer. It's buzzing with noise outside, people trying to tame the busy pavement, either heading back to work after lunch, or leaving work early, cars and taxis everywhere, horns beeping. It's a big tourist spot, so I'm not surprised it's packed right now.

I stop at the front doors, digging in my bag to find my mobile phone. I need to turn it off before I go into the meeting. I find it, but trying to turn it off, swipe, and hold my handbag and folder at the same time is difficult. I slide my folder under my arm, and try to squeeze it there in place while I use both hands to turn my phone off.

As I do, my folder slips against the silk of my blouse and falls to the floor, a few papers swing out, but thankfully it's not a total disaster: most remain inside the folder. I put my now-silent phone back in my handbag and I'm about to bend down to pick it up when two black boots step into my view. I'm looking down, and see a man in black jeans and heavy black boots bend down before me. I can see he is wearing a leather jacket, holding a black helmet and has a thick head of inky black hair. I can't see his face as he is looking down at the ground.

I begin to tell him not to worry about it, but he looks up at me and my brain-to-mouth neurotransmitters — or whatever they are called — decide to stop working altogether. Fuck... I can't come up with anything right at this moment. I'm frozen, I can't think beyond those blue, blue eyes staring at me.

He slowly rises to his full height; our eyes are locked the whole time, and then all of a sudden I'm staring up, way up, at the motorcycle guy's face. God, he must be a foot taller than me, and I'm wearing mega heels today. I'd guess maybe six foot four inches.

His face is just too pretty to be real... like one of those men in the motorcycle ads in magazines; you know, the ones that women drool over and men want to be.

He is looking at me so intensely, like he can read my thoughts, and for a second I try and stop thinking — just in case he actually can read what is going on inside my usually intelligent brain. My eyes have a mind of their own and roam his face. The utter perfection I see is frankly disgusting; no one should be that good-looking, and I've seen many good-looking guys.

Blue eyes the colour of the Mediterranean are staring at me, framed with the blackest lashes and eyebrows you have ever seen. His nose is perfectly straight and perfectly shaped, coming to a slight point; it's cute, but fits his manly face at the same time. His lips are plump and kind of pouty, they look soft... are they as soft as they look? Wait... What am I thinking? I stop staring at his lips and look up again. I think my face is giving me away, and I'm so embarrassed. Am I blushing? This doesn't usually happen to me.

His hair is cropped shorter on the sides; a thick mass of black hair, longer on the top, is flicked to one side, like he ran his hand through it after he took his helmet off, and why am I thinking about doing that exact thing right now? Get yourself together, Brooklyn! I drag my eyes away and make to grab the folder he is holding between us. I look down and mumble a 'thank you' — the best I can do under the circumstances — and when I look up he is still staring at me, his eyes boring into my face like he has seen a priceless artwork at the Louvre.

He still hasn't spoken, not uttered a word; maybe he has a hearing impairment? I mean, he could, right? I'm not sure, and I don't want to assume anything… so I look at him again and mouth 'thank you'. I don't think any sound came out, just the movement of my lips, but it makes him look down at my mouth, then back up, and he smiles. Fuck! Again my brain is misfiring like a rusty farm tractor. I close my eyes and take a breath. He is still in front of me. I grab my folder and tell my brain to tell my legs and feet to start walking or I'm going to be late.

I side-step the motorcycle god in black and see a shiny black and chrome motorcycle parked on the pavement, as I head into the peace and quiet of the Houston Hotel.

What the heck was that, Brooklyn? Get a grip. You have a very important meeting today.

I give myself a little pep talk and walk over to the reception desk. An attractive brunette in uniform is sitting behind the desk.

"Hello, Brooklyn Barrett here for a meeting with the manager of The Wave," I say, getting my mojo back.

"Oh yes, Miss Barrett, Daniel has asked me to send you up; to the first floor, take a right when you exit the lift. You will see the front entrance to The Wave; he will be inside. I think your manager has already arrived."

I thank her and head over to the lifts on the other side of the grand lobby, my peep-toe heels clicking all the way over on the shiny marble floor. As I enter the lift and press the button for the first floor, I look back out into the lobby and see his beautiful face still watching me. Just inside the front entrance is motorcycle god — arresting me again with those ocean-blue eyes.

I try to look away, but it's useless; it's like I'm in a trance or something, because neither of us moves until the doors shut, and I let out the huge breath that was lodged in my chest. What the fuck happened? I need to shake it off and get my mind back in the game. The lift pings its arrival on the first floor. I smooth down my top, make sure it's tucked in nicely, and step out, turning right and heading straight for The Wave, with my confident, determined steps. Girl, you got this.

I walk up to the front entrance of The Wave, a security guard speaks into a little microphone and opens the door for me to walk in. My heels hit the polished timber floor, and I look around. I'm stunned, impressed with the atmosphere The Wave immediately exudes. Calm, luxurious yet welcoming at the same time. It's a larger venue than I expected; the photos don't convey the size — I bet it holds two hundred people. I see a stage off to the left with a stunning grand piano, black and glossy, just sitting there very stately looking.

I hear Mel call my name and I turn around.

I walk over to the couch where Mel is sitting, I presume, with the manager, Daniel. They stand when I arrive. "Hi, Bee, so glad you found it. Amazing, right?" She doesn't wait for me to answer. "This is Daniel Thompson, General Manager of The Wave. Daniel, this is Brooklyn Barrett, your new star attraction," she states, beaming.

Daniel is smiling. I catch a quick flick of his eyes over my outfit, and back up to my face. I am used to that, I can't deny that I am an attractive girl; men look, but as long as they don't linger too long, making me feel uncomfortable, then I'm fine with it. Daniel extends his hand and I take it, shaking firmly.

"It's a pleasure to finally meet you, Brooklyn. I have wanted to have you perform at The Wave for some time now," he says confidently.

"Thank you, I'm happy to be here," I reply, smiling. He lets go of my hand.

"I caught a couple of your shows at the Cavendish. Impressive. I believe you will be an asset to the Houston Hotel." I detect a slight Scottish accent in his voice.

"Great, I'm happy you had a chance to see Will and I perform in person." I sit, and so do Mel and Daniel.

I wasn't wrong: the seat feels like a cloud. I settle in and cross my legs.

"Would you like a drink? I can have the staff make tea, coffee, cold drinks?"

"Water is fine, just room temperature, if that's OK?" I ask. I'm still trying to calm my nerves after the motorcycle god incident downstairs, but I don't think Mel or Daniel pick up on my weirdness.

He signals the waiter over and orders drinks for us.

Mel, the little bulldozer she is, gets right into the details.

"Daniel, Bee has decided that four months is more to her preference in terms of performance duration. I'll amend the current contract — with a clause that it can be extended if she feels like lengthening the time later. Let's see how this goes first, shall we?" She looks at him expectantly.

He is still looking at me, not sleazy or such, like he is studying me, a little transfixed, then turns to her and agrees.

"Of course, I would like to lock down the full six months, but if that is not possible at this time, we will take whatever you offer," he says and takes a sip of his drink.

"Great," Mel nods. "Now, I have added all the details in the contract with the personal requirements for Bee and her musical partner Will Stanton. I'm sure your staff can handle those."

He nods, and Mel continues, "With the wardrobe, we would like to know what you propose. Is Bee expected to source her own attire, or are you covering that?" Direct as always; god, I love her.

"Of course the Houston will cover all the wardrobe and styling requirements; we have a stylist on hand. There is no need for Brooklyn to do anything other than turn up an hour before each show; our stylist will have everything ready — she sources the best British fashion designers, of course.

"Hair and make-up will be included," he adds, smiling at me. "Just send Brooklyn's measurements over via email and I will forward them to Vivian, our in-house stylist, and she will take care of the rest."

"Thank you, it's much appreciated," I pipe in. It's a huge expense they are carrying, especially considering the hefty fee Mel has got them to agree to pay me. It's a win-win for the three of us: Will and I get paid well for the next few months, and Mel gets her manager's fee doubled.

I don't doubt this place can afford it, though, the glassware alone looks like it's Royal Doulton!

"Are there any songs in particular that you would like on the set list?" I ask Daniel, and open my folder to take notes.

He responds, "I will email a list — but I'm sure you and your musical partner are more adept at reading the room. We are happy with letting you decide the song choices; maybe just mix it up, some classics and some modern music. Our crowd varies, some mature patrons, but mostly we get the young professionals through."

I nod, smiling and making a couple of notes. I have some ideas with songs already swimming around.

"So we can all agree, Bee will start on the twentieth of the month?" Mel chirps. "That's in two weeks."

"Yes, it gives us time to get everything ready and also add the necessary information to our website and social accounts that Brooklyn will be performing," Daniel says, clearly very happy with the arrangement.

Mel agrees to have everything drawn up and sent over for us all to sign as soon as possible.

Just as we are about to stand and take our leave, a handsome man walks over, smiling and looking expectantly at the three of us. Daniel stands, and so do we. "Brooklyn, Mel, this is Christopher Houston; he is here to annoy me into hosting a birthday party for his brother." He laughs. "Of course, he wants to open the rooftop exclusively for it." He smiles and shakes Christopher's hand.

Christopher looks well-maintained, wearing navy slacks and a crisp white shirt. I'm not sure what he does, but he has the Houston name. He looks youthful, maybe mid-twenties, clearly well-to-do, the expensive watch on his wrist just screams money, but not in your face over the top.

He shakes Mel's hand and then takes mine. Daniel goes on to say, "This is Brooklyn Barrett, our newly signed artist at the Houston, and her manager Mel Adams." Daniel gestures to Mel.

Christopher nods at Mel, then looks back to me, and, what's with blue-eyed gods lately? His eyes are crystal blue, his smiling face is taking me in, he is very handsome, in a cute 'I'm a naughty boy' kind of way — you know he would get whatever he wants just by smiling. Straight teeth, clear skin, a jawline to cut glass.

His hair is styled in a clean-cut frat boy style; He is tall, about six foot three inches, and very lean; not overly skinny, but healthy, no bulk on him at all.

'Houston?' I ask. "As in this hotel?" I cock my head to the side.

"The one and only," he admits. "But don't hold that against me!" He smiles as his eyes meander over me.

Mel pipes in, "Well, thank you so much, Daniel, it's been a pleasure doing business with you. Bee and I will let you two conduct your party business. Lovely meeting you, Christopher." She smirks and holds a hand behind my back to encourage me to move along.

"B?" Christopher asks as I'm about to walk away.

"It's a nickname; most people call me Bee," I say casually.

"B for Brooklyn?" he continues.

Mel jumps in when I don't answer. "Actually, it's BEE, as in Honey Bee."

"Well, that's intriguing... How did you get that nickname?" Most people don't ask, they just assume the B is for Brooklyn or Barrett. Mel can see that he is getting a little personal, so she decides to go full lioness.

"I gave her that name when she was fifteen. She loves honey, she loves flowers and if you get on her bad side, she will sting you like a motherfucker." Mel states this with a perfectly straight face. Oh my god! I'm trying so hard not to poke her in the ribs right now. Did she go there?

YES… she used the word motherfucker in a sentence! Why am I surprised? This is Mel. Somehow, with her tiny frame and innocent face, she gets away with it.

The guys are silent for a second. Then Christopher bursts out laughing. I give him an awkward look that I hope says 'sorry'. They are both laughing now, looking at us.

"Well, I will definitely make sure not to annoy you in any way, Bee — I'm allergic to bee stings!" he says, still laughing; and I laugh, too.

"I can't wait to see you perform soon. It was a pleasure to meet you both, and if Daniel doesn't cater to your every whim, then please come to see me personally, and I'll make sure you have whatever you need." He is glowing, smiling with perfect teeth, and an adorable face that would melt hearts everywhere.

Is everyone around here a Tommy Hilfiger model or something? Even Daniel is handsome; older — maybe late thirties — with dark blond hair and gold natural highlights, dressed very professionally in a suit and tie, but he has more of a rugged face, like maybe he played rugby or something. A stocky solid frame.

"Thanks again, and see you in two weeks." I nod, and Mel and I head out the door. I take a last look around The Wave: it's sensational, and I can't wait to start performing here.

We get to the lift and I turn on her. "Motherfucker! Really? You can't go one meeting without using the word motherfucker in a sentence?" I'm pretending to sound angry, but in reality, I'm dying of laughter inside. Mel makes no apologies: she grew up with four brothers, and I inherited her vocabulary style while living with her as a teenager. It's not like I don't know her.

She just shrugs, with a little smile on her face, as the lift opens in the lobby and we exit together.

"You know Katie is going to start school and you will have to attend the principal's office weekly when she constantly uses the word 'fuck' in her school work." I'm imagining that right now, shaking my head. "Can you imagine her teacher asking, 'Kate, where is your homework today?' and she replies, 'It's in my fucking school bag, miss'." We are both cracking up now, eyes watering at the thought of gorgeous little fluffy-haired Kate saying the F-word to her teacher, her little innocent face looking up.

"Gosh," Mel breathes, trying to catch her breath, "I have a few years to prepare for that. I don't think Simon would find it very amusing... Maybe I need to start watching what I say at home," she muses, putting a finger on her lips.

"If you can," I retort. "Getting you to stop using the word 'fuck' is as easy as making me wake up at seven a.m. every morning — not going to happen!" We look at each other and burst out laughing again. I dab under my eyes with my fingers. We hug and she gives me a little kiss on the cheek and blows out the doors into the fray of bustling city traffic.

I take a breath and head out the door to find a taxi, then notice the shiny black and chrome motorcycle from earlier is still there… catching the sun and glinting its shiny parts at me. Just like the ocean eyes of its owner did earlier. Both captivating me in a way that's never happened before. I put it out of my head. I'm going home to change into something comfortable and hang with my bestie Anton; after all, it's Margarita Monday's bitches. Here I come.

Chapter Four

MARGARITA MONDAY

I make it home in good time, despite the crazy Monday traffic. I decide to get dressed in something comfortable, so I head to my wardrobe, grab some black gym shorts and a matching crop top, and then cover my top half with a soft cotton singlet. It's still warm in early August. My legs are bare, I rub some lotion on them and slip my feet into my fluffy pink Ugg boots. I tie my hair up in a messy bun and head out of the room.

I realise I haven't eaten since breakfast, so I make some sandwiches to take to Anton's for Margarita Monday. I need food in my stomach before I suck down the sweet fruity drinks, and boy, after my meeting and the motorcycle guy freak-out, I really need a few. I make a platter with hummus dip, cut-up cucumber, tomatoes, and carrots, add some bread sticks, and make a few healthy chicken and salad sandwiches. I cut them up into little triangles, and place them on the plate.

When you live alone, you learn to be self-sufficient. Mel is not the best cook; I appreciated her attempts at cooking while I lived with her and Simon, but honestly, we ate more take-out than home-cooked meals. My mother never cooked: I was literally brought up on packet cereal, ramen noodles and potato crisps.

I learned to prepare simple meals, I'm no Nigella, that's for sure, but I can handle a small dinner party without embarrassing myself. Tonight, I don't feel like cooking, so this will have to do.

I knock on Anton's door. "Honey, I'm home," I sing.

Anton answers the door in cotton sweatpants and nothing else. He looks clean and showered. "And you bring healthy food! Honey Bee, you are the perfect girl. I wish I was straight some days," he says, smiling with those perfectly straight teeth.

"You don't, and besides, I like my freedom. No man is going to come between me and my ice-cream," I walk in and place the platter of food on his coffee table. I sit down, make myself comfortable and put my feet up on the edge of the table.

Anton goes back into the kitchen and finishes making the Margaritas. "Trey can't make it tonight, he has to work late. I wish his boss would give him a break; he thinks junior lawyers don't have a life outside of work," he complains. He walks over and hands me a frosty glass of frozen goodness, with lots of fresh lime, just how I like it.

"How was your meeting today, Honey?"

I take a few sips before I answer him. "Mmmm, so good," and I go back in for another sip. "It was great. I'm signing a contract to the Houston Hotel; you know, the one on Park Lane, super glam."

Anton takes a sandwich and starts eating. Talking around the food in his mouth, "Oh, wow, yeah, I went there for drinks a while back; stylish, very prestigious." He takes a piece of cucumber and dips it in the hummus. I decide to nibble, too, getting a few pieces of carrot and a bread stick.

"My first show is on the twentieth; can you make it?" I ask while I nibble on the bread stick.

He takes his phone out and starts typing. Music starts to play from his speakers: Adele starts crooning 'Hello'.

"The twentieth?" he asks, while looking at his phone.

"Yes. Will and I are playing at The Wave, level one. Let me know and I will get your name on the door list."

"Locked in, Honey Bee, I wouldn't miss it for the world," and he gives me a little kiss on the forehead, putting his phone on the table.

"YAY! It's been so long since you came to a gig; you have been working too hard lately," I say. I'm about half way down my first Margarita already.

"I know. Trey is complaining a lot lately, but it's the nature of the beast: I need to pay rent and eat, too," he says, rolling his eyes. I know the life of a performer is all or nothing, you are either working or you're not, and working is always preferred over being out of work in London, especially knowing how expensive it is to just survive here. It's not a cheap city to live in. But the demand is here, the art scene is off the charts.

"Something happened at the Houston today," I say... with a little hesitation, because, honestly, did something actually happen? Or was my brain just making it all up? I'm not sure now.

"Oh, juicy, by the look on your face. Give Uncle Anton all the details," he laughs, and I hit him with a soft scatter cushion.

I settle back down and decide to lay it all out.

"OK, well, when I arrived today, at the front of the hotel, I was turning my phone off and dropped my folder." I take another sip of my drink. 'Annnd…" I drag it out.

"Annnd what, Honey Bee?" he asks, drinking his own frozen Margarita, looking at me curiously.

"There was a guy…" I stop there, shutting my eyes. Probably for the drama, but really because saying this out loud makes it feel real.

"Hmmm, really, a guy? Well, that doesn't sound out of the ordinary; you see many guys on a daily basis, it's not hard to distinguish males from other species on the planet," laughing, he pokes me in the leg.

I groan and look back at him. "I'm not talking about a regular guy and you know it. This one… well, kind of took my breath away." I say it like it's painful to admit, screwing my face up like I just ate something disgusting.

Anton is now really laughing at me. "Oh my gosh, Honey Bee, are you telling me a man made an impression on you, so much that you couldn't breathe?" Laughing eyes are staring into my face like he can read my thoughts.

"MmHmm," I mumble, nodding my head. I hold up my empty drink, and he stands up, taking the glass to get me a refill in the kitchen.

"So explain, and I want every little detail," he says from the kitchen, so I take a deep breath — here goes.

"He picked up my folder and handed it to me, and when I looked at him, it was…" I pause, looking for the right word to describe the scene. "Electric. Anton, I can't describe it; our eyes connected and just held." I rub my fingers over my mouth, feeling the cold chill on my lips from my frozen drink.

"It looked like he had just arrived; he was wearing a leather motorcycle jacket, and carrying a helmet," I explain.

Anton returns to the couch and hands me my drink. "Ah… a bad boy," he smiles wistfully. "Sounds like chemistry to me. Doesn't happen often, Honey Bee. Did he say anything to you?"

"No. I could barely get a 'thank you' out. It's not like I could stand there staring at those stunning blue eyes all day. I had a meeting to attend."

"So what happened?"

"Nothing. I side-stepped the motorcycle god and hightailed it into the hotel." I chuckle… this second drink is hitting the right spot. I better eat a couple of sandwiches, so I lean over and take one from the table.

"Honey Bee, if it's fate, then you'll see him again; if not, you have enough visual material for your personal pleasure time, if you know what I mean." He waggles those perfectly sculptured eyebrows at me.

"Oh my god, Anton!" I hit him right in the face with the pillow. He leans over and starts tickling me silly, and we end up falling into fits of laughter on the couch.

He gets his phone out again and Adele stops singing. Then the theme from *Dirty Dancing* begins to play, and Anton stands up, offering me his hand. "My lady, will you do me the honour?" He gives me a graceful bow from the hips.

I extend my hand and stand up, kick my Ugg boots off, and move towards him.

"Why yes, kind sir," I answer, both of us moving away from the couch and coffee table as a deep male voice starts to sing.

I place my hand on his shoulder and he holds my other hand in a strong, confident grip, our bodies close but not touching. Just like they do in the movie. This is our song. I asked Anton to teach me this dance months ago, and it always makes me so happy to dance with him. We never do the lift — I'm not that confident — but the dancing is so much fun. We smile at each other. And that's how the rest of Margarita Monday goes: us drinking, dancing, laughing… and just enjoying being young and free.

Tuesday morning, I wake up to a familiar sound, my phone barking at me with 'Who Let the Dogs Out?'.

For a second, I pretend I'm not going to answer, but then I remember it's Mel, and she knows I will get more irritated listening to this stupid ringtone than I will talking to her. I roll over and answer my phone.

"You know this call is cutting it fine," I answer, looking at the time: it's eleven thirty a.m.

"Good morning, Little Bee, I'm your favourite person, so I know you will always forgive me," she says, probably smirking, the bitch.

"To what do I owe the pleasure of this call at the arse crack of dawn?" I ask, not really mad, just pretending to be.

"Arse crack?" she says. "It's almost lunchtime for the rest of us." She loves giving me shit, it's her life motto.

"Honestly, why do we have clocks anyway? Why do we even look at the time? We should all just work whenever we want, with no time restrictions; people would be much happier... I am," I state proudly.

"Well, Bee, you are unique; not many people have your talent, so the rest of us are destined to live normal lives," she says, "Speaking of talents, I got a call from Daniel at The Wave. The contract is all done; I emailed you both copies to sign."

"Great. I'll sign it and send it back to you this afternoon," I reply.

"That's not all. He has a special request: he is hosting a party at the Houston on the twenty-first, the night after your first gig, and begged me to ask you to sing. They are opening the rooftop bar, exclusive for the party. I told him you don't take commissions outside of your contract, but because it's for the Houston Corporation, the same venue, I assured him it wouldn't be an issue." She continues, "The fee they offered is much more than you usually would settle on, so what do you think?" Her voice is chirpy today.

"Singing two nights in a row is not ideal, but I can do it. Sure, the Houston has been amazing so far, it's the least I can do really," I say.

Mel replies, "I have already sent Will an email; we need a full band, so he is hitting up Lenny, Rick and probably James this week. You can arrange a rehearsal day next week. I know you and Will rehearse every Wednesday anyway, so maybe just invite the gents over and go through some songs to play. They want up-beat, something people can dance to."

I nod, thinking the same thing. "I'll handle it; nothing we haven't done before, and I will make a set list of songs and put them to Will tomorrow when I see him,"

"Great, then it's settled. Oh, and Daniel said the stylist they have for you at The Wave will be attending and she will have a dress ready for the event. They think of everything! This job is a dream, Little Bee," she breathes.

"It sure is," I agree happily. "Now let me go so I can get my coffee fix before I start melting like the Wicked Witch of the West."

"Yes go, get your disgusting coffee fix before you melt... Oh, are you free for a family dinner on Thursday night? Kate is busting to show you her new obsession... I'll let you guess what that could be," she says, laughing, probably rolling her eyes on the other end.

"Yes! I haven't had a Katie fix for so long. I'll bring the dessert,"

"Let me guess, ice-cream?"

"Is there any other kind of dessert? I mean really, Mel," I huff over the phone.

"OK, just don't bring the fucking nut one again. I wasn't a fan... Maybe something with strawberries," she states.

"You will have to wait and see. Bye now," and I hit the end call button.

I do a little stretch, feeling surprisingly well after four... no, five Margaritas last night. I smile. It's always so good to hang with Anton; we haven't had much time together since this last performance contract, eight months of regular shows and Saturday matinee times left him exhausted. It's good to have him back. Hopefully, his auditions coming up will be successful. They will be rehearsing for months before the ballet opens, so I know I have time with him before that happens. He will crush it, I smile to myself, he is so talented. Life is good. It's perfect. I hop out of bed with a skip in my step, heading into the kitchen for my fix.

Wednesday afternoon, I'm heading downtown to the rehearsal studio Will and I use every week. It's our regular booking; we test out new songs, write some tunes that have been stuck in our heads, and just practice to maintain the perfection that is he and I playing music together.

I arrive and Will is already set up in the room. I hand him the black tea I purchased a few doors down, and he thanks me, standing up and giving me a bear hug, squeezing me so tight. He has faded jeans on with a blue sleeveless T-shirt, showing off the tattoos on his upper arms and shoulders. He has great arms. A black watch sits on his left wrist, and he has a couple of thin leather bands around the other wrist.

He looks exactly like a rock musician should: hair hanging around that attractive face in perfect waves, just hitting his shoulders.

"Hey, you," I say, and take a sip of my lemon tea with honey. Whenever I sing, I only drink water and herbal tea: the honey is soothing to my vocal cords and helps to keep me healthy, raw honey especially is so good for the immune system. This is partly why my closest friends call me Honey Bee... I'm kind of addicted to the stuff — that and ice-cream, of course.

"Hi, Honey, you look good," he says, taking me in. I'm just wearing navy skinny jeans, ballet flats and a cropped white band T-shirt, showing a little slither of my smooth, pale, stomach.

"I am good, thank you," I smile at him. "Did you receive the email from Mel about the extra rooftop event at the Houston Hotel?" I ask.

"Sure did, and that's fine. I have arranged for the guys to attend rehearsal next week — so we can go through the set list. Just email it to me over the weekend and we will be ready to jam next week," he says, smiling at me.

He is so easy to work with, never an issue; we are still the perfect musical partnership after all these years. "You are awesome, Will." I take a deep breath. "Now, let's do this," I say, getting the microphone stand in front of me ready. This is my favourite thing in the world. Just doing what I do best... Sing my heart out.

The rest of the fortnight flows by so fast, in between rehearsal with Will and the full band, going to Mel's for dinner and spending some much-needed Katie time — smooching her little chubby face, laughing at her new obsession.... bees. She looked so adorable in her bee costume, running around Mel and Simon's flat. I don't really have time for much else. Anton got me to the gym and busted my arse numerous times, so I worked up a good sweat. Keeping my body in check is an important part of my job. I basically came home and collapsed.

We enjoyed another Margarita Monday, and this time Anton's boyfriend Trey attended. I was so happy to see him; he is such a perfect fit for Anton. Trey is cool, calm and collected; a young lawyer, he attended Oxford University, is mega-intelligent, and one day will make an amazing partner in the firm. Trey keeps Anton grounded; he is not as flamboyant and outspoken as Anton is, but he has a quiet confidence about him. Born and bred in England, he is the epitome of a London Gent. I love that Anton drags him out of the seriousness of the legal business into his world of performance, art, music, and style. Like I said, they complement each other so perfectly.

Now it's Friday, and my nerves are a little jittery today. I don't usually get nervous before a show, but this is the first one at The Wave, and for some reason, I just feel unsettled. Will and I are solid; we have been performing for over ten years together, and we rarely make any mistakes. We are a well-oiled machine when we play. Both being professional musicians, it's our job to put on a great show. This is no different than what we have done in the past. Why am I feeling a little weird, then? I take a few grounding breaths and start to dress.

I'm wearing a fitted black skirt and a matching jacket. The skirt is a little short for day wear, but it's still a professional night-time look nonetheless. I pair that with a grey cami underneath. I have put on a strapless bra, just in case the stylist dresses me in a strapless gown for the show. My breasts are pretty full and keeping them contained in a strapless bra can be an effort, but this one holds the girls nicely, giving me a peep of pale cleavage under my cami. I keep my hair in a smooth ponytail, and just add a touch of mascara and pink lip gloss, so the stylist doesn't have to remove too much from my face when I arrive.

I find my pale pink Valentino rock-stud pumps and sit on my bed to put them on. They are equal parts elegant and edgy, and coated in smooth blush-hued leather, they give my outfit a rock star aura. I spray Jo Malone Nectarine Blossom and Honey perfume on my body, spritzing around my neck and down my front. You can never go out without a signature scent: it leaves an impression on people when they remember how nice you smell.

That, and I am obsessed with nice-smelling things, fragrance and fresh flowers especially. No wonder Mel gave me the nickname Honey Bee all those years ago. I love to fill my flat with fresh flowers on the regular. I guess growing up I never had that house and garden lifestyle.

Nothing to cheer me up, just stale smells and old stained furniture. My home is my sanctuary now, and I love nothing more than to have it smelling fresh. The flowers brighten my mood and bring a little touch of nature into my world.

I take a deep breath, looking at myself in the vanity mirror. I'm ready, I'm going to crush this performance with everything I have. Let the Houston Hotel see their money is well spent on Will and me.

"I'm going to give them a fucking show," I state out loud, as my hot heels walk me out the front door.

Chapter Five

THE WAVE

I arrive at The Wave early. Daniel meets me at the door himself, dressed in a ridiculously smooth three-piece suit, fitted navy trousers, waistcoat and jacket, paired with some shiny Oxford shoes, but no tie: I guess he took it off. He has left the top button open at his neck. The switch from day to night is evident, and he seems relaxed and assured.

"Brooklyn, perfect timing. Vivian is waiting for you in the dressing room; let me show you the way and introduce you," Placing his hand on my lower back, he guides me across the room and to a hallway. I can see the sign for the restrooms, a door that must lead to the kitchen at the back, and then we stop at the last door with the sign 'Private' on the front.

"Thank you. Will and I are looking forward to tonight. I hope you enjoy the show," I say, smiling at him.

He nods and opens the door. "Brooklyn, I have no doubt we will all love the performance; you are truly breathtaking when you sing." The glow of appreciation is evident in his eyes, and I smile back.

We enter the room; it's a beautiful space, similar to the styling in the main room, very Art Deco, a lush couch in the same blue ribbed velvet against one wall, with a gold side table, and wall lamps give the room a golden glow.

A stunning woman turns around when I enter. She was setting up make-up and brushes on the vanity table, a large gold mirror on the wall in front of her. She sucks in a breath when I smile, her eyes going wide in her lovely face. She is wearing a white cocktail dress, simple and striking, the dress features a high neck and fitted skirt in a custom lace fabric, and she wears chandelier earrings and cream stilettos.

With dark glossy hair, perfectly straight to her shoulders, and a modern fringe that just touches her eyelashes, her skin is olive and tanned like she just came back from a trip to the Greek islands; she is tall and willowy, very statuesque. She smiles at me with gleaming white teeth and plum-coloured lips.

"Wow, Daniel, I had heard Brooklyn was beautiful, but that word doesn't seem enough."

She looks at me, a slow perusal from my toes to my hair, and remarks on a breath, "Dazzling... What more can I say?" Her words bring a little pink to my cheeks.

"I'm Vivian, stylist and general wonder woman at your service while you enjoy your stay here at the Houston." She extends her hand to me.

I take her hand and give her a little squeeze in thanks as I shake it. Her praise embarrassed me.

"Well, I'm sure dazzling will be more apt once you work your magic on me. Thank you, though, and it's lovely to meet you, too, Vivian. Call me Bee." I let go of her hand

"Daniel, you can leave us, thank you; Bee and I have magic to make together," she says, smiling at him, standing at the door. Daniel nods, gives me a little wave and closes the door, leaving us girls to get down to business.

"Honestly, Brooklyn, I'm so excited to work with you. I have heard such amazing things about you already, and well, look at you!" she exclaims, with a finger under my chin. "You are a dream to style, and this face…" She breathes a sigh as her eyes examine my face up close. "Your eyes are… unique."

"Thank you again, Vivian, just let me know what you need me to do; I'm at your command."

"First, let's choose a dress for tonight, then I'll work out the hair and make-up to complement the outfit." She points to the back of the room and I turn around with a gasp. A huge rack is standing in the corner, full of the most beautiful dresses I have ever seen! There must be twenty hangers at least, and from what I can tell, they look expensive and very glamorous. Shoe boxes are packed in rows on the floor next to the rack.

I quietly take it all in, not knowing what to say. I just look at Vivian with surprise all over my face.

"I know, right," she says with a knowing smile. "The Houston family went all out for you. I had the time of my life shopping for you, Bee; I was in absolute heaven. I'm just happy to have another female around again. Mr and Mrs Houston are in New York, running the hotel there, and the boys handle the UK site. Don't get me wrong, shopping for menswear is great, but it's nothing compared to styling a beautiful woman, especially one that will be the star of the Houston for the next few months," she touches the fabrics then runs her hand over the dresses.

"Boys?" I ask her.

"Yes, the brothers, Jarrod and Christopher, manage this hotel. Nothing but trouble, those two," she says, laughing. I can tell she means they are a handful.

"Oh, I met Christopher a couple of weeks ago when I came in to meet Daniel. I can see what you mean: that smile and those eyes could get him in all kinds of trouble," I agree with a knowing look.

"You have no idea!" She rolls her eyes at me and we both laugh.

"Let me see, with your natural blonde hair, I'm thinking of going bold tonight, kick the night off with a bang. What do you say, Bee, go all out?" she asks me, with her head tilted to the side.

"Why not? Let's blow them away," I answer, grinning back at her.

We go through a few dresses, and Vivian pulls out a stunning and slightly risqué red two-piece number. It's blood-red satin, the bottom half is a fitted floor-length, high-waisted skirt that has a slight fish-tail train behind, and the top half is an asymmetrical midriff style, off the shoulder, that leaves one arm bare, and the other arm has a full-length sleeve. It's gorgeous, it's sexy, it's a show-stopper. It doesn't actually show too much skin, but just enough to push the limits of evening wear, leaving a bare shoulder, arm, and my upper stomach exposed. Thankfully, I've been hitting the gym this week — I must remember to thank Anton for forcing me into those ab crunches!

"Try this on. I think it's the perfect opening night outfit for you, Bee, and I can tell you, no one is going to be looking anywhere other than at you!" she exclaims with excitement.

Vivian helps me get dressed; she hands me some silver strappy stilettos, not that you see them with the length of the skirt, but it gives me some height, showing off the magnificent train. I look in the full-length mirror on the wall and gasp when I turn around and view the back of the skirt.

It has a V cut into it, dropping from the hips to the base of my spine, almost like an arrow pointing down right between my cheeks, the ruched detail giving my bum a peachy shape and drawing the eye right to that asset.

"Oh, wow!" I breathe. "Is it too much?" I ask her.

"Are you kidding?" she laughs, fixing my top and making some adjustments. "There is making an impression, and then there is this dress on you. Girl, you are a walking fantasy!" She finishes her fussing and turns me around by my shoulders. "Now, let's dress this face. I'm thinking silver on the eyes and a bold red lip... Sit, relax and let me paint my Mona Lisa."

Over the next forty minutes, she does paint me like a masterpiece. My hair is styled like an old Hollywood movie star, subtle blonde waves frame my face, and my make-up is perfect. The classic red lips just make the whole outfit pop. I'm sipping some room-temperature honey tea when there is a knock at the door.

Vivian calls out, "Come in."

I turn around to see Will take a step in. His eyes go round as he looks at me slowly, up, down, then back to my face. "Honey Bee, I'm not sure I want anyone else to see you like this; I'm a musician, not a bodyguard." He is smiling, but I think he is somewhat serious.

I laugh and walk over to give him a gentle hug, not kissing him with my red lips. "I'll take that as a compliment, then?" I ask, smiling at him.

"Oh god, how am I going to concentrate on playing tonight when you look like that? Every guy in the room will be thinking about... well... things they shouldn't be thinking," groaning he looks up to the ceiling.

I smack his arm playfully. "Shut up, Will... When you start playing, no one will even look at me."

"Oh, sorry, where are my manners? Will, this is Vivian, the stylist here at the Houston, and I can already tell we will be fast friends." I gesture to Vivian.

Will speaks first. "Nice to meet you, Vivian; you have certainly outdone yourself looking after Bee tonight," he says, holding out his hand.

I look over to Vivian, who for some reason is just staring at Will. It takes her a moment, and I see a slight blush creep into her cheeks before she realises she hasn't spoken yet. She moves to take his hand.

"Oh, yes, nice to meet you, too. It's umm... it's nothing, just doing my job." She sounds a little breathless, and I can tell Will notices, a smirk creeping over his face. He gives her a quick once-over, obviously liking what he sees. Then he clears his throat and looks back at me.

"OK, Honey Bee, we are on in five minutes. I'll see you out there," he nods to Vivian before he leaves.

"Jesus Christ Almighty, is that your guitarist? I'm going to pass out right here," she breathes, holding a hand over her heart for dramatic effect.

I laugh. "Yes, guitarist, pianist, multi-talented rock star and amazing guy... who just happens to be single," I say with a knowing look.

Vivian chuckles, looking into the mirror and fiddling with her hair, then rubbing her fingers around her lips to make sure nothing has smudged.

She turns around to me when she has finished her touch-up, "Right, this is it, it's show time. Go and bring the house down, Bee." She air kisses my cheeks and walks to the door, holding it open for me.

Here we go, it's time.

The venue is packed. I guess Daniel's social media and website advertising really did gain attention. As I enter the vast room, I look around; the atmosphere is electric, I'm so excited and feel the familiar adrenaline start to kick in. Daniel and Christopher arrive at my side, striding up next to me. Christopher takes my hand and brings it to his lips, giving me a look under his lashes as he kisses my hand.

"Bee, wow, you look amazing."

"Thank you; nice to see you again, Christopher," I say, smiling. He releases my hand and just stands there staring at me. I let out a little laugh, shaking my head.

Daniel gets my attention, "OK, Will is ready for you, Brooklyn; head up to the stage," he gestures to the platform. Will is sitting at the grand piano, looking handsome in his black trousers and black shirt, hair tied back in a messy low bun only he can get away with, ready for our first song. I have chosen a classic to open with: hopefully, it sets the mood. Will gives me a hand up the step and escorts me to the microphone at the front of the platform. He then sits back down, waiting for my cue to begin.

"Good evening, ladies and gentlemen, my name is Brooklyn Barrett, and this fine gentleman is Will Stanton." I gesture my hand over to Will and he gives a nod to the crowd. "It will be our pleasure to entertain you tonight. Sit back and enjoy." I smile out to the crowd.

I turn around and nod to Will, and the haunting sounds of the grand piano start filling the air.

I've chosen the song 'Killing Me Softly', singing with just Will at the piano and my voice, smooth like honey, flowing out into the room.

As I sing and look out to the crowd, I notice the mesmerised looks on people's faces, the wonder and awe they feel when they hear us play. I know we have that effect on people: it's why I was given a recording contract so young. I just have one of those hypnotic voices.

As I'm singing and looking out into the audience, something catches my eye, I look over to the side of the magnificent marble bar and my voice goes a little breathy... Nothing noticeable to the public, but my note just comes out a touch airy because standing right there, leaning on the bar with a drink in his hand, is my motorcycle god. His gaze is arresting me, no less intense than the first time I looked into those depths, ocean blue, gleaming at me from across the room. He is wearing all black again, fitted dress slacks and a black button-down shirt, open at the neck, no tie, and the sleeves rolled up on those hard-tanned forearms.

Fuck, if I don't look away soon I will forget the words, and that is not what I want for my first night at The Wave.

He is just too much. I look at him one last time; he knows I can see him, and his stare is penetrating my whole body. I look away to finish the rest of the song. When it's over, there is a collective quiet around the room and I worry that everyone could read my thoughts. Did they notice my distraction?

But then the whole room breaks out in applause, people who were sitting, stand clapping, and I look at Will with a smile. He winks at me, then we flow into the next song like we have done hundreds of times before.

Our set list is a good one tonight: we mix it up with some old-school tunes and more modern songs, I sing an Adele classic that gets the room excited, and I sing from the heart with a Lady A love song called 'Need You Now', then sing a song by Rita Ora called 'Let Me Love You', with Will just playing on acoustic guitar.

I can tell the crowd loves our choices; the room is buzzing, my voice is on point, and Will plays with amazing grace, perfectly swapping between the guitar and piano with professional ease.

I look out and see Anton and Trey in the back, Anton blows me kisses each time he catches my eye.

I haven't looked back over to see if my motorcycle god is still there. I can't, I will mess up, he just does that to me — he makes me forget my mind — so I force myself not to look over that way for the rest of the performance.

Will and I end the set with a favourite song of mine, Will playing the piano perfectly to Christina Perri's 'A Thousand Years'.

I sing about a girl who has waited her whole life for love. A thousand years of waiting for him, and she would wait forever more if she had to.

As I sing this final song, I can't help but look over. Ocean Eyes are locked on my face, his mouth a little open, like he is breathing faster, and I melt inside. I sing directly to him, the last few lines of the song.

I don't know why, because I don't even know him, but I feel like this song is somehow for him. When it ends, I look down, just to break the contact and give myself a break from the intensity of his face. Will and I stand at the front of the stage and while he gives a slight bow, I dip into an elegant curtsy. The room explodes with applause.

Smiling, we stand there a little longer, because people are still clapping for us, then Will hands me down the step and escorts me off the stage. Christopher and Daniel are waiting off to the side, and I'm smothered in a big hug by Will, who kisses my cheek, telling me how beautiful I sang tonight, his eyes shining at me with emotion. Christopher pulls me into a hug next. I didn't expect it, a little thrown with his embrace. He is a hugger, I note.

"Bee, you were absolutely smashing." He is beaming at me, and he turns to Will and offers his hand. "Will, that was something else. I'm Christopher Houston, welcome to The Wave. That was a memorable start."

Will shakes his hand. "Thank you for having us, but Bee did most of the work tonight," he says, looking down at me, his eyes shining with pride.

"Come, we have a VIP area sectioned off for you; order some drinks and relax, soak up the atmosphere." Daniel escorts us over to a seated area. A waitress brings a bevy of cocktails to the table and asks if she can get us anything else. I just ask for my usual gin and tonic with lime; Will takes a beer from the tray.

Anton and Trey come over and I'm squashed between them in the biggest man sandwich ever. Laughing, I kiss them both. "And what did you think? I'm so happy you both came," I say excitedly, squeezing Anton's hands in mine.

"Honey Bee, no words can describe what happens when you sing. It's pure perfection," he says.

"Bee, you are mesmerising!" Trey comments next.

Vivian comes over to join us, sitting next to Will, I notice. She keeps smoothing her glossy hair. I can tell he doesn't mind, but he is still keeping an eye on me. I give him the 'I'm fine' look over my shoulder.

Introductions take place, and everyone enjoys the tasty cocktails on display. Background music is playing and the bar is full. I'm so happy that the first performance is over; now I can relax a little and just soak it all up. I look around, but can't see the object of my thoughts; he is gone. I can't say I'm not a little disappointed; well, maybe a lot disappointed… My heart hurts just a bit.

Vivian leans over to talk to me. "Don't forget to arrive early tomorrow. I need to dress you for the rooftop party; it's going to be the event of the year," she exclaims with a huge smile, giving a little side-eye towards Will, and back to me. He nods and I notice his eyes drop to her legs before he looks away, taking a sip of his drink.

"Yes, Master Da Vinci," I say, smiling, "I can't wait." I give her a wink.

But my eyes keep roaming the bar, looking for that elusive someone who hasn't even spoken to me once.

Chapter Six

THE PARTY

I arrive at The Wave early. Vivian and I exchanged numbers last night, so I text her to let her know I'm riding up in the lift. She meets me at the doors with a big hug.

"Are you ready to blow the roof off the Houston tonight, Bee?" she asks, "I received a special delivery today for you; come and see."

I follow her into the private dressing room. She is all jittery and bubbly today, and I wonder if that's because of the party, or maybe knowing Will is playing again tonight. I can't hide my smile. She looks sensational in a long black fitted strapless dress with split, hugging her willowy frame, and with large white gold hoops in her ears. Vivian is an understated picture of elegance.

"Look what arrived for you this afternoon," she says and opens a large box with a black ribbon on the table. Vivian lifts the lid and I see a sparkly gorgeous dress; it looks to be strapless, silver shimmering everywhere, then she takes out a smaller box and opens it, and when I look inside I can't hide my gasp, my hand going to my throat.

It's a stunning platinum choker necklace, with probably eight rows of diamonds. Well, they look like diamonds, but it's most likely costume jewellery — it has to be. I touch it delicately and look up at Vivian.

"What? Whoa! This is too much. Tell me it's just costume jewellery, Viv?" I ask surprised.

"Umm... no, Bee, we don't do costume jewellery at the Houston," she laughs like it's nothing. "It's a gift; these are separate from your Friday night wardrobe. A gift from the birthday boy personally, a thank you for singing tonight. Aren't they just exquisite?" she beams.

"The birthday boy? I haven't even met him! I cannot accept this — fuck, it's way too much." I'm beginning to feel light-headed looking at the dress and diamond choker.

"You can, and you will; it's his way of saying thank you. Plus, you are the headlining act here for the next few months, and it's not like you're not worth every penny." She makes a little 'pfft' sound. "Now, let's get you ready for tonight, baby girl. It will be a night to remember," she states, as she begins to help me remove my clothes. I mumble a response and start doing as she asks. Let's get this show on the road.

An hour later, I'm looking at myself in the full-length mirror. Vivian is fixing my hair at the back — she left it out tonight, hanging down past my bare shoulders in a wavy mass. I look at the dress and think it's just so perfect, dreamy, a shimmering beaded silver strapless bodice with a sweetheart neckline, which merges into a nude flowing tulle skirt. It's short, showing off my legs, and she gives me nude stilettos to complete the look; they lace up to mid-calf, and she ties them off with a little bow. It is amazing on its own, but adding the diamond choker takes it up another level. The diamonds sparkling in the light, my neck surrounded by such extravagance, it is kind of erotic, intimate, not the usual kind of jewellery a man would buy a woman unless he knew her — all of her. I try not to read into anything; he is probably just some wealthy spoiled womaniser anyway — most wealthy men with money and power are in my experience.

My phone starts grooving to Bruno Mars' 'You Can Count On Me'. It's Will. I hit the accept button and place it on speaker phone.

"Hello, Rock Star," I answer.

"Hi, Honey, we are all set up; are you ready?" he asks me.

"Yes, Viv and I will head up in five minutes; see you soon." I smile and end the call.

"I like your ringtone; cool song," Vivian remarks.

I explain my little phone game to her. "Well, that's just Will's song. I assign a song for each person on my contact list; it's a little game of mine," I say, smiling at her.

"Oh really, and what song did you assign me?" she asks me with a smirk.

"You will have to call me and find out," I grin back.

She grabs her phone and taps on the screen; the next second, my phone comes alive with the sound of 'Pretty Woman' by Roy Orbison.

"Oh my god!" She laughs "You gave me a prostitute's song?" Her face is mock horror.

"What? No," I say, laughing with her. "It's Vivian, the beautiful rags to riches Cinderella story; besides, I think it's Julia Roberts' best work!" We both crack up.

"Well then, I accept that you think I'm pretty woman worthy!" she says, as she opens the door and leads me out.

We take the lift up to the roof, and when the doors open, Vivian and I are hit with loud music playing. I can see a DJ on the other side. The rooftop is massive, with people mingling everywhere, a central bar undercover, silver balloons covering the ceiling, tables and seating scattered around the place, candles flickering in the night. Outside is exposed on this warm night, and you can see the stars twinkling already. Some outdoor heaters are placed around here and there just in case it gets chilly later. I can see the band finishing the set-up: it's just about time to rock this rooftop, literally.

As we head into the crowd, we get many eyes swinging our way, appreciative glances, following our slow walk through the crush of bodies. Vivian holds my hand, leading the way. She stops when she reaches someone and starts talking. I look over her shoulder and see Daniel and Christopher.

"BEE!" Christopher yells over the crowd, then comes over to hug me, and I'm swallowed up in his embrace. "Wow, you look... you look like a princess." His eyes roam over me, slightly glassy.

"Are you pissed already?" I ask, laughing. "It's only early."

"What, me? No, I'm pacing myself. I have a whole night to get shit-faced," he laughs.

Daniel gives me a nod and takes my hand, squeezing it. "Brooklyn, you look amazing, and thank you for doing this on such short notice." He kisses my hand.

"It's nothing, honestly. I'm happy to sing for you all tonight. Besides, where is the elusive birthday boy I'm yet to meet?" I ask, looking around.

Christopher turns around and I see him grab a guy in the crowd behind him who was talking to a group of people. I see the back of him as Christopher drags him over, and when he turns around to face me, my heart stops. I think it just stopped beating because the breath left my body with a punch. My hand goes to my chest, just to check my heart is still keeping me alive, and I look up into the bluest ocean eyes of my motorcycle god.

Shit! My stomach is now alive with a thousand butterflies.

"Brooklyn, this is my big brother, Jarrod Houston, who is thirty today, older but not wiser, and definitely not as good-looking as me. Jarrod, meet Bee," Christopher says proudly, albeit a little slurred.

I'm trying not to make it obvious that I'm about to faint; probably, it's that or swoon like one of the Regency Misses in period romance novels. Fuck, he is gorgeous up close. Like a carved marble statue: perfect features, the face of an angel — or devil, I can't decide which — long black eyelashes that look striking against the blue of his eyes, and that dark hair, expertly combed back off his face for a more formal look tonight. He is dressed in all black again: a tailored suit, black shirt, waistcoat and silver/grey tie give him a dangerous edge. He takes my hand, and the contact sparks up my arm. I wonder if he can feel the electricity.

"Brooklyn," he murmurs, staring into my eyes with a force, while he kisses the back of my hand. The hand I'm not going to wash again. Never. Fucking. Ever.

His voice is cultured, smooth, low, perfectly fitting for a dark and dangerous motorcycle god — who happens to be disgustingly wealthy and whose family owns this bloody hotel I'm standing on top of.

He is still holding my hand. I have again been rendered speechless, so I try and get my brain to snap out of the Jarrod-induced trance and speak like the adult I am.

"Nice to meet you, and thank you for the…" I let go of his hand to motion over my outfit, which I now realise was gifted by him, making it all the more personal.

His eyes roam over my body, sparkling like an ocean in the moonlight, and they finish on my neck, where the diamond choker is sitting. His mouth parts and I see him take in a breath before his eyes flick back up to mine in a silent promise. Of what, I don't know, but the heat coming off him is starting to hit me, and my hand goes to my throat, touching the diamond choker.

I look away, just to get back some equilibrium; the air is so thick, that I can't even feel a breeze up here. "No thank you necessary, the pleasure is all mine, Brooklyn, trust me," he states in a low tone.

I look back and he is giving me a full megawatt smile. I can see perfect white teeth, slightly longer pointy eye teeth, like he is part wolf or something, waiting to consume Little Red Riding Hood, who just happens to be me, by the look of it. I smile back, hoping to give him a little punch of what he is giving me. I think it works because he looks away from my face and runs his hand through that inky black hair.

Daniel breaks the connection by saying, "Brooklyn, the band is ready; would you like to start now, or do you need a drink first?"

I look over to him, grateful for the intervention. "No, I'm ready, thank you. Can I have a bottle of water on stage? I'll head over now," I walk towards the stage, not looking back to see if blue eyes and sharp teeth are following me.

I reach Will and the guys, who all give me big bear hugs, exclaiming how lovely I look. Will takes my hand and kisses my cheek gently: he knows not to mess up the face Vivian so expertly painted.

"Honey, you look amazing," he says, his eyes doing a once-over, and I smile.

"Thank you, so do you. Are you ready to rock this rooftop?" I ask. "Because I am."

"I want nothing more than to see you do that, Bee. Let's go."

He leads me up to the microphone and the guys take their places. It's time.

I take a sip of water that the waiter left next to my feet and approach the microphone. The DJ stops playing his music and all eyes swing our way.

"Good evening, I hope you are enjoying your night. I'm Brooklyn, and these handsome gentlemen behind me are London's finest musicians; Will, Lenny, Rick and James. Let's have a little fun together," I say with a cheeky smile. I nod to Will, and the band kicks in with our first song, 'Diamonds' by Rihanna.

The room erupts in cheers, with couples flocking to the dance floor, moving and dancing: it's a beautiful sight. Silver balloons float around the space, candles are lit everywhere, and the atmosphere is dynamic. As I'm singing, I look around, my body moving to the music, and I see him. At the bar, like last night, a drink in his hand, those eyes giving me blue flames of electricity, it's humming through my body. A very attractive woman is speaking to him, but his eyes are on me; she tries to bring his face towards her with a hand on his cheek, her face showing annoyance, but he just removes her hand with a flick of his wrist, giving her a hard look, before turning back to look at me.

The rest of the night goes perfectly. I try to avoid looking at Jarrod too much, it throws me off my axis; I need to work, and it's hard to do that with his eyes on my face the whole time. We play a mix of songs again, but more upbeat over the dulcet tones I sing at The Wave. We mix some originals in there, too, songs Will and I have written over the years. I don't play anything from my youth, those songs are in the past; besides, I don't want to be recognised as that young teen star any more; I'm a different person now.

The crowd is very relaxed, drinks flowing, people looking a little sweaty and less polished than they were a couple of hours ago. We are about to sing our last song for the night.

I take the mic off the stand and hold it to my mouth. A slight breeze comes through the open doors, cooling me down, and blowing my hair a little.

"This is our last song tonight." The crowd groans, and shouts of "No" and "More" get called out. I find Jarrod in the crowd, our eyes connect and hold. I take a breath, pushing my hair off my shoulders, maintaining eye contact the whole time. He is watching my every move.

"I just want to wish the birthday boy a very happy thirtieth. Jarrod, I hope all your dreams come true... on a night like this."

The band starts playing, and I start dancing, swaying my hips to the music: Kylie Minogue's 'On a Night Like This'. The guests all crowd the dance floor, shaking their bodies to the music, but I barely notice. My eyes are locked in an embrace like the tide pulling me under. The beat pounding out from the stage is tangible.

I'm looking directly at him as I whisper the first line into the microphone about being kissed, being touched. I sing about her fantasy, falling for him, calling for him.

The atmosphere is hypnotic. With the last note, the room erupts in clapping and cheering. I drag my eyes away and thank the crowd, giving a graceful curtsy and blowing kisses. I turn around: the guys all look happy, ready to partake of the open bar, no doubt. Will takes my hand and escorts me off the stage to where Vivian and Christopher stand.

I'm a little out of breath, and yet it has nothing to do with the two hours of singing and dancing. It's the crazy feeling that blue eyes are following me around the room. The intense connection is something I can't shake. Do I even want to? Yes, it scares the fuck out of me. I never let anyone really see me. I'm damaged. It feels like he is looking into my soul. It's shaken me up.

"Bee, that was so amazing!" Vivian hugs me. "I'm in awe, your voice is angelic," she compliments me.

Christopher hands me a glass of champagne, his face beaming, and I take a sip. "Thank you, I needed that," I say, smiling.

Will gives me a little hip bump, looking into my eyes. "You good, Honey Bee?" his eyes travel my face. I think about that: I feel... overwhelmed. I'm not sure how I feel. It's all surreal, like I drank a freaky magic potion or something. This night, the dress, the diamonds, the music... him watching me.

"Yes, just a little tired. I will stay for a drink and then head off, but you guys enjoy it." I look over at Vivian with a wink and turn back to Will. "Enjoy the rest of the night, you earned it." I kiss his cheek and pat him on the arm. I would normally stay longer, and enjoy it myself, but I'm feeling a little tender right now. Too open.

Christopher takes my arm and places it around his, walking me through the crowd to a seating area. Many people come up to give me praise for a fantastic performance; I thank them graciously.

Sitting down, he leans over. The DJ is now pumping some tunes into the speakers, and drunken revellers dancing. "Bee, I don't know how to thank you. That was amazing, you made our night," he speaks into my ear, and I smile, taking a sip of the cool bubbly.

"I was worried I wasn't going to come up with a decent gift. What do you get the brother who has everything?" he asks, shaking his head.

"A fabulous party with free booze?" I ask, laughing, clinking drinks with him. "Cheers."

"Well, yes, but that's hardly enough." He looks at me, amused. "I got him you!" His drunk face beams at me and I just look into my drink, not sure if it's the alcohol heating my face.

"He wanted you to sing, that's all he asked for." I think Christopher is embellishing a little, in his inebriated state.

"Well, I hope expectations were fulfilled," I say looking back up.

"Are you kidding, Bee? God, you have no idea."

Thankfully, he changes the subject. I look around and see Will and the band at the bar, having drinks and laughing. I smile. Vivian is not far away, and she keeps looking over at Will. I must remember to have a chat with him about her: I think she is very interested.

"Bee," Christopher gets my attention and I look back at him. "Are you free Tuesday? I have tickets to an exhibition and no one to go with. Rolling Stones — it's the most comprehensive and immersive insight into the band's fifty-year history. You like the Stones, right?" He looks at me expectantly.

"Umm, yes, of course, I love the Stones, but I don't think it's a good idea to mix business with pleasure, if you catch my drift," I say, shaking my head.

"Oh, no, I didn't mean it like that, Bee; just as friends. Jarrod and I play — well, he is super-talented, I pound the drums when I get time off, but I just want someone to go with, someone that can appreciate the music, you know?" he says, nodding at me.

"Most of my friends just want to party, drive fast cars, drink, that kind of thing. They wouldn't appreciate the history and music. I know someone like you would," he says confidently, waiting for my answer.

"Well, in that case, sure, why not?" I smile. "Two friends going to see a music exhibition is fine," and he grins at me like I just gave him a gift.

"Capital! Give me your number and I'll text you the details." He holds up his phone. I give him my number; my phone is back in the dressing room downstairs.

I decide it's time to call it a night. I don't want to bother anyone, so I hug Christopher goodbye, telling him I'm beat and need to head home. I ask him to say goodbye to the others for me. He nods like it's no problem. I suspect he is going to get shit-faced now, as he dances off into the crowd, women following in his wake.

I shake my head, laughing at his antics, as I head towards the lifts. Slipping away, I arrive back to my dressing room a few minutes later. I text Will that I'm leaving, saying I will see him Wednesday at rehearsal, giving him kiss emojis.

I start to get my bag and clothes from the couch and hear a knock at the door; it's probably Vivian coming to help me out of the dress.

I open the door, and my eyes convey surprise, because standing right there, with no jacket, no tie, an open black shirt showcasing a nice expanse of skin, and his arms outstretched, gripping the door frame, is Jarrod. Blue eyes sparkle at me while I stand there with my mouth slightly open.

"You sing to me like that and then just leave?" His voice is low, smooth, and sexy. I ignore the comment, because yes, I did sing to him, for him, and then I left. He is right.

"You're missing your party," I say, looking up at that beautiful face. He looks casual, but there is an edge of something, his hands not moving from the door frame, straining a little, like he wants to let go, but can't.

"I don't care, the best part is over now anyway." He takes a slow look at me, from my toes to my hair, tilting his head to the side, like he is trying to figure me out, like I'm a puzzle.

"May I come in?" he asks me, so politely, despite the look he just gave me, which was more like a big bad wolf. My heart starts to beat a little faster now. I'm not sure why I trust him — in the past this kind of situation would have me in a panic, remembering a time when I was young, trusting, and when my innocence was taken from me without my consent. He must read something on my face because he places his hands in his pockets, and very gently says, "I won't hurt you, Brooklyn." It is a statement, a fact. He looks right into my eyes, I can't say why, but I do believe him. I just nod, my voice staying silent. He can read me so easily.

He takes a few steps in shutting the door. Looking around, he takes in the room, all the dresses, shoes, and make-up. Jarrod looks back at me, confident, hands still in his pockets. I relax a little.

"How are you finding everything at the Houston so far, Brooklyn?" he asks while taking a step closer.

I look around, like he did, and look back, catching his eyes on mine. "Great, amazing. It's a dream job; I'm happy to be here. Thank you for all of this." I motion to the dresses and the room. "It's too much," I say with a breathy laugh, trying not to show my nerves with him so close. And god, why does he have to smell so good? My perky nose is just dying to lean forward and sniff him more. I'm a freak — get a fucking grip, Brooklyn.

"You're too much," he murmurs, taking a strand of my hair in his fingers, slowly twirling it around, looking into my eyes, then back to my hair. Shit. Shit. Shit! I don't say anything: I can't while he is still playing with my hair, touching me.

"I'm not going to ask permission, but I won't do anything you don't want, all right?" He looks into my eyes with the most intense expression, as he slowly moves his head forward, his eyes flicking down to my lips. I don't move. He isn't rushing it, he is giving me a moment to understand what is happening; yet I feel that if I said no, he would stop immediately. He is waiting, just holding me there, breathing slowly, watching my face.

I give him a little nod, barely a tilt of my head, and I feel his hand leave my hair and slip around the back of my neck, feeling the diamond choker I have on, and sliding into my hair, while he slowly brings his lips to mine.

His mouth is warm, wet, and delicious. I taste the champagne on his tongue as he slowly parts my lips and slips it inside my mouth. No rushing, just slow and sensual, he is consuming me with only his mouth on mine. His tongue is doing things to me the rest of his body wants to do, I can tell. I've kissed before, but this is different, it's like a rolling wave that keeps hitting me, not letting me up for air. I don't want it to stop. His other hand grips mine, entwining our fingers, squeezing me, connecting us more.

I'm lost in the feel of him kissing me so slowly, so languidly, so patiently, that I barely hear the knock on the door. "Bee, are you in there?" I hear Will's voice at the door. Fuck! Jarrod releases my mouth with a growl, breathing faster than he was earlier. He touches his forehead to mine for a brief moment, looking at me, then steps back.

Letting go, I immediately feel the heat dissipate, leaving me cooler. He goes back to putting his hands in his pockets — I think it's his way of keeping them off me.

"Come in," I call out a little shakily.

Will opens the door, and the smile he had for me freezes and then drops, taking in the two of us alone in the dressing room. His eyes scan me, looking for any sign of distress; then he looks at Jarrod, and they stare at each other for what feels like minutes, before Will turns back to me and asks, "Are You alright, Honey Bee?" concern in his voice, maybe a little anger.

"Yes, I'm fine. Just about to change and head home. I'm beat; playing two nights in a row has me exhausted. I was just telling Jarrod it was a wonderful party," I say, a little breathy, a little too fast.

Will flicks his eyes to Jarrod and then back to me. "I just wanted to make sure you were good. I'll see you Wednesday at rehearsal," he states, and opens the door, giving Jarrod an expectant look.

"You know I'll be there. Now go and have fun, I'm going home to a tub of black raspberry ice-cream," I say, smiling brightly, and Will just looks at me rolling his eyes.

"Mmm, black raspberry... sounds delicious," Jarrod murmurs, looking at me, then casually strolls out the door. I close the door after them, my head hitting the timber with a soft thump. Of course, the only words he utters in those uncomfortable few minutes have to be something that sounds like sex. Turning my ice-cream fix into something else entirely, like sex, and Jarrod, and sex… with Jarrod. Fuck. My ice-cream addiction just got interesting, because when I go home and put that delicious dessert in my mouth, I'm going to be thinking of him.

Chapter Seven

THE TROUBLE WITH BLUE EYES

Sunday and Monday went by so fast, that I needed a good rest after the big weekend at the Houston. I especially needed time to process that kiss. What happens now? I'm not sure. I don't have relations with anyone I work with; that has been a hard and fast rule for me since I was young, but Jarrod is making me question that rule in a whole new way. Maybe it was just a one-night thing; it was his birthday, drinks flowing… God! I don't know what to think. I decide to just let it be for now.

I tell Anton all about it on Margarita Monday.

"I had no idea he was one of the Houston family when I first saw him," I complain, sipping my frozen drink. "And now it's going to be a big fucking mess. I have to perform for four months; what if this goes badly, Anton?" I ask with a sulk in my voice.

"Honey, what did I tell you about fate? Your motorcycle god is actually a hotel heir. Just go with the flow, Bee; but I will say be careful, men like that can be hard to tame, if you know what I mean. Bad boys are great for a short time, not a long time. Have some fun, you deserve it, just don't let your heart get involved." He finishes on a sombre note: "I don't want to see you get hurt." He looks into my eyes more seriously now. "It's been such a long time since you let your guard down and got involved with anyone, but I think you can handle it, you are stronger now," he kisses my head.

"I'll think about it. But who knows, he probably got drunk and doesn't even remember kissing me," I laugh.

"Not likely, you are not easy to forget," he tells me, offering me his hand. "Now shut up and dance with me, my little Honey Bee." The *Dirty Dancing* soundtrack begins to play on the speakers, and I squeal with glee!

Tuesday arrives and just as I am checking my phone, a text comes in from Christopher:

Hi, Bee,

I will pick you up for the exhibition today. Send me your address, be ready at 3pm. Chris.

Oh gosh, I almost forgot that was today. I shoot him a quick text back with a thumbs up and my address.

After my morning coffee ritual, I take a shower and head into my wardrobe to choose my outfit. What to wear, I think. I guess casual is fine for a Rolling Stones exhibition. I decide on black fitted skinny jeans, and black Valentino ankle boots, with a block heel and studded leather buckles. I find a vibrant yellow halter-neck top: it's modest at the front, covering me from neck to waist, but the back is open, just a little bit naughty. I put on some hoop earrings and tie my hair up in a messy bun, making sure to leave a few wisps of hair around my face.

I decide to put on minimal make-up today, just a little lip gloss, dusty pink blush and mascara for my lashes. I look fresh, but a little edgy; it's a rock and roll exhibition, after all. As I'm sliding on my leather jacket, I hear the buzzer. I spray my favourite perfume around my body, very theatrical-like, and run to answer the intercom at my door.

"Hello," I answer breathlessly into the intercom. "I'll come down."

"Hi, Bee, actually, can we come up? I need to use the loo?" Christopher answers.

"We?" I ask him, but he doesn't answer, so I press the button to open the front entry door.

As I put my phone and keys in my black handbag, I hear a knock at the door. I open it, and just like every other time I've seen him, he takes my breath away. Standing next to Christopher is Jarrod. Motorcycle god, business suit-wearing, hotel owner, and stealer of slow kisses.

My mouth hangs open a little; they both look incredible, dressed casually in jeans and T-shirts, Jarrod is dressed again in all black, giving him that edge of something dark, whereas Christopher is wearing blue faded jeans and a Rolling Stones T-shirt. My eyes take them in, together... it's sickening. So bloody beautiful, the both of them. Where did they get their DNA? The Disney

Prince sperm bank? I muse to myself as I shake my thoughts away.

"Um... hi," I manage, still holding the door open.

"Hello, Bee, can we come in? I seriously have to take a leak," Christopher says with a grin.

Where are my manners? "Oh, sure, of course, come in." I move away from the door, and they both walk in.

It's like I'm offering the flat for sale: they both walk in and immediately start looking around, taking everything in, my home, my personal space; it feels a little smaller with these two giants scoping out the place.

"The bathroom is down the hall, last door." I point towards the hallway for Christopher.

"Great, thank you," and he jogs off leaving us alone.

Jarrod looks around, hands in his pockets, his bare arms looking all toned and tanned — he works out, you can tell. As I'm giving him a once-over, his eyes meet mine in that same way, waves crashing in the surf. So intense and direct.

"You have a nice flat, Brooklyn,"

"Um, thank you. I didn't know you were coming along today," I state the obvious. He just smirks at me. "I can tell. I hope you don't mind?" he answers while taking a step closer to me.

"No, of course not. I'm sure it will be a great exhibition. Did you enjoy your birthday party?" I ask, looking away. I walk over to the couch and start folding the throw blanket, to give my hands something to do.

"The party was tolerable," he reflects with a smile in his voice, "but something else was much more enjoyable." He moves closer again, and I don't turn around, because I know I will drown in those deep blues.

"Well, of course, you had the best musicians in London playing." I smile as Christopher walks back into the room.

Christopher turns his head, looking around my flat with interest, "Bee, this is one stunning pad you have here. Do you live alone?" he asks, more curious than snooping.

"Yes, why do you ask?" I question him.

"I know you're talented, but this is next level; it must be worth a mint," he states appreciatively.

"What can I say, I have a fantastic manager; she invested for me when I was young." I leave it at that. I don't want to get into all the details.

Jarrod was watching my face the whole time. He didn't comment, but I can tell he has questions. "Um... so, do you guys want a drink before we leave?" I ask, remembering my manners.

"No, thank you, Brooklyn," Jarrod answers. Christopher is too busy looking at the frames on my sitting room wall. I have photos framed of my concerts, a young me on stage, Anton and I pulling stupid faces on the beach in Brighton last year, family portraits of Mel, Simon, and Kate, and a stunning black and white photo of Will and I on stage performing a couple of years ago. That was one of my favourites — he is looking at me while I sing.

"If it's OK, may I also use your bathroom? Chris and I just drove back from Cambridge; we came straight here," Jarrod tells me. They must have been in the car for an hour and a half. I wonder what had them driving out there.

"Yes, of course," I answer, and motion in the direction of the hallway, and he disappears around the corner.

My brain is quickly computing: Did I leave it all clean? I think so. I use the bathroom in my bedroom, so it should be in reasonable shape. No one else has been over lately.

Christopher moves to the window and looks out at the street below, taking it all in. "What side of London do you live on?" I ask him.

"What do you mean, Bee?" He looks back at me with a smile. "We live at the Houston, of course."

"Oh! I had no idea; you live in the actual hotel?" I ask, surprised.

"Well, we have a family wing, separate from the hotel, of course, but yes, we live there. It makes it easier when needed, we have to be available; the hotel runs twenty-four hours a day."

"I can imagine," I remark. I wonder what that's like having to work and live in the same place. It's a very luxurious place, mind you. But would you ever get privacy?

"You will have to come up and see it one day. We have a music room you'd love," he tells me with a bright smile.

"You do? Wow, that's something I would love to see," I comment, but I'm distracted, wondering why Jarrod is taking so long.

I walk down the hallway to check and see him standing there, staring into my bedroom, his taut arms holding onto the door frame above his head, like he is holding himself back. His black T-shirt is lifted just enough to show me a flat, hard stomach and the start of a trail of fine dark hair that disappears into his low-rise jeans.

God, he is delicious to look at. He messes with my head, electricity seems to run through my veins when I look at him. He turns his head and our eyes meet. I can't look away, the heat radiating off him is almost setting me alight. I feel like he just took a mental Polaroid of my space, my personal space: where I sleep, I get dressed, I go to bed… thinking about him. Does he know that? I feel he can read my every thought.

He doesn't say a word, he just stares at me. So I walk slowly down the hall towards my bedroom. He removes his hands from the door frame and places them in his pockets again. I lean in close to him, my arm brushing his body as I reach for the door and slowly close it, keeping my eyes on his, the whole time.

"It's a mess. Don't you know it's not nice to snoop in a girl's bedroom," I stare into his blue flames.

"It smells like you," he says, leaning forward and slowly putting his nose in my hair, breathing in.

Fuck. He did. Yes, he just sniffed me. I'm dying.

"Hey, hurry up, you two, or we are going to be late," Christopher yells from the sitting room, effectively breaking the spell I'm under. The wolf next to me steps back, and I hear him take a deep breath. Good, at least I know he feels a little breathless, too. It's not just me.

"Let's go, Brooklyn," Jarrod puts a hand on my back and gently guides me down the hallway. This is the part where I tell my brain to tell my legs to cooperate and start walking. Duh!

I grab my bag, we walk out of the flat and head downstairs to the car parked in front of my building. "Wow, flashy," I comment, as we walk up to a sleek black Mercedes-Benz.

"It's one of Jarrod's babies, it's an EQE," Christopher says, like I even know what that means. All I know is that it's a very nice ride. A sound beeps and the doors unlock.

"You ride in the back, Chris," Jarrod tells him and gives him a shove away from the front passenger door.

"Tosser," Christopher mumbles, as he opens the back door and gets in with an eye roll at Jarrod.

I get in and look around; it has that new leather smell. It must be a recent purchase. All sleek and sophisticated interior, black leather, a massive flat screen sits in the middle of the dash, no buttons or dials anywhere — it looks like a spaceship computer. I don't want to touch anything.

Jarrod leans over me to secure the seatbelt, killing me with his scent, like some kind of woody, citrus aftershave. I try not to make it obvious that I want to sniff him back.

Fair play. I can manage a seatbelt myself, but I like the contact, so I keep my mouth shut. He just gives me a little smirk and clicks in the belt.

"Thanks," I mumble. My cheeks feel a little warm. I'm thinking payback for that is going to be a bitch. I have my own tricks, you know. Jarrod starts the car, and it's so quiet; I realise this car must be electric.

We drive into traffic, just making general conversation on the way to the exhibition building. It's not that far, but the usual city traffic is hectic. It takes us fifteen minutes to arrive and find a park, somewhere that Jarrod is comfortable with, knowing no one is going to hit his car when we leave. Christopher teases him ruthlessly about it from the back seat. I just laugh at them both. Boys and their toys.

We enter the building and go through the security entry. I guess fifty years of memorabilia is worth a lot.

As we walk into the first room, Christopher lets out a deep breath. "Fuck, this is amazing," he comments in awe.

The exhibition embraces all aspects of art and design, sound, film, video, fashion and performance, encompassing more than five hundred original artefacts from the band's personal archives. Clothing, albums, musical instruments, it's all here. I didn't expect it to be so phenomenal. We walk around for a bit, just taking it all in.

Jarrod follows behind me, not saying much, just observing. My phone starts to ring; it's Mel, because my phone is barking like a dog. Luckily, it's not too loud. I take my phone out and answer.

"Hi, did I forget we had plans today?" I ask her.

"Hello Bee; no, it's all good, I just wanted to say that an entertainment reporter is coming to your show Friday night. They are doing a piece in the paper. No pressure, I just wanted to give you a heads up," I wander around while she talks, looking at the frames on the gallery wall.

"OK, thank you for letting me know. I'll let Will know tomorrow. I'm at an exhibition, so I have to go. Kiss Katie for me."

"I will. Love your face, bitch," she says, hanging up.

I slide my phone into my back pocket and turn around. The guys are behind me, Christopher giving me a quizzical look.

"What?" I ask as take off my leather jacket. It's getting warm inside. Jarrod leans over and takes the jacket from my hands and I look at him, tilting my head to the side in a silent question.

"I can hold it for you," he says casually.

Before I can answer, Christopher speaks up. "Why do you have that god-awful ringtone, Bee?" He screws his face at me, and I laugh, before telling him my little phone habit — this is going to be fun.

"That's my manager's ringtone; Mel, you met her. I assign a song to all my personal contacts; it's just what I do. It's my special talent."

"Really? Then what song did you give me?" Christopher asks, beaming at me like it's a surprise gift, he puts his hands on his hips, waiting.

"I can't say, it's a secret." I give a cheeky grin and look at Jarrod. He is smiling at me now, too. I think he can see the glint in my eye. God, that smile is breathtaking. We stare at each other for a heartbeat. I don't see Christopher take out his phone, but my back pocket starts vibrating and playing a very amusing song: The Offspring's 'Pretty Fly (For a White Guy)' kicks in right with the drums.

Christopher's jaw drops open. "What the fuck! Bee!" he exclaims in horror. Jarrod is almost bent over with laughter, trying to catch his breath, looking at his brother's face. I start doing a little dance to the beat, singing to him, mouthing the words "Pretty fly for a white guy".

Jarrod and I are laughing so hard, someone hushes us from the back. Christopher's face is hilarious: he looks annoyed but tries not to laugh at the same time, his arms are crossed in front of his body.

"You are going to pay for that one, little Bee. My revenge will be swift and painful," he says, putting his face right in mine. I still can't stop laughing, but I blow him a kiss and spin around, walking off and whisper-singing the song. We are probably disturbing the visitors.

I hear a grunt, and Christopher mumbles in a low voice, "Arse-hat, what was that for?"

I turn around and Jarrod is staring at me, like a statue, not moving, just blue piercing eyes blazing. Christopher is rubbing his side. "What happened?" I ask, looking at them both, side by side.

"Nothing," Jarrod mumbles, while Christopher says "Cramp" at the same time. I look down; he is rubbing the side of his stomach.

"Oh, I get cramps sometimes, when I stand up singing for a long time; you just need to give it a little massage," I lift my hands to his side. Christopher looks at Jarrod and a huge grin appears across his face, eyes gleaming. That naughty boy look is back.

"Did you hear that, Jarrod? Bee wants to rub my boo-boo!" He looks at his brother with a wicked smile.

"Do you want another one, dickhead?" Jarrod asks and takes my hands before I can help Christopher.

"What's going on?" I say to them both. Two pairs of vibrant blue eyes look at me like innocent little boys, and I don't believe them for a second. Vivian was right — these two are trouble with a capital T.

"Brooklyn, what are you wearing?" Jarrod asks me and releases my hands. I look at him and realise what he means. Ahh… well, maybe he is getting payback, after all. My bare back is exposed, and he just got an eyeful of my smooth skin, the tattoos down my spine visible as well. I smile. Two can play this game.

I put an innocent expression on my face and shrug. "A top and jeans, nothing special," Then I turn on my heels and saunter over to the next room, looking over my shoulder just to make sure my little display is working. Both brothers stand with mouths agape, and eyes glued to my back. Take that, Jarrod, you deserve a little retribution for the bedroom incident earlier. Smiling to myself, I forget them for a while and just bask in the amazing rock history of the Rolling Stones. I wonder if Will has seen it; he would love it.

After a couple of hours immersed in the exhibition, we leave and head home. The car stops in front of my building and the brothers get out and meet me on the pavement.

"Thank you for coming with us, Bee, it was a great afternoon, despite being humiliated by that song, and getting punched in the ribs," Christopher says, rubbing his side.

I laugh at his sulky face. "You get a song upgrade when you earn it. I'll have to put you on notice," I hug him, giving him a little squeeze. "It was a fun afternoon, thank you for inviting me, Christopher. See you Friday night."

"I'll walk you up," Jarrod says, as I look over. I don't know why I can hug Christopher so easily, but when it comes to him, I get all nervous. I feel it wash over me instantly.

"Uh, OK." I turn around and press the code to open the front door of my building. We walk up in silence; he is right behind me, I can feel the heat on my bare back. When we get to my front door, I pull my keys out, looking down. Jarrod puts a finger under my chin, lifting my face to his, and immediately I feel the electricity again where he touches me, just zapping its way through my body like a lightning bolt.

His eyes are serious, deeper blue now, just holding my own green and amber gaze. "You know what I want, don't you?" he asks me quietly, eyes roaming my face.

I'm not sure how to answer that, so I try for honesty. "You want to... fuck me?" I ask, surprised at my candour with him. My cheeks are heating under his gaze, but I don't look away. I know what men want when they look at me that way. But with Jarrod, it feels different, not like all the others.

"Christ, Brooklyn... Yes," he breathes, looking away from me for a second, and then his eyes land back on me with such ferocity that I have to swallow — he scares me. Not in a physical way, but in an emotional way.

"I won't be anyone's one-night stand, Jarrod, I can't. That's not who I am." I speak from the heart. He doesn't know what it feels like to be used, abused, or hurt. I can't go there again. Not even for a single night with him.

"That's not what I mean, fuck. You make my head spin, Brooklyn." He takes a deep breath in, steadying his eyes on mine again. "I want more with you. Can you give me that?", his voice is low and gravelly.

"I'm not sure," I say because I don't fully know what he means by 'more'.

"My job is important to me, I don't want to mess that up for a fling. I don't do casual," My eyes tell him just how much that means to me.

He lets out a breath, closing his eyes for a heartbeat "I understand, I do, but I can't walk away from you." And that's all I get before he leans down and kisses me breathless.

He is more desperate this time, crushing his mouth to mine, his tongue sliding into my mouth like hot lava, his hands sliding up my bare back and pressing me against him. He lets out a groan, right into my mouth, like he can't stop himself, touching me, kissing me. I lift my hands and grip his hard shoulders. I feel him, his neck, his arms. I can't stop myself, either. I don't know how long we are kissing before someone clears their throat, loudly.

Jarrod breaks from the kiss but doesn't let go. "Fuck... this can't be happening again," he whispers. He takes another breath, then lets go of me. We both turn and see Anton standing in the doorway of his flat with a huge shit-eating grin on his face.

"Honey Bee, you're home. I'd ask if you've had dinner, but I can see that you have something very delicious home-delivered already." He is cracking up, trying not to laugh, his eyes roaming all over Jarrod in awe.

"Anton, this is Jarrod Houston... Jarrod, this is Anton, my nosy neighbour." I roll my eyes at him.

They shake hands, Jarrod giving Anton a nod. Anton just stays put, a big smile on his face the whole time.

"I'll see you Friday night, Brooklyn." Jarrod leans down to give me a soft kiss on the lips, keeping his eyes on mine the whole time; then he turns around and disappears down the staircase.

"Well, Honey Bee, you in trouble, girl," Anton states with an exaggerated Caribbean accent, fanning himself with his hands.

I slump back on my door, hands holding my heated cheeks, and I look at Anton. "Yes, I'm totally fucked, aren't I?"

Chapter Eight

ICE-CREAM

I enter rehearsal on Wednesday with my standard hot tea and I hand one to Will as I walk through the door. He always arrives early to set up. Looking like the typical rock star, today he is wearing faded, ripped black jeans and a fitted V-neck top, giving his arms a nice tight fit.

"Hello, Honey, how's things?" he asks, as he takes the cup from my hand, giving me a gentle kiss on the cheek.

"Great. I'm excited to try some new songs. I've been working on originals lately, too," I take a seat on the stool opposite Will.

"Brilliant. Whatever you want Honey, we can work on it." He takes a sip of his tea. "The weekend was a big one; have you recovered well?" he asks, and I think I know the part he is insinuating because he's looking at me with that look, like he knows something.

"Yes, it was," I agree. "Umm, so, Jarrod kind of kissed me," I say quietly, suddenly shy.

"I know," he looks down at his tea, picking at the edges of the lid with his fingers.

"You do? Was it that obvious?" I laugh a little to try and make this not as awkward as it feels.

"Yes, we spoke when we left your room." Will takes a breath and looks back at me.

"Oh, you did?" I ask surprised. "What did he say?"

"It doesn't matter. Look, Bee…" He takes a deep breath again. "I just want to make sure you know what you are doing. Be careful. I don't want to see you get hurt." His eyes convey such pain and love for me. Will knows everything that happened to me back when I was a young recording star, and my last short relationship. But I'm sensing something more now.

I take his hand and look right into his eyes. "I know, and thank you for looking out for me, being there for me, always," I say with feeling. "But I'm a big girl now. I have to fight my own battles. Besides, I'm not even sure about him yet, so let's just concentrate on the shows and see how it all pans out. Yes?" I nudge him with my knee, smiling to lift the mood. "Vivian is totally into you, you know," I smirk over my tea.

Will rolls his eyes at me, shaking his head. "Honey Bee, it's time for singing, so stop talking now," I let him off the hook, and I do the thing I do best. Sing.

Friday night turned up faster than I anticipated. I hit the gym Thursday night with Anton, making sure to get my quota of pain in for the week. No slacking off when Anton is around. I went home after and soaked in a hot bath, my aching muscles slowly unwinding, the room filled with soft music coming from the speakers, and vanilla bath salts permeating the steamy room. I needed that, just some quiet time to myself.

I arrive at The Wave early, and head over to the private room where Vivian turns me into a goddess, no matter how dishevelled I look when I walk in.

"You're here, perfect. How was your week, Bee?" Vivian asks, as I place my takeaway tea on the table. She looks stunning as usual, wearing a blue turtleneck dress, with long sleeves, and a short ruffled skirt with a waistband and cuffs. The fabric looks light and flowy. Her long legs are the star of this confection. I lean over for a hug, careful not to mess her hair and make-up.

"Great, and I'll be even better when you paint me like one of your French girls, Jack," I say, pouting my lips at her, hoping she gets the *Titanic* movie quote.

"Honey, you are the real gem here. The heart of the ocean diamond is a pebble compared to you!" she answers back, totally getting my quip, and we laugh, eyes sparkling at each other. "Now, let me turn you into a sparkling emerald tonight," she comments, and holds up the most stunning emerald-coloured dress I've ever seen, and my eyes light up with gems of their own.

An hour later, I'm inspecting Vivian's masterpiece in the full-length mirror. The dress is covered in emerald crystals, it has a very short skirt, with a fabric tie at the front that hangs down, giving a nice shape to the waist. It has elegant long sleeves and an eye-catching sultry plunging neckline. I had to take my bra off, but Vivian assured me the tape would hold the dress in place, making sure no boobs flashed during my performance.

My hair is up in a sexy high ponytail, sparkly dangling earrings hanging from my lobes. She gave me a pair of black painted leather pumps; classic, and they don't detract from the dress. It's a little risqué, but eye-catching nonetheless. I have come to realise Vivian likes to push the boundaries with stage fashion. My lips are neutral, my eyes vibrant and bold with smokey charcoal and emerald eye shadow, blended perfectly in an ombre style. God, she makes my eyes look so striking, I think, as I look in the mirror close up. Big green orbs.

A knock sounds at the door, and Vivian opens it. Of course, it's Will, he is ever so punctual.

"Wow, Bee, you look..." He takes a breath, as his eyes roam over me. "Is that dress going to be a problem on stage if you move?" he asks, looking a little worried.

Vivian just laughs, getting Will's attention. "No, Will, I can assure you I have used secret 'fixings' to make sure it won't budge. Trust me, it's unmovable. An old Hollywood secret women have used for decades," she says, as she eyes my barely-covered boobs proudly.

"OK, well, Vivian, you are the master, I'll take your word for it." He grins at her, and her cheeks go a little pink. "Five-minute call, Honey Bee," he winks, walking out the door.

"Be still, my beating heart," Vivian says, dramatically falling onto the couch in a flustered heap.

I just laugh at her antics. Poor Will, he is going to have to put her out of her misery soon. I think they would make a beautiful couple.

"OK, I'm ready, Viv," I say, smiling. She nods in agreement and opens the door.

We start to walk out and I stop immediately. Jarrod is leaning back on the opposite wall, hands in the pockets of his black tailored trousers, dark blue shirt open at the top, looking all casually delicious. His eyes widen when they see me, but nothing else moves, just those blue depths dragging me under. He looks over me slowly, from my feet to my hair, and his eyes finally land on my face.

I think he can sense my heart beating from the short distance between us. It feels like it's beating out of my chest. The chest his eyes are looking at again. Vivian clears her throat loudly.

"Ahem… Hi, Jarrod, Bee has to be on stage now," she tells him, looking directly at his face with a stern expression. I can't look at her, she will see my blush; my cheeks feel hot. The look he is giving me is melting me from the inside out. I curse my fair complexion around him: my cheeks seem to hold a permanent pink flush.

He brings his eyes back to mine and stands up straight, keeping his hands in his pockets. "I know, I just wanted to wish her good luck tonight." He looks at Vivian and back to me, then takes a deep breath. "Brooklyn, will you have a drink with me after the show…? Don't run away again," he states with a smile, waiting for me to reply.

"Yes," and that's all I can manage. I have to get my head in the game. Vivian pushes past him and grabs my hand, leading me down the hallway. I look back over my shoulder and see him standing there, not moving, just watching me walk away.

Will escorts me to the microphone again, and this time I hear clapping and whistles coming from the crowd. I put on my best smile, grab the mic and introduce us. "Thank you… that's some welcome. My name is Brooklyn, and this fine musician next to me is Will. Please, enjoy the show."

Will starts strumming his guitar in an acoustic version of Harry Styles' 'Adore You'. I start singing and Will sings backup harmonies into his mic.

I find those blue eyes in the crowd and sing to him, because that seems to be our language. I can hardly say two words to him in person, yet everyone else in the room disappears and I sing… to Jarrod.

The set goes perfectly. The room is packed tonight: no space left to move, it's a crush. I thank the crowd, giving my little curtsy at the end before Will leads me off the stage. As we leave, an older gentleman comes up and approaches us. Daniel is next to him and introduces us.

"Brooklyn, Will, this is Patrick Garfield from the *London Arts and Entertainment* magazine. He is doing a piece on your performance at The Wave." Patrick offers Will his hand, then takes mine next. He looks to be about fifty years old, and he is wearing a grey suit with a white shirt and blue tie. He is smiling at me with a slightly pudgy face, and black slim-framed glasses.

"So great to finally meet you, Brooklyn, I have followed your career for some time now. Do you have a moment to speak with me? I have a few questions for the article," he asks very animatedly.

I look to Will, and he nods, leading me over to the VIP seating area that is kept separate from the rest of the bar patrons. We sit down, and Patrick gets out a pen and notepad from his top pocket. He looks at me, smiling, his eyes wandering over me, a little too closely I feel, but I maintain my eyes on his face.

"Brooklyn, that was an amazing show tonight. I did see a few you did recently at the Cavendish Hotel; sterling performance from both of you, I might add," he says, looking at both Will and I.

"Thank you, we loved performing there, it's a first-class venue," I say, as he looks down at his notepad for a second.

"How long are you here at the Houston?" He looks back up at me.

"Four months, and if all goes well, we may stay on a little longer," I answer, smiling politely.

He nods and scribbles in his notepad. "And how does singing in these establishments compare to being a recording artist and touring large concerts, you know, like you used to do?" he asks expectantly, looking at me with interest. My breath catches a little. I don't like the way he is looking at me now.

"We prefer to stay local. Brooklyn and I are not inclined to play large concerts any more. We feel the smaller, more intimate venues suit our style better," Will answers, putting a protective arm around my back.

"Oh, I'm sure it's tremendous to play places such as this," he says, as he waves his hands around the opulence of The Wave cocktail lounge. "But come now, Brooklyn, for such a successful child star, don't you miss the big shows? The recording industry?" he pushes again.

I look at Will, a little shocked that this is happening right now. I don't want to talk about my past; why is this guy bringing it up? Fucking wanker. He is making me feel uneasy. We are supposed to talk about the shows here.

"Actually, no," I say firmly, "I don't miss anything, and I'm very content singing here right now. The Houston Hotel staff and its patrons have been amazing, and very welcoming, I'm so lucky to be given this opportunity," Hopefully he gets the hint and moves on. I feel Will's hand moving on my back, gently giving me strength.

"Of course," he agrees with me, writing something down in his stupid notepad. "What happened when you were fifteen to leave the stage in the first place? I mean, you just disappeared and stopped making albums. Can you tell me about that time in your life, Brooklyn?" His eyes bore into mine with determination.

I look over at Will, who is gritting his teeth, looking like he might murder this tosser, when Jarrod appears from thin air; he must have been behind us, because I didn't see him when we sat down.

"Brooklyn has another engagement tonight," he says coolly, "and she is already late. Please excuse us, won't you?" he looks down at Patrick with flaming eyes, as he holds his hand out to me.

I take his hand and give the fuck-face a polite smile, Will stands up behind me. Patrick decides to press his luck even more — what is with this guy?

"My apologies for keeping her too long, and you are?" He stands up and inspects Jarrod up close.

"The owner of this hotel," Jarrod states. "Daniel can show you out; thank you for attending tonight's show," he says smoothly and looks at Daniel standing a few feet away, giving him a nod.

Jarrod squeezes my hand and leads me away from the bar. I take a deep breath; this has ruined my night, and I just want to go home now. Open my ice-cream and eat the whole damn tub!

We arrive at the door to my private dressing room and Jarrod walks me in, Will close behind him.

"Honey Bee, are you OK?" Will asks with concern etched on his face, his big hands on my shoulders, looking into my eyes. He flicks his eyes to Jarrod, and back to me. I know what he means: he is trying not to say too much in front of him, not give away anything too obvious.

"I'm fine. I just want to go home now. It's been a busy week," I lean in for a hug. Will gives me a big bear hug, squeezing the breath out of me, kissing me on top of my head.

"I'll take her home," Jarrod murmurs quietly next to us.

Will pulls back and looks into my eyes. "Is that all right with you, Honey, or do you want me to call a taxi and take you home?" he asks, not caring if Jarrod is standing right there. He wants me to voice my choice out loud.

I look at Jarrod; I can see concern on his face, but he remains silent, his eyes on mine, waiting for my answer. "Sure, Jarrod can drive me home. I'll be fine, I will text you," I say, and kiss Will on the cheek.

Will nods and looks back to Jarrod. "Take care of her." It's a warning. I can feel his apprehension, but he lets me go. "I'll talk to you soon, Honey Bee," he adds, and he leaves us alone, shutting the door gently on the way out.

I don't bother to change here. I grab my bag and phone and look over at Jarrod, who is quiet, just watching me. "Here, give them to me. Let's use the service lift; my car is parked underground," he says, and he takes my bag, grabs my hand, entwining our fingers, and leads me out of the room. I'm grateful he doesn't ask me any questions. I gather he can tell my mood is sombre and I don't feel like talking now.

We drive the short distance to my flat in silence, low music playing in the car: James Bay's 'If You Ever Want to Be in Love' playing through the speakers in the background. I love his music, I think, with my head back on the headrest, in this comfortable new car, the seat heating my bare legs, warming up my back.

We arrive at my front door. I don't feel like being alone right now, but I'm nervous about asking Jarrod to stay for a while. I decide to go for it. "Have you had dinner? Do you want to come in for a bit?" I ask, looking down at my keys. I'm nervously twisting them in my hands.

He puts a finger under my chin to lift my face, looking into my eyes, reading my thoughts, it seems. "Yes, I want to come in. No, I haven't eaten yet," he says, and he smiles at me, something I really need right now, I smile back. I like that he is direct; he doesn't mess around with unnecessary words. Definitely not an over-talker.

"OK, we can order something," I turn around to open the door. We walk in and I click on the wall lamps, with just enough lighting to see around the room at night, but not enough to be overly bright.

My blinds are open and the street lights are filtering through the window.

"Make yourself comfortable. I'm just going to change and wash this makeup off," That sounds so cliché, and I mentally slap myself in the head. But I don't entertain hot men in my flat very often, really never, so I'm not sure what to say. He scatters my brain every time I look at his captivating face.

Jarrod gives me that look, like he is capturing the image of me in this dress before it's gone for good. "What do you want to order? I have the app, I'll just order while you change," he pulls his phone out from his pocket.

"Umm, there is a great Italian place around the corner; just order whatever you like from there. I love their food. They're called Florentino," I say, walking over to the kitchen island. I get a box of matches from the top drawer and light a vanilla-scented candle. He watches my every move, those eyes following me around the room. I shoot off a text message to Will, letting him know I am home safe.

I enter my bedroom and close the door. I remove the dress and hang it up. Kicking off my shoes, I rub some lotion into my legs and feet. I walk into the bathroom, take out the make-up wipes and begin to remove the heavy eye makeup Vivian artistically painted on me. It's a shame to take it off, because she did a stellar job tonight, as usual.

I wash my face and add some face cream. I look at my reflection: I look younger now, fresh-faced and scrubbed clean. I put on some white cotton shorts and matching tank top. I'm not trying to entice him tonight, I just want company. So I decide against anything 'sexy' and just go with comfortable.

I walk out to find Jarrod with his back to me, hands in his pockets, just looking at the pictures on my wall. His shoes are beside the couch, sleeves of his shirt are rolled up in that casual way that men do when they unwind from work.

I watch him for a moment, just taking a second to breathe him in without him knowing. He must realise I'm in the room, because he turns around and just stands there looking at me. Taking in my casual look, his expression doesn't change; he doesn't give much away, but his eyes give me heat.

"Drink?" I ask, and walk over to the kitchen. "I have white wine if you like?"

"Sure. The food will be here in twenty," he stands by the window, observing my every move.

I pour two glasses of a crisp white Pinot Grigio and walk over to the couch. I hand him a glass and turn around to sit down. I turn on the TV with the remote and channel surf to find something interesting. Jarrod walks over and sits next to me. I can feel the heat from his body immediately, radiating across to me, making me feel warm. I take a sip of the wine, loving the feel of the smooth fruity flavour going down my throat, soothing my vocal cords with a cool trickle.

I find the movie channel and decide on *The Wizard of Oz*; it is a classic I haven't watched in years. I love Judy Garland, her voice was so regal. We watch in silence for a while. I'm so nervous to even move.

I smile when she starts singing, linking arms with the scarecrow and skipping down the yellow brick road.

"You're adorable, do you know that," I hear him say quietly, and I look over. Jarrod is watching me again, not the movie. I don't answer, but I smile and sing him the words that Dorothy sings.

I stay like that, looking at him for a heartbeat.

"I have to kiss you now," and he doesn't give me any thinking time before those soft lips are on mine, tasting like chilled wine, slowly yet forcefully taking my mouth hostage. We are both holding our wine glasses, but I feel a hand gently grab the nape of my neck and bring me closer. His mouth's not cool any more, it's hot, and his tongue is asking mine to dance, so I give him what he wants. I slide my tongue into his warm hot mouth, and he groans, tightening his hold on my neck a little bit more. We kiss for what seems like endless minutes, Dorothy chattering away in the background. Then the buzzer to my flat sounds, effectively breaking the spell in the magical world of Oz.

Jarrod slows down the kiss, moving away and resting his forehead on mine with a deep breath.

"I swear, soon I'm going to kiss you without interruptions!" he says in a frustrated tone, then smiles, shaking his head.

I smile and take another sip of wine. "I'll get the food; we can sit at the kitchen island to eat," I get up and walk over to the buzzer to let the delivery driver up, trying for total calmness on the outside, but inside I'm a wreck.

I mouth "Oh my god" to my front door, my heartbeat pounding in my veins like a massive lambeg drum.

Once I have the food, plates and wine bottle on the island, we sit across from each other and enjoy the meal. "This looks amazing. I'm starving; I worked through lunch today," he remarks while taking a big forkful of pasta. He ordered two kinds of pasta, a basil and tomato pizza, and a fresh garden salad. It goes perfectly with the wine. I'm actually hungry now, too, so I dig in.

I ask him about his work, what he does at the hotel, and what he likes to do when he isn't running the Houston with his brother.

"I work long hours — it comes with the territory, I ride my motorcycle, I love the freedom," he says, taking another bite of his food. "Mmm, this is so good." He closes his eyes and I take a second to appreciate his face without him knowing.

"My passion is music. Christopher and I play when we get a chance; it takes my mind off work and other stress. I guess you know what I mean."

"What do you play?" I ask as I take a sip of wine.

"Guitar. Chris plays the drums. I would have majored in music, but my parents wanted me to concentrate on business studies, family legacy and all that," I detect a tiny hint of disappointment in his tone.

"You can play for me some time," I say, finishing my food and putting my plate in the sink.

"Maybe, if you're lucky," he tells me with a cheeky smile, like he is hiding a special secret.

"I'm done, thank you." Jarrod stands up and takes his plate to the sink, rinsing it under the tap.

"How about dessert?" I ask.

"What are you offering?" He eyes me across the island bench with a smile, wolf-like teeth peeking out under his top lip. God, that smile gets me warm in all kinds of places.

"Why, Jarrod, are you suggesting there is anything other than ice-cream for dessert?" I ask with mock horror. "Ice-cream is king. Nothing else comes close," I open the door to the freezer and ponder my selection for a minute, not sure what I feel like. My finger on my lips, tapping my mouth while I think it over.

I take out a tub of mint chocolate chip. I don't bother with bowls, I just eat right out of the tub. It's the weekend, after all: I get my treat with no guilt. "Do you want some?" I ask, showing him the tub.

"Yes. But I think my ice-cream fantasy is a little different to yours," he flicks his eyes between mine and the container I'm holding. I can see his eyes heat, blue flames sparking at me, and my face flushes, despite holding the freezing ice-cream in my hands. I look down and grab two spoons from the drawer. We head back over to the couch and sit down close, arms and legs touching. Dorothy has now made friends with the Tin Man.

I hand him a spoon and then help myself to a big spoonful of minty goodness, keeping my eyes on the movie. "Mmmm," I moan, dragging the spoon from my lips. "So good, right?" I ask; but when I look over, he isn't eating, he is watching me. His eyes are on my mouth, he's breathing faster, and then he takes my spoon with the ice-cream container and places them on the side table next to the couch.

A chill goes through me. I feel my nipples harden, and I don't think it's the cold ice-cream I was holding.

"I want to taste you," My insides melt, like holy shit. I can't escape his heated gaze — I don't move. He leans over, gently pushing me down on the couch and moves over me, holding up most of his weight on his arms, flexing through his shirt. Jarrod leans down and takes my mouth, just like he did earlier, but with a desperate passion I haven't felt before.

"Fuck, you taste so good," he mumbles into my mouth. I put my hands in his hair; I've wanted to feel this hair since the first moment I saw him, so black, it's soft and silky, just as I imagined.

"I told you the ice-cream was good," I say into his lips.

"Brooklyn, it's not the ice-cream," he kisses me senseless. His body relaxing into mine, he allows the full weight of it to fall onto me, and now I really feel him, his solid chest, firm thick thighs, and something very hard digging into my pelvis.

"Jarrod…" I break the kiss, breathing heavily — I'm not sure how to broach the subject.

"Brooklyn, look at me, what is it?" he asks, concerned, he leans back a little.

"I'm just… I don't want to give you the wrong impression, that's all. I'm not a casual sex person. I didn't have the best experience in the past…" I leave it at that. I don't want to completely ruin the night.

He takes a minute to look at me, holding my face while he searches my eyes, weighing up what he is about to say to me. "I know. And this, us, it's more than casual, do you understand me? I told you before, Brooklyn, I want more." He leans down to kiss me, gently, like I'm precious. "I want more with you."

He keeps his eyes on mine as he lowers himself to me again. I feel his full weight on me. This time I get the full force; I think he was holding back before, because now, he is showing me what he means. His warm hand moves from my hip, sliding under my cotton top and spanning my stomach, moving over my skin with reverence, like he has to touch me.

I feel his breathing change, and his hand slides up to cover my breast. God, I can't think, he is making me forget everything, all the bad in my past, the relationships I've had. All gone; it's just us, like starting over new.

His hand glides over my breast, his tongue in my mouth, sliding in and out, and I begin to move my hips; the feeling of rubbing against him is a fire in my blood. His hips grind in time with mine, his hardness rubbing against me, hot and firm, I can feel how much he wants me, his body showing me without words.

Jarrod breaks the kiss, opening his eyes, and staring as he gives me a slow roll of his hips, making me feel what I'm doing to him. Then he moves down my body, keeping his eyes on mine the whole time, reading my reactions. He sits back on his heels and takes hold of my shorts, gently pulling the soft material down my legs. I don't stop him, I don't think I can.

He drags them down slowly, watching me before he does the same with my underwear. He throws them over the side of the couch. He leans over to the ice-cream and takes a mouthful from my spoon; it's softer now, sitting out on the table this long. I just watch him, mesmerised, his movements leisurely, like he has all the time in the world. Then he lowers himself and I realise what he is about to do.

He grips my legs, placing them over his shoulders, and lowers his head between my thighs.

The first touch of his mouth on me shocks me. "Fuck!" I breathe out. The cold chill from the ice-cream on his tongue and the heat of his mouth jolt me, my head flies back and my back arches, pushing more of me into his mouth. He sucks with passion on my clit, then moves his mouth from my sensitive spot and licks everywhere. He is everywhere.

I grab his hair, anything to hold on to, and I feel him release a growl; he likes it when I do that. He is eating me like I'm the best dessert, as if I'm his favourite ice-cream. I can't stop the heat from flushing through me. I feel it coming up fast, like flames washing over me... My head is shaking from side to side, I'm moaning now, letting my voice out, I can't keep it quiet any longer, and then it hits.

I'm crashing, my whole body shakes and I dig my nails into his scalp. I don't know if I'm hurting him, but I can't stop, my thighs squeeze his shoulders. "Fuck! Fuck!" I breathe out... "So fucking good!"

His mouth on me slows, he is gently sucking my clit, and I can't take it. "Please, Jarrod," I say, wanting him to stop, yet not stop at the same time.

He keeps going and I'm getting warm again; the first orgasm has barely faded and I'm pushed over the edge a second time, not a big explosion like the first, but a gradual slow ripple running through my whole body. My legs start to shake and I cry out. I can't hold it in. I grip his shoulders and softly push him away. He kisses my thigh, licks up my leg, then places my legs back down on the couch. I lie there for a moment, just catching my breath.

I open my eyes to see him leaning over me, looking at me with such heat and awe, like I gave him something special. Yet he gave that to me; I haven't done anything.

"You're so fucking beautiful, Brooklyn," he whispers, leaning down to kiss me gently. I taste him, I taste me. I feel his erection through his trousers digging into my hip and I look down, then back up to his face. "Can I do something for you?" I ask, watching him.

He smiles, removing a strand of hair from my face, and traces my lips with his finger, his eyes following the movement.

"Tonight was about you Brooklyn. That was the best damn ice-cream I've ever tasted," I laugh out loud. Fuck, I'm never going to eat ice-cream without this memory again!

Chapter Nine

MORNING BATHS

Saturday morning arrives with diffused soft sunlight filtering through my bedroom window. A warm finger is tracing my spine, working its way around the curves and lines of my back tattoos. My cotton tank top is lifted to my shoulders, my lower half wearing my shorts again, legs tangled up in the sheets.

"What do they mean?" he whispers to me, knowing I'm coming back to awareness now.

I groan. I'm warm and comfortable and want to sleep longer. "They're Runes," I answer with a sleepy mumble. My face is turned away from him, I can't see his expression. I didn't realise he stayed over: I assumed he would have left during the night. I am a heavy sleeper: once I hit the bed, I'm out; but I would have been disappointed if I woke up and he was gone. I need to think about that later. For now, I put my feelings in the vault.

His fingers keep tracing the lines on my back. "Like Viking symbols?" he continues.

"Mmm, somewhat yes." I don't elaborate, because it's too early for talking. I haven't had my coffee fix.

I decide I need a visual of Jarrod this morning, so I turn my head around to face him. Seriously! How good can a person look in the morning, he should be on a movie set somewhere. I, on the other hand, probably look a mess, my hair fanning out on the pillows, a disarray of knotted waves. Luckily I scrubbed all the make-up off last night.

"There she is," he says, smiling, he removes the hair from my face with a soft touch. I look at him for a minute. His bare chest is killing me, lying on his side with one arm under his head, the other one touching me.

All golden skin, smooth and firm, his sculptured chest and stomach begging me to touch, just a little bit... I drop my eyes and see the top of his black boxer shorts above the sheets. I have vague memories of a warm body next to me when I was sleeping. Not what I am used to after sleeping alone for so long.

I reach a hand out, just a couple of fingers touching his chest, running them down his hard abs and into that trail of black soft hair I got a glimpse of the other day. He sucks in a tight breath, his ocean eyes watching mine. He takes my hand, removes it from his body, and kisses me on my fingers.

"If you keep doing that, we won't make it out of bed." His eyes are serious, but his mouth is smirking with a wolf-like grin, all sharp teeth and soft lips. "I'll be back. Don't go anywhere," he tells me and rolls out of bed. I get a delicious view of his tight arse in black shorts as he leaves the room.

I lay on my back, eyes closed, trying to fall under again, but knowing he is here, so close, I just can't sleep. My mind is conjuring up all kinds of hot thoughts, especially after last night. He took care of me, and he didn't expect anything in return. I've never had anyone do that for me in the past. Most men just want a hot body to use.

Aside from my initiation into sex in the most horrible, twisted way possible, I've only had a couple of partners. There was James, who I dated while at university, he was sweet but it wasn't love. He respected me, and we were friends, then it ended and we went our separate ways. As I got older and developed into a woman, men just seemed to crowd me, to stalk me. I felt like they didn't want me, just my body. Call it paranoia, but when you have been raped, you essentially don't trust anyone any more.

My record producer drugged me at the age of fourteen. I was supposed to attend a meeting in his office.

My mother, Sam, dropped me off and left. I later realised she knew what he wanted. By the time it was over, I could barely stand up and walk out of the office, the ketamine and Rohypnol making me incapable of controlling my body. That's how Mel found me. She was a young talent agent, recently employed by the label.

She took me to the hospital and called child protection services. What ensued later was twelve months of court appearances, charges, and finally my emancipation from my mother. Mel was my angel, my knight in shining armour, my saviour. The details of my case were kept closed, due to being a minor. No one outside of the legal team and police knew what happened. Everyone just assumed I left the music industry because I lost my record deal. No one outside of my bubble knew the truth. The arsehole rapist got two years — that's what power and money can buy. Less time, and no public shaming. It was all kept hush-hush.

My last partner was Oliver. We met at one of Anton's performances. He was suave, good-looking, the perfect gentleman on the outside. We dated for a few months. I tried to fall for him, I liked him, but something kept holding me back from really letting go.

He got horribly jealous of my time with Will. That's not something I will tolerate. Will is like a brother to me; yes, we are affectionate, but we have known each other for a decade. I won't allow someone to come in and tell me I can't spend time with him. Will is my family.

Eventually, it got too heated and I had to break it off. Will means more to me than someone who flies into a jealous rage whenever I mention his name. Needless to say, Will was ecstatic when Oliver left: he threw me a 'Thank Fuck He's Gone' party with Anton and Mel. We all got shit-faced drunk and ate ice-cream.

It's been a while now. I've been happy doing my own thing. I haven't needed to be with anyone, but now... I'm not so sure. I'm wary of starting something new, especially with Jarrod, as I work for his company. Yet I just can't ignore the connection we have. I've never had this with anyone else. I have to watch myself with him.

My eyes are shut, and all of a sudden the bed dips then I'm lifted into strong arms, my eyes fly open, and I grab Jarrod's neck in surprise. "What the…?" I squeak.

He smiles down at me as he carries me over to the main bathroom, and I see he has filled the tub. The room is warm and steamy, vanilla fragrance surrounds us. He gently puts me down on the tiles, his hands on my hips in a firm steady grip, making sure I am holding myself up.

"Brooklyn, will you join me?" he asks, and he nods his head towards the full bathtub, eyes on mine the whole time.

I look around: he has put clean fluffy towels next to the tub, used my favourite bath products, and lit a scented candle. Well, heck, how can I say no to this? I look back and give him a small smile, nodding my head. He moves to the hem of my cotton tank top, slowly lifting, giving me plenty of time to stop him, but I don't. I lift my arms and he removes my top. I guess I'm really doing this. God, this is a dream; am I even awake?

His eyes are like heated ultramarine gems, taking in my body, lingering on my creamy, pale, full breasts. His stare is making my breath catch. I reach down to remove my shorts. He seems transfixed, not moving, just watching my slow movements. I kick them off and stand there, my hands resting on my thighs.

Jarrod looks up finally and takes my face in both his hands, his thumbs moving over my mouth. Looking into my eyes, he breathes, "You're fucking perfect," and kisses my mouth in the softest way I've ever been kissed.

"I'm not usually so gentle, Brooklyn, but with you, I have to be, I need to be," he confesses.

"Thank you," I respond as he kisses my lips again.

He lets me go and reaches to slide his own shorts down, and when he stands up again, I take him in. He is hard. I can't look anywhere else, because his erection is sitting there straight up to his abdomen, firm and hot and fucking huge. My eyes can't look away, because seriously, that thing is going to be a challenge. His body is so fit, like a Calvin Klein underwear model. I don't have words at this moment.

"Shall we get in before the water cools?" he chuckles and picks me up again. I squeak and wrap my arms around his neck for support. He lowers us into the hot bath; at first, it gives me a little sting, then the heat settles in and I moan with the soothing feel of being surrounded by water and Jarrod's big body behind me.

It feels so good, too good. My muscles start to relax and I recline back against Jarrod's hard chest. His chin is on my shoulder, arms trailing water and soap up my arms, and down onto my stomach.

He reaches over to the side and I see him holding the washcloth. He dips it in the warm water and starts to wash my body gently, hands roaming over my heated chest, my breasts, around my navel. It feels so good. I shut my eyes and enjoy the feeling of him washing me for a few minutes.

I look down at his strong legs surrounding mine. I touch my toes to his, putting my foot next to his colossal one. "You have big feet," I say, smiling, and measure my smaller foot next to his.

"You know what they say about men with big feet," he comments into my ear, and I can hear the smile in his voice.

"Yes, they say it compensates for other smaller appendages," I respond laughing, and the next thing I'm being tickled mercilessly. "Stop! Jarrod! OK, I take it back," I breathe between laughing, trying to stop his hands from touching me. He takes my hands and entwines our fingers together, wrapping them around my body so neither of us can do more damage.

I take a few breaths... still smiling, calming myself. I can feel his deep breathing behind me too. I move forward and he releases me slowly. Turning, I kneel between his thighs. Our eyes lock, and I decide to take the lead. I'm not ready for sex just yet, but I want to give him something.

"I want to touch you," I whisper. He doesn't say anything, but his body reacts and I can tell he wants me to, very much. His eyes glow and his pupils dilate. Jarrod reclines back in the tub, arms casually resting on the sides; he is letting me take the lead. His stomach muscles flex and tighten as my hands leave his thighs and take hold of his hardness. It's firm again now, filling my hands completely. I take some vanilla body oil and start to rub it all over him.

Jarrod reclines his head back with his eyes closed. His breathing starts to increase as I massage the oil around him. I'm gentle at first, not sure how he likes it. It's been a while since I had one in my hands; well, a real one, and not my battery-operated one, used only when absolutely necessary.

"Brooklyn, you're killing me," he breathes, his eyes open and stare into my own. I watch him; he looks down at my hands, gripped around him tightly, sliding up and down, then he closes his eyes again, like he can't help it, "Fuck, angel, you're going to make me come."

I speed up, gripping him tighter, using one hand now. The other hand I smooth over his lower abs, rubbing the oil on his body. It's slick and slippery with the oil and water mixing. His breathing turns into panting now, his knuckles going white as they grip the sides of the tub. His hips pump into my slick hold and I kick up the pace, giving him the full slide, from root to tip, squeezing him at the top as I glide my hands over him.

Jarrod lets out a loud groan, "FUCK!" I look away from his beautiful face and watch as his come spurts out, thick and hot, surrounding my hands and his abdomen. I slow down and ease my grip, rubbing him softly now. His eyes are still closed, his head back, his face is flushed with heat, his chest dripping with condensation from the warm water. He looks magnificent. I gently move my hands away and massage his body, soothing him after such physical pleasure.

I take the cloth and clean him while he gets his equilibrium back. His eyes open and meet mine. I know that feeling, too — he gave me that last night.

"Today was about you," I repeat his words from last night back to him with a bright smile.

"Come here," he commands, his big hands gripping my hips as he drags me on top of his wet body. "I need to kiss you now," and he does. He kisses me like I'm the most delicious strawberry ice-cream sundae.

With the weekend almost over, I wake alone on Sunday morning. Jarrod had to leave yesterday for work, and very reluctantly departed after our sensual hot bath together. He was already late and had stayed to spend more time with me. I don't want to overthink it, but I get the feeling we are both in deep water.

I feel for my phone on the bedside table to check my messages and turn up the ringtone volume.

I have three text messages, one from Will, making sure I was well. I reply and let him know it's all good.

I answer Mel's angry, sweary text message — she obviously heard about the wanker who interviewed us on Friday night — and then one from Vivian, asking if I was free tonight: she is getting a group together to go out for drinks. She casually asks me to invite Will and my neighbour Anton with his partner Trey. I send her a text in response:

Sure Viv, I'm in. I will let the boys know, send me the details.

A minute later, my phone chirps; she has replied already.

YES! We are going to have so much fun, baby girl. She adds a link to a bar and I forward that to Will and Anton with the message:

Vivian is taking us out on the town tonight boys, get ready, and I press send.

I spend the rest of the day doing a quick clean and once-over around my flat. I skip the gym but end up doing some yoga on the sitting room rug, trying to make up for all the carbs on Friday night.

My phone starts to ring — no ringtone, it's a private number. "Hello?" I answer cautiously.

"Hi, Angel," Jarrod breathes deeply through the phone like he is doing something strenuous. "I'm in the gym now, and have some work to finish, then I will pick you up tonight, all right?" he asks me. I can hear music in the background.

"Yes, that's great. I wasn't sure if you were coming out tonight," I say, happy to hear that he is.

"Of course I am," he laughs like it was obvious. I haven't known him long enough to know his routine with work hours, and especially his routine with women. How often does he date? Hook up? See the same woman during the week? All these questions fly around my brain as I contemplate that.

"Can you fit Anton and his partner Trey in the car too? We may as well go together."

"Whatever you need just ask, your wish is my command, Brooklyn," he states, laughing lightly into the phone. It's nice to hear him laugh; he is usually quiet and brooding. Christopher is the extrovert in the family.

"Hmmm, then I'll have to think up a really extraordinary wish, Jarrod," I breathe out. "Send me your number, so I can save it in my contacts list."

"I'll do one better," he ends the call. What? Smart-arse. He hung up on me!

Next thing I know, a photo message comes through with a number, and I click to open the image.

I catch my breath. Jarrod sent me a photo of him lying down on rubber gym mats, ear pods in, bare chest covered with sweat and a huge wolf-like grin on his face. Fuck, my brain is fried.

I take a minute to look at him, glorious blue eyes laughing at me in the picture, black hair damp from his workout, hard body, one arm reaching out to take the photo and the other one resting on his taut abs. God, he is a Disney prince, with a bad-boy edge. I save the image. I'll be looking at that often — that smile is breathtaking.

It takes me a few minutes to respond, because shit, that photo messed me up. I lie down on my bed, my hair fanned out around me. I'm wearing my red yoga crop top and shorts. I reach over to my bedside table and open the top drawer, taking out a bright purple vibrator and holding it to my chest. I'm teasing him, I know, but I can't think after that image he sent me, and I want to shock him a little. Have some fun. I've never done this, ever!

I take the photo, one arm outstretched to show him a view of my body, and the other one holding the toy against my chest. My face is laughing at him in the picture. I press send and wait.

Five minutes go by, I begin to wonder if the photo was received. Then my phone starts ringing. I will have to set a song for him when I think of an appropriate one later, I smile at the thought.

"Hello?" I answer

"Brooklyn," he practically growls down the phone at me.

"Yes, Jarrod," I say innocently… trying not to laugh out loud.

"Christ, I had to walk out on my gym session. I'm harder than a fucking rock right now!" He takes a few deep breaths… "I don't think you comprehend the risk, tormenting me like that, Angel."

I smile to myself, his voice is doing all kinds of things to me. "I don't know what you mean, Jarrod. I'll see you tonight," and end the call. Let him deal with that, He does the same to me.

I jump out of bed and head into my wardrobe. My most pressing concern is, what the heck am I going to wear?

Chapter Ten

𝒦𝒜𝑅𝒜𝒪𝒦𝐸 𝒢𝒪𝒟

Tonight, at Anton's insistence, I dress seductively in a very short black leather skirt. I paired that with a set of hot red heels and a cropped band T-shirt. I put silver bangles on my wrists and wear large hoop earrings. I leave my hair in long waves, and my face fairly minimal except for the ruby-red lips. The bar we are going to looks a little rock and roll, so I chose to grunge it up tonight.

I spray my usual perfume, doing a little twirl, making sure it settles over my body. I walk into the bathroom and grab the vanilla body oil, applying it to my legs for a nice glow, remembering exactly what I was doing with that oil the morning before. Gosh, I'm never going to forget that memory of Jarrod, all hot and wet, coming over my hands, slick with vanilla body oil in the tub. I have to stop thinking about it, or I won't make it out the door tonight.

I hear knocking, and I open for Anton and Trey.

"Wowsers!" I say, checking them out. "You two look like the most delicious chocolate and vanilla ice-cream dessert I've ever seen. Yummy!" My eyes dance over them. I lean over and air kiss them both, careful not to mess up my lips.

"And you look like a naughty band groupie who is getting lucky on the tour bus tonight," Anton states with a huge grin, holding my arms out and inspecting my look for tonight.

"We'll see…" I quip back. "Come in, Jarrod is picking us up shortly. Have you been to this bar before?" I ask, and they both shake their heads.

"No, I've never heard of it, but I don't get out often, as you know," Trey states with a smile, looking so handsome in his casual jeans and shirt, smart modern glasses giving him a clean-cut businessman appeal.

"Well, Vivian chose the place, so it should be *Trè Chic*," I say in an exaggerated French accent. Just then, the buzzer sounds. I walk over and press the intercom. "We'll come down."

I hear Jarrod through the speaker, "Okay."

"Let's go, boys. It's fun time!" I say as we head out of my flat.

Jarrod is waiting downstairs, leaning back on his Mercedes-Benz, hands in his pockets. The very picture of male perfection. I need to get over it already; I can't keep being this affected, it's not normal. Black fitted jeans surround those strong legs, his usual black T-shirt hugging his body, black boots, and an expensive-looking watch on his wrist.

That face, with his black hair flicked to one side, like he was running his hands through it seconds ago, matches perfectly with his long eyelashes that give his ocean blue eyes a 'pretty boy' look. Those mesmerising eyes look up as we step out and he smiles, no wolf teeth this time, just lips.

"Oh, Honey Bee, you are fucked tonight. I mean that figuratively and literally — just look at that specimen!" Anton whispers loudly to me. I'm not sure if Jarrod heard, but I don't think I care, because my brain is mush.

Trey coughs into his hand, trying to hide his laugh, and I suspect Anton was not as quiet as he intended.

Jarrod takes a minute to check me out, his eyes travel over my body, my legs, the bare strip of exposed stomach, my face, and finally my red lips.

He closes his eyes, still leaning on the car, and throws his head back, breathing out a puff of air into the night. "I'm dead," he states, then looks back in my direction. He straightens and walks towards me.

"Yes, peach, you are. But remember to tread lightly, she is precious." Anton walks up and taps him on the shoulder. Jarrod nods and turns around to open the car doors for us.

I smile at him as I bend down to get into the passenger side, his eyes on me the whole time.

We make general chit-chat on the way to the bar, Trey telling Jarrod about his work at the legal firm. He seems very interested in what area of legal Trey works in.

We arrive at the venue and find a parking spot just a few doors down. As I exit the car, Jarrod takes my hand, linking our fingers, and walks with me to meet the others at the front of the bar.

I look down at our entwined hands and back at him. OK, then, he's a hand-holder. It's sending a message to the others, I can feel it. As we get close, I spot Christopher talking to Will, Vivian by his side, and three other people I've never met.

Two guys, probably Christopher's age, mid-twenties, and a very attractive brunette. Come to think about it, she looks familiar, and I recognise her from Jarrod's birthday party. She was the woman trying to get his attention while I was singing.

As we arrive, all eyes turn to us. I look to Will first, his eyes catching mine, then he glances down, seeing my hand entwined with Jarrods. Jarrod gives me a little squeeze, and I look over at him, not sure what he is trying to convey, but I just smile, and we share a silent moment between us. All right, I'm doing this.

Vivian lets out a squeal and rushes over to give me a big hug. "Bee, so glad you could make it; we are going to have a bloody entertaining night," she says happily. "And you look... flaming hot, I might add." Her eyes roam over my outfit. She is a stylist, after all; of course, she notices all the little details.

"And you, my pretty woman, look spectacular yourself, Vivian. Edward would be sporting a massive stiffy for sure," I say with smiling eyes, and she cracks up laughing, getting my *Pretty Woman* pun. What can I say, I have a thing for old movies, especially romance.

Vivian is wearing a red dress, fitted in all the right places, stretchy material, with small cap sleeves and a round neckline. She may not have the boobs I have, but she has the legs, and they are on full display tonight. Her hair is pulled back into a sleek ponytail with just her fringe out, it floats above her eyes. She looks stunning. Her olive skin looks so tanned against the red of her dress.

She leaves me to greet the others and I let go of Jarrod's hand to give Will a big hug. He lifts me off the ground and does a little spin, before putting me back down gently. "Are you well, Honey Bee?" he whispers into my hair.

"Yes. Promise," I say, and squeeze him. He leans over to shake hands with Jarrod, a silent look passing between them.

Christopher hugs me next, and then introduces me to the other guests. Jarrod steps back to my side and takes my left hand again, keeping it firmly locked in his. "Bee, these two tossers are my friends from University, Thomas and Henry." I shake their hands, their eyes appreciating me very conspicuously, I note. Christopher gives them both a light punch on the shoulder. "That's enough," he tells them, and they complain, but remain smiling.

"Bee, this is Henry's sister Elizabeth," he says by way of introduction, and I hold my hand out to be polite. Elizabeth is a very attractive brunette, my height, with long wavy locks, brown eyes and a very lovely face. She is wearing a black dress with a gold belt around her waist, black sandals and a few gold rings on her fingers.

She takes my hand briefly, eyes looking over my face like she is looking for some kind of flaw. "Nice to meet you, Elizabeth," I say.

She murmurs "Hello," and then her eyes immediately slide to Jarrod. "Jarrod, I'm so glad you came tonight," she gushes, putting a hand on his shoulder and leaning over to kiss him on the cheek. He doesn't move, he just stands there. "I haven't seen you since your birthday party; that was such fun, wasn't it?" her hand remains on his arm. "We had a little too much to drink, didn't we?" she adds and then looks at me with a smirk on her face. Finally, that hand drops from his body and I relax. I'm not a jealous person by nature, but that was blatant bitchiness on a platter.

They totally fucked, I know the look she is giving him. The 'I want to fuck your brains out again' look.

"My party was sensational because this Angel sang for me," he says, squeezing my hand. I look at him and catch his blue gems watching me and smile. I'm not here to get into a bitch fight tonight, I want to enjoy myself.

Vivian speaks up loudly to get our attention. "Everyone, we have a table booked, we can all head inside now." We turn around and go through the front door after a security guard removes the rope for us to walk in. As we enter, the heat hits me, warm bodies, music, noise, and the smell of alcohol in the air.

I look up and see a stage with a large screen. What the fuck? "Is this a Karaoke bar, Viv?" I ask over the noise.

Anton cracks up laughing behind me, as Trey is having a panic attack. "OH MY GOD, no way! I'm not getting on that stage!" he shouts to Anton. The look of absolute terror on his face makes me laugh.

I look over to Jarrod. "Did you know?" I ask, and he shakes his head.

"I had no idea," but strangely he doesn't look panicked. He doesn't seem the type to get up and sing in front of all these people, so maybe he is chill because he will just sit back and watch everyone else embarrass themselves.

We find a huge booth, with bench seats surrounding a round table in the centre. Jarrod moves me before him, and I sit next to Will, who has Vivian on his other side.

Anton and Trey slide in next to Jarrod, while Elizabeth slides in next, her face sour, probably because she is quite a distance from Jarrod; then Christopher and the boys take the final places. Vivian waves the waiter over, giving everyone drinks menus.

"What would you like to drink, Brooklyn?" Jarrod murmurs to me over the music, his warm hand moving to my bare thigh, just resting it on my leg. I feel the connection immediately. I am surprised he is so affectionate in public; I didn't expect him to be, but maybe he is showing a certain someone that he is unavailable.

"Umm, I'll have a gin and tonic, fresh lime," I answer, looking at the drinks menu. I'm not fussy.

"Good choice. I'll have the same." Jarrod and everyone else order drinks and we sit back and watch the show. Music pumping, coloured lights criss-crossing the room, it's an elegant-looking place, not like the usual dive bar you would expect for Karaoke. We chat over the table, laughing at the performances on stage. God, they are funny fuckers. Some great voices — you know they come here to impress — and others so awful you just have to clap them for courage alone. Liquid courage, mostly.

After about an hour, we are all feeling the drinks, and Anton stands up. "OK, let's do this, motherfuckers," he says loudly and kisses Trey as he walks towards the stage.

Christopher is jumping out of his seat, watching and laughing as Anton dances his way over, looking every bit the professional he is. "This is going to be good," Trey says and smiles at me. He knows Anton has a decent voice; he does sing for some stage performances when required, he's the whole package.

"Are you going to sing, Bee?" Vivian asks me over her drink.

I shake my head. "I don't think I should. I'll let you all take the stage tonight," I tell her.

The table breaks out in shouts of "No way!" and "Come on", Christopher stands up and points his finger in my face. "No way, Bee, I'm getting my payback for that ringtone incident," he practically yells at me.

"I'm choosing a song for you," he states with an evil grin on his face, evil but adorable nonetheless.

"Oh shit, Brooklyn, you poked the bear!" Jarrod laughs next to me.

I turn to him and say, "If I go, then you go, Houston," and air kiss his lips, trying not to get red lipstick on his face.

His eyes are smiling, looking down at my red pout and back up to my sparkling eyes. "Sure," he answers, and my eyes widen.

"You are actually going to get on that stage," and I point over, "in front of everyone and sing?" my face hurts from smiling so hard. He just tilts his head and nods, giving my leg a squeeze under the table. OK then, I am suddenly very into this, I think as I take a sip of my drink.

Everyone starts yelling "Anton is on," and we all turn to the stage to watch him. Gosh, he looks amazing, wearing casual jeans, a fitted pink shirt, rolled up to the elbows, two buttons open for that hint of smooth chest, and glowing rich skin. You got this, my friend.

The music begins and Anton starts singing, dancing practised moves on the large stage. He chooses 'Raspberry Beret' by Prince, his vocals sounding great.

The crowd goes wild, people singing with him, dancing in front of the stage. He even hits the high notes well. We all stand up, dancing to Anton's performance. I'm having fun, Vivian is dancing, Will giving her side-eye looks, not making it too obvious. He catches my eye and we do a little dance together, as he spins me around.

The song ends and we clap like mad, Anton gives us a wave from the stage. Trey is beaming love eyes. "OK, Little Bee, it's payback time," Christopher says, holding out his hand to me.

I roll my eyes at him. "Seriously? What song?" I ask.

"It's a secret." He spits my words back to me, laughing. Fuck, I really did upset him with my ringtone.

Jarrod gives me a little nudge and I look over my shoulder. "I have faith in you, Angel," he kisses my cheek smiling.

"Fine, let's get this over with," I say, and take Christopher's hand. We make our way to the DJ booth, and Christopher whispers something to the guy, who looks at me and smiles, a thumbs up. Great, I think. I give Christopher the stink eye and walk over, next in line after the girl who is currently murdering a Madonna song.

When her song is over, I accept the microphone and walk up on stage. Shouts and whistles fill the room. I laugh, because they are probably getting an eyeful of red lace underwear: my short skirt was not a problem till now, I realise. I give a little curtsy, and wait for the song to pop up. I look over and blow a kiss towards our table.

I see the song choice, and the music starts, electric guitar screeching through the speakers before the drums kick in. Def Leppard's 'Pour Some Sugar On Me'... Oh, you're dead, Christopher! I shake my head.

"This one is for you, Christopher," I speak into the microphone and start dancing, my red heels clicking across the stage as I move my hips. The crowd goes crazy, people shouting at me from below. I get a clap going because this has to be the cheesiest thing I've ever done.

I start to sing. I'm working the room, pointing to the crowd, razzing them up, and the audience sings with me during the chorus. OK, I'm having more fun than I expected. Christopher is going down. I smile and keep singing: "Pour some sugar on me."

I look over to our table. Christopher is standing on the bench seat, arms in the air, singing and laughing. Everyone is on their feet, entertained I'm sure. Jarrod is standing there, toned arms linked behind his head, with a massive grin on his face, like he can't believe I'm actually doing it. I run my hands over my body, going full eighties rock star on them.

When the song is over, I'm literally out of breath. I give a bow, my hair flicking over my head, then back up. The crowd shouts as I head back over to the table. Will reaches me first, laughing so hard, hugging me. "Honey Bee, you smashed it!"

I just laugh. "You're next, big guy." I look to Vivian. "Make sure he gets up there," I say to her.

"Oh, I will," she takes his hand, leading him over to the booth with a smile.

Christopher gives me a sweaty hug, kissing my cheek. I think he has sucked down a few drinks by now. "Christopher, you arsehole, I can't believe you did that to me," I say in a huff… He is holding onto my shoulders.

"Bee! My god, that was the best thing I have ever seen… You killed it!" his face beams at me.

"Well, you better get up there tonight or I'm never speaking to you again," I threaten him.

"I will, don't worry, I have the perfect song to pull the ladies in… It's going to get me laid for sure," he says with that classic naughty grin. I just roll my eyes. The others congratulate me, telling me how well I sang.

Elizabeth remains silent, her face in a perpetual scowl. I see her mumble something to her brother, but he just shrugs.

Jarrod is staring at me, hands in his pockets, those eyes following my every move. As I reach him, he places his hands on my waist pulling me closer, I rest my hands on his chest as we share a moment. "Brooklyn," he breathes, his nose touching mine, "you consume me." I feel the heat and think, fuck the lipstick, Brooklyn, I kiss him. I kiss him like he is my favourite ice-cream, my favourite song, my favourite everything. I hear whistles as I slowly detach my mouth from his perfect face.

His eyes are like deep blue pools. It takes effort to turn around and see all the faces looking at us. *What?* I think. What is so strange about two people kissing in a bar? But they are staring at Jarrod like he has done something weird. "Why are they staring at you like that?" I ask and wipe his lips with my finger.

He looks back down at me and smiles. "Ah... because I never do this kind of thing," he shrugs.

I tilt my head. "Like kiss a girl in a Karaoke bar?" I ask, laughing.

He looks deep into my eyes and says, "Like turn up with a girl, hold hands, kiss in public, all of it... Never." He takes a breath to consider his words. "Before you... I ate out, I never brought the meal home, if you know what I mean." I just look at him. I understand what he is talking about, but why? "I told you, Brooklyn, I want more with you," he whispers, touching my face with his fingertips. I just nod, because what can I say…? I'm fucking gone.

Christopher starts to yell and we turn around. Will and Vivian are on the stage together, the song starts and I start clapping. Jarrod stands behind me, arms wrapped around my waist, a hand on my bare stomach, rubbing me as we sway to the music. The song they choose is 'I Want It That Way' by the Back Street Boys. Will's perfect pitch is carrying Vivian; she is pretty good, not a professional singer like Will, but she can hold her own in this song. Will sings the main verses and Vivian comes in on the chorus. The crowd singing with them is brilliant.

Everyone else takes turns up there, except Trey, who is happy to just spectate tonight. Anton gets up and does another number, crushing Madonna's 'Vogue' with all the moves to match. It was scintillating. I notice Elizabeth doesn't get on stage, either. Her sour face is constantly looking over at me. I do my best to ignore her.

I'm taking another sip of my cool drink when Christopher gets up on stage. "Here we go, he's such a wanker," Jarrod laughs behind me. I smile and clap, waiting to see what his 'I'm getting laid tonight' song is.

The music starts up and I burst out laughing. "Oh my god, you are kidding me! This is the song that gets him laid?" I crack up.

"Umm… he hopes it will. I don't think it actually works," Jarrod laughs.

Christopher starts playing air guitar when the music starts up, then switches to drum hands when the beat kicks in to AC/DC's 'You Shook Me All Night Long'. Oh Jesus, he is dancing, shaking his arse on stage, pointing at the ladies in the front row. He is cute, I'll give him that, his voice is not bad either; maybe he will take home a catch of the day with this song after all. We are all screaming and clapping for him. This young hotel heir, shaking his arse for the crowd and loving every second.

When he's finished, he gives us rock hands, then points to our table and drops the mic. As in a 'Mic Drop Moment'. Dickhead, but an adorable one at that. I think he downed about eight drinks to drum up the courage to perform with such confidence. Plus, he looks like a prince; I don't think the ladies would care if he was a bad singer. I giggle.

He comes back to the table, a huge grin on his face, and of course, we all tell him how amazing he was. Christopher sits, taking a few gulps from his drink to cool down. "Your turn, bro." He points at Jarrod, then towards the stage.

I do a little happy dance, my face breaking out in a huge smile. "Yeah, let's see what you got, Houston," I say, and smack him on the butt. Jarrod rolls his eyes at his brother and then gives me a peck on the lips. "Brooklyn, this one is for you, Angel," and he heads off towards the booth.

I watch him walk away with confident, carefree strides, and I wonder how he can be so cool under pressure.

We all know getting on stage and singing to a room full of people is nerve-wracking, even for us professionals.

"How bad will this be?" I ask Christopher, and he looks at me with a smirk on those pretty lips.

"Oh, Bee, you have no idea, do you?" he says, then looks back towards the stage. "Prepare yourself, my big bro is going to get mobbed after this" — and I wonder what the heck he is talking about.

The current singer finishes a torturous version of '500 Miles' by The Proclaimers, and Jarrod walks up to the mic. I move away from the table, more into the centre so I can see him properly. He takes the mic and speaks. "This is for Brooklyn," our eyes find each other in the crowd. The music starts playing, a familiar guitar riff, and I realise instantly what song this is: 'Iris' by the Goo Goo Dolls. It's one of my favourite songs ever. Released about twenty years ago, but still so relevant today. One of the most beautiful rock love songs ever written.

Jarrod starts singing, and I stand there stunned. Gobsmacked. Holy Fuck. I can't breathe.

The lyrics resonate across the room, straight to my heart. He sings about giving it all up just to touch her. He is willing to give up his own immortality to spend it loving her. It's intimate, it rips me open for all to see.

Jarrod's eyes never leave mine: oceans of blue sparkling under the stage lights, making him look angelic, like he is some kind of archangel on earth. His voice is luminous, husky, perfect pitch; he sounds like a professional singer in a band, his voice carrying through the room. Fuck, he is technically better than John Rzeznik, lead singer of the Goo Goo Dolls.

My mouth hangs open the whole time. With his black hair, black clothes, and stunning face, he looks like he belongs on stage. And he is singing to me, looking at me, consuming me.

Christopher and Anton appear at my side, watching my face closely.

"Christopher..." I breathe out in a whisper.

"I know, Bee, talent like that is wasted at our hotel," he says with a sad tone and squeezes my hand before he walks back to the table.

"Honey Bee, I was wrong about him. I thought he was like all the others, but..." Anton trails off; no words can convey what is happening here.

"Girl, if you don't tap that tonight, I might have a crack," he continues, making me almost choke on my drink before he walks off.

Jarrod finishes the song with roaring applause. Yes, every female in a ten-mile radius was orgasming to his voice. I think I saw a pair of panties thrown at him. Jarrod takes a bow and walks off the stage. Christopher's prediction comes true, because he is absolutely mobbed by women as he tries to get back to me, trying to be polite, but not stopping. He looks up and his eyes hold me in place with just a look.

"He just wants to fuck you; he won't love you." I turn around like a whip to see Elizabeth standing behind me with a nasty smirk on her face.

"Because that's what he did to you? And now you can't get over him?" I answer back, her face turning red, she looks at me with such hatred and storms off.

I take a deep breath and shake it off. What a cow.

Jarrod finally reaches me and I pull him close, looking up into his face, taking my own mental snapshot of him in this moment, I breathe into his mouth, "Jarrod you consume me." I give his own words back to him.

"Stay with me tonight," I say — knowing he understands exactly what I'm asking. No more words are necessary, then he kisses me like I'm his favourite song in the world. The kiss leaves me beyond doubt, the answer is yes.

Chapter Eleven

NO GOING BACK

The night out is a hit. I think we all enjoyed hanging out and having fun: no work, no responsibilities. Even Will looks like he had a great time. He is usually more of a quiet reserved guy.

Christopher and his friends leave to dance and peruse the banquet of beautiful women in attendance. I don't think his stage performance of 'You Shook Me All Night Long' has much to do with his success; rather, it would be the fact that he is a stunningly gorgeous man with a bright smile and charisma in spades. I doubt very much Jarrod and Christopher have to try hard in that department anyway. Jarrod sticks to me like Velcro the whole night, effective enough to keep the bevy of hot, willing women circling him at a distance.

Elizabeth is left at the table on her own, not talking to anyone and stewing in her own jealousy. I ignore her, and much to her chagrin, so does Jarrod. When it is time to leave, somewhere around two a.m., she decides to make one last effort to get Jarrod's attention. The boys had ditched her earlier, most likely not sleeping in their own beds tonight.

"Jarrod, I need a lift home; you can take me." She tries for a seductive note, but it comes out whiny.

Jarrod holds my hand as we walk outside towards the street, the others chatting away and following behind. "Apologies, Elizabeth, my car is full, but I'm sure Vivian can be of assistance," he says, giving her a firm stare.

She pouts, letting out a huff of breath, her eyes sliding over to me with deadly hatred. God, what is wrong with some women, why such hostility towards me? I don't even know her, but I guess I have what she so badly wants.

Jarrod pulls Vivian aside and has a word with her. I don't know what he says, but I think, regardless of his feelings for Elizabeth, he is still making sure she will get home safely. Vivian just nods, not exactly jumping for joy at the cause, but she doesn't argue. Will hails a taxi for the three of them, coming over to give me his big warm bear hug, the hug that makes me feel safe and loved.

"Did you have fun tonight, Honey?" he asks me, caramel eyes sparkling at me.

"I sure did," I say, smiling up at him. To anyone who doesn't know us, we might look like a couple in love, but it isn't like that. It is the love of a person who has known my worst pain and heartbreak, yet thinks I am still the strongest person he knows, Will is my rock.

"You looked happy tonight, Bee. I love seeing you happy, it's everything," he kisses the top of my head before letting me go.

"I... am, I think. I feel happy," I wonder why that feels so strange to admit but good at the same time. "Now go, and I'll see you Wednesday for rehearsal and dinner," I say, letting him go. I turn to hug Vivian and she, still looking fresh and amazing after hours of sweaty singing and dancing, gives me a genuine firm squeeze back.

"Thank you for this, Viv. I needed a night out, away from work," I say, still holding her hands.

"I'm so glad, Bee. I couldn't be happier to have met you; having another female around the Houston dulls some of the testosterone if you know what I mean," she smirks. "And... it makes me happy to see Jarrod so confounded over you... He doesn't know what hit him, literally."

I blush and have no comeback to that. I don't know if Jarrod is acting any different than he normally does; I take it from the looks tonight that maybe he isn't behaving as he usually would. Vivian heads over to the waiting taxi and waves goodbye to everyone.

We lost Christopher and his friends a while ago, and now it is just the four of us left. The drive back to my flat is a little more subdued than earlier: I think Anton and Trey have hit their party limit, looking tired in the back seat.

"Anton, your performance of 'Vogue' tonight was incredible. I hope it goes viral tomorrow. I saw so many people in the audience recording it," I say as I look back at him. He is holding Trey's hand in the back seat, sitting close and comfortable together.

"Honey, I'm Madonna's love child; that shit better be trending like a Kardashian sex tape tomorrow," he replies, and we all crack up laughing. Anton is bold, unapologetic and utterly unique. I love this man.

As we pull up to the building, my nerves start to kick in. I know it's been a while, and that's natural, but this feels different, surreal, like I am in some kind of strange dream. It feels more important, more intense, something... just *more*.

Jarrod parks his sleek car and we all exit. I have been avoiding looking at him for most of the car ride, just to tame the nerves a little. Anton and Trey give Jarrod a handshake and thank him for the lift. He murmurs a quiet "It's my pleasure," and the boys head into the building. Before he closes the door, Anton turns around, watching my face, waiting for a heartbeat to check I'm OK, and then winks and pulls Trey up the stairs.

I'm really starting to question my bold statement from earlier now, but I know I do want this, whatever this is...

"Brooklyn, look at me." The softly spoken words tug at my heart, and I finally swing my eyes to his deep blue depths. "We don't have to do this tonight. I can wait until you are ready" — just that comment alone takes the edge off, making me finally take a breath for the first time since we left the bar.

He takes my hands in his, linking them together. I'd normally wait longer before getting so intimate, but Jarrod is *sui generis* — unique, unequalled.

"No," I say, my eyes watching his, "I do; I'm just nervous." I let out a shaky laugh... "I'm not um... I haven't had a lot of partners, if you know what I mean," I say, embarrassment tingeing my cheeks pink, and I curse my fair complexion for always flushing my emotions for all to see.

"I don't care about that, Brooklyn, that's not what this is about," he says, tucking a piece of hair behind my ear. He is being so patient and tender with me, it's almost like he knows my past, like he knows I'm damaged and he needs to be gentle.

"What is it about?" I ask him earnestly. "Because I'm… I'm complicated when it comes to sex, and I don't want to get into something if you can't handle that. I need a connection," I do need to make it clear. I think he did hear me the other times I've mentioned casual sex doesn't work for me, but I give him one last chance to bail.

Jarrod smiles at me, that adorable, hot, wolf-like smile that stops my breath as he kisses my mouth. A full lips, tongue, wet, hot, panty-melting kiss that makes me think I've swallowed a potion from Professor Horace's classes in *Harry Potter*. Some weird concoction that will wear off eventually and it will all be a dream.

"Brooklyn, I can handle complicated, and I'm pretty sure you can feel the connection we have together," he says, smiling at me, holding my face now so that I can't look away. "I want this… I want you," and those eyes give me no room for privacy; the intensity is rolling off him and right into me, I have no escape. He speaks to me without words. I can feel his intentions, as strange as that sounds.

"Jarrod," I barely whisper, taking a deep breath, and placing my hands over his on my face, "will you stay the night?"

"Yes," he kisses me gently, like feathers over my lips. I take his hand and we head inside.

We enter my flat and I tap the wall lights on low. It's almost three a.m. now, and even though my nerves are still there, I don't feel as shaky as I did earlier.

"Would you like a sparkling water? Wine?" I ask as we enter.

"Water is fine, thank you," he answers, and that gives me something to do with my nervous hands.

I pour two glasses and we sip in silence at the kitchen island. I try to read him, but I can't. He seems to read me so easily; it's like he can hear my thoughts.

He takes my drink, places it on the countertop, and pulls me to him slowly. I want him to take the lead: I have no idea how to start this, and I want him to show me.

He walks us to my bedroom. He has slept here before, but this is different, this is taking the next step. To where I'm not sure yet, but it feels right.

Jarrod sits on my bed, looking like a large black-clad divine being, watching me silently as I take off my jewellery and place it on my vanity table.

"Give me a minute?" I ask, and he nods, as I head into the bathroom. I take a much-needed breath, just looking at myself in the mirror. 'Stop being a nervous kitten, Brooklyn,' I say to myself. I'm not one to panic in my everyday life, but sex, and physical intimacy, intimidate me, especially the first time with someone.

I have worked hard over the years to shake that fear and anxiety from my past, but it still creeps in occasionally. It's something you never forget, you can never erase. I just hope I am good enough for Jarrod, I hope I don't disappoint him in any way; but I don't want to linger on negative thoughts. I take my make-up off, gently rub my face cream in, and then spray floral rose water on my face and body, hydrating me after a night of drinking and dancing.

I walk back into my bedroom and find Jarrod still sitting on the bed, his boots off to the side, looking all casually perfect and calm. Ahh... how can he be so serene when we are about to do the deed...? Which makes me laugh... Do the deed... Knock boots, funny business, hanky-panky... How many euphemisms can I think of to say? We are actually about to fuck. Yes, I'm going to have mad hot sex with Jarrod Houston in my bed!

"What's so funny, angel?" he asks me with a quizzical smirk on his face, taking my hands and pulling me between his long legs.

"I was just thinking you look so calm and confident, and I'm over here like a dork in gym class," I say, and we both laugh.

"Trust me, you are definitely not a dork." He kisses my hands as he stands up. He takes my top and slides it over my head, then sits down on the bed again to unzip my leather skirt, letting it fall to the floor, leaving me in my red lace underwear.

"Fuck, Brooklyn, you are definitely not in dork territory wearing red lace underwear and those heels," he exclaims, looking me over as I step out of the skirt. I kick my very sexy shoes off to the side and let him look his fill, because, frankly, I'm totally going to be doing the same thing to him in a few seconds.

He runs his hands over my body, my hips, my stomach, and the tops of my thighs as if he needs to feel me everywhere. He pulls me closer, running his face over my stomach, back and forth, breathing me in. Then he starts kissing me, and holy hell… everywhere his kisses land goose bumps erupt, he's heating my skin like a furnace.

His hands smooth over my back, then slide down, cupping my lace-clad arse with firm pressure. I place my hands on his broad shoulders because I'm not sure I can stand on my own with him doing this to my body.

"God, you're beautiful," he says into my stomach, kissing his way up to my chest. His eyes look up and hold mine; I'm totally lost in them like I can jump into pools of dark water. Holding my gaze he takes my nipple into his mouth, right through my lace bra. My breath hitches, making me hold him tighter. I moan, and that's all it takes. Jarrod stands up and starts to remove his clothes like they are a barrier that needs to be removed urgently. His top is first, leaving his tan-toned chest and hard stomach on full display. I try to touch him now, but he keeps going, unbuttoning his black jeans and dropping them to the floor.

My breathing accelerates, looking at him like this, dressed in only his black boxer shorts that bluntly stretch around his very sizeable erection, barely containing his equipment in the soft material.

He bends down and takes something out of his pocket and then places it on the side table next to my bed. I look over and realise they are condoms. Yes, we are doing this now, Jarrod Houston is going to get naked with me, and why haven't I fainted already?

His body is created like a marble statue, it deserves to be worshipped. You can tell he puts in hours at the gym: he is all hard muscle and soft skin.

Jarrod puts his hands on my back, and I feel my bra come loose.

I let it slip down my arms, then drop to the floor. We are even now, just the underwear left on. "Come here," he practically growls at me, the wolf is not hiding any more, he is ready to pounce.

He bends down and lifts me, like I weigh nothing, and places me on the bed, then covers me with his body, warm, hard, he swoops in taking my mouth in a hot kiss.

I don't know how long we kiss, I don't even know if you can call it kissing; he uses his whole body to consume me while his mouth does the work. I don't think I am even breathing at this point.

My hands explore his bare back, feeling the firm muscles, and the smooth skin. I feel him press harder against me, grinding his body into mine with heavy pressure. I can't stop kissing him; even if I was drowning and needed to come up for oxygen, I wouldn't move my mouth away, I let my hands traverse the shape of him. Delving down into his shorts, I feel his naked arse, feel him flexing as he moves. This feels amazing. I'm so heated, that I can feel the perspiration dampening our skin already.

Jarrod moves to the side, a hand skimming over the front of my lace underwear. He keeps kissing me, sucking on my lips, my tongue, like he can't get enough. Suddenly, he is gone, and my body feels a cool wash of air as he sits up. He watches my eyes as he slowly takes the sides of my lace underwear and drags them down my legs. They end up on the bed, or the floor, I don't know where, but I'm totally bare for him now, and his eyes roam over my body with heated lust and need.

He gently opens my legs with his firm hands, giving himself a full view of my most intimate parts. I don't cover myself, because, well, he had his face right in there recently. I lie still and wait for him to make the next move. Just watching him look at me like this is getting me even wetter, while the awe and admiration on his face shakes me up inside.

He lies down on the bed next to me, one hand under his head, like he is casually modelling for an underwear commercial, all sexy and patient. I'm practically panting like a dog, and he is Mr Cool.

The other hand starts at my neck, making circles and touching me lightly, heading down my chest. I watch him, waiting for his next move. He flicks his eyes up to me, giving me blue flames, and I'm about ready to combust.

His hand keeps going, circling my nipples, his eyes tracking the movements. Jarrod is slowly torturing me with every touch down my body, swirling around my stomach and heading south. I feel him taking deeper breaths now, the closer he gets to my wet heat, his chest moving with every breath he takes.

When he makes it to the final destination, he touches me so reverently, so softly, I break. I moan, my eyes closing; my breath holds and I can't even think. I feel him slowly slip a finger into my body, not all the way, but just enough that he feels me, how wet I am. And he moans, leaning over to take my mouth in a hot, luscious kiss.

"Fuck, you are so hot, so wet and ready for me, Angel," he whispers into my mouth. I can't answer; I just lift my hips for more and he responds by sinking a long finger into me, palm hitting my clit, rubbing at the same time that he pushes into me, in and out, slowly, but with purpose. I can't stop the whimpers I make, I can't stop my ragged breaths. I'm going to come with just this, just him kissing me like I'm a fantasy, and his expert fingers pumping into me.

"Fuck, I have to taste you again. I've been thinking of nothing else all night," he sighs as he takes his hand away. I feel lost; I was so close, and my moan of disapproval must have been louder than I thought, because he gives a short laugh as he drags my hips down the bed, placing his shoulders in between my thighs.

"Don't worry, Angel, I'm going to give you what you need" — and he does! His hot mouth comes crashing down on me, like a tsunami on the beach, way too powerful to stop. I grab his hair and hold on. I don't even know how hard I'm gripping him, but I can't help it; his mouth is killing me in every way, sucking on my clit, making it so sensitive and raw, tongue lapping at my opening, delving into taste me like he wants to have me for dessert.

I can't take it. My thighs tremble, my hands move to his shoulders and I feel my nails rake against his skin. Jarrod groans, the vibration moving up into my core, and I explode.

"Holy... FUCK... I can't..." I can't open my eyes, my body convulsing like it just exploded from the inside... I turn my face into the pillow, biting down to ride out the most powerful orgasm of my life.

He is still kissing me there, softly now, letting me come back to reality, but not taking his mouth off me just yet. I shiver, trying to relax my legs and feet so they don't cramp, and my muscles start to loosen again.

Jarrod moves up my body, leaving a trail of kisses as he goes. "That was the most beautiful thing I've ever seen... you shattering like that," he says, kissing me with that luscious mouth that just worked me into a mind-blowing orgasm to end all orgasms.

I smile. "You are beautiful," I hope he likes that because my brain is fried and I'm in orgasm heaven right now. His blue orbs penetrate my emerald ones, and he stares at me for what feels like minutes, just watching me, as if he can see all my secrets in there. Then, still keeping his eyes on mine, he leans in to kiss me, a kiss that tells me everything: he wants me, he desires me, but more… like he is going to hold me, keep me forever.

Jarrod leans over to the bedside table and brings a wrapper to his mouth and tears off the top. He pushes his boxer shorts down and kicks them off, then rolls the condom on his very hard, very ready, very enormous erection. I clench in anticipation. I will be feeling this for days, no doubt.

He moves over my body, holding his weight on his toned arms as his eyes return to mine. He doesn't ask for permission, he once told me that, but he can see that I'm ready, that I want this; he reads me like no one else can. I widen my legs to take his hips in invitation, and he smiles, like I am giving him the best ice-cream flavour on the menu. I smile back and trace his face, and his lips with my finger. "I want you," I whisper, I really do.

"You're mine, Brooklyn," he whispers back leaning in to take my mouth with his. I feel his body drop to mine, hard and ready at my entrance now, wanting to slip into my heat.

Jarrod flexes as he enters me slowly, just a bit, he takes in a sharp breath, holding there for a second as his eyes close and he stops kissing me. I let him take his time, not moving, and then he opens his eyes and they lock onto mine as he pushes in all the way. I gasp, because he fills me so much, like there is no more room in there. So complete.

Jarrod lets out a low groan, his body tightening and flexing as he holds himself inside. "Brooklyn, fuck, you are so tight, so hot… I'm losing my mind." He starts to move, his body withdrawing from mine and sliding back in, right to the end. I feel a tiny tinge of pain as he pushes in all the way, but then it's gone, my body adjusting to his size.

Jarrod leans down to kiss me and I can't take it. I move my hips up to meet his every thrust, I kiss him and attempt to breathe at the same time, he is stealing every particle of air I have. This connection, whatever it is we have, is taking over. I grab his tight, firm arse and I pull him closer with every thrust, he uses one arm to hold himself up and the other lifts mine above my head.

Entwining our fingers in a firm grip, he holds me there and pumps harder, his breath fanning my face. Our eyes lock, and I watch the emotions on his, he can't hide in this raw moment for both of us, I shatter again, with him looking right into my eyes, so personal, so private, I can't look away. I know I can't hold back with Jarrod, whatever comes out of my throat is carnal.

My body grips his: I can feel it pulsing and squeezing him as he rubs himself against me. He takes my other hand, holding both now in his tight grip, and he lets go, thrusting so hard, like he can't stop what his body needs. His mouth smashes down on mine, bruising my lips a little, but it's a good pain. His hips slam into me, and then he breaks. God, what a beautiful sight. Head thrown back, inky black hair around his perfect face, cheeks flush, and those soft pouty lips open as he comes inside me with a deep growl ripped from his throat.

We are both breathing heavily now. Jarrod dips his head down, touching his forehead to mine, breathing the same air as we recover from the high... from the magic of whatever just happened between us. Because, holy fuck, that was some kind of experience. I've never had sex like that before, I've never felt someone inside me like he's part of me. It's kind of unbelievable and incredibly mind-blowing all at once.

I don't want him to leave me just yet, so I squeeze his hands in mine. His eyes open and search my face, and we just stare at each other for a moment. This is the way we communicate: no words can even come close to what that was. I know he feels it, I can see it in his eyes. He leans down to kiss me, so gently, with so much emotion behind it.

Jarrod slowly withdraws from me. I know he has to discard the condom, but I wanted him to stay in me longer. He rolls over to dispose of it in my bin and comes back to me, holding himself over me.

"Brooklyn, you amaze me. That was.... Fuck, I don't know what to say," and I get the most beautiful smile I've ever seen on a face before. Awe, shock, maybe astonishment. His midnight eyes observe my own reverence on display.

"You amaze me, too, Jarrod. Thank you... Thank you for giving me something to erase all the bad memories, because now I have something so much better, something beautiful," I say as I feel a tear slide down my cheek.

"Brooklyn," he whispers, his fingers tracing that tear as he holds me, his large warm body encasing me like a cocoon, his face in my hair, his chest to my chest, and I feel like I'm finally healed.

Chapter Twelve

NEW BEGINNINGS

A solid weight contains my thighs and a warm finger traces the lines and symbols down my bare back. My face is buried in my fluffy pillow, sunlight softly glowing in from the window. I breathe in deeply and exhale: his scent is all over my bed.

"What do they mean?" he murmurs into my neck as he moves my hair away and kisses me there. I have a feeling of *déjà vu*... Have I been in this dream before?

"Mmmm, coffee," I mumble into the pillow. His hand and mouth touching me, both relaxes me and burns me at the same time.

"Soon, I promise," he whispers, while he keeps up his gentle assault.

"Rune means a secret thing, or something mysterious," I tell him, my voice husky, as I feel those soft warm lips move to my ear lobe and he starts sucking. Jesus, I can't think.

"But what do these Runes mean?" he asks again, continuing to slowly and gently render me speechless with his hands and lips.

"Well, Jarrod, it wouldn't be secret or very mysterious if I told you," I feel his leg shift over, and then his whole body is sitting on mine as he traces the tattoos I have. I hate that he stopped kissing me, sucking me. I was enjoying that, but he begins to gently massage my back and shoulders, firm warm hands exploring me.

"I've wanted to do this since I saw your naked back at the exhibition," he tells me. I'm a little shocked at his honesty, and openness about his thoughts. "You drive me crazy, do you know that?" he continues, and I close my eyes and just breathe for a few seconds. He is working his way over my back slowly, and I feel like I can't escape him, his smell, his body, his words attacking my brain, and I'm not ready for this onslaught — I haven't even had my coffee!

"I think you're too much for me, too much everything," I answer because I don't know how to convey this with words. He doesn't respond, but I know he is thinking about my comment. I give him what he wants, what he asked me earlier, just to change the subject.

"They are symbols and depictions of the Aesir Gods; they are considered the heroic or 'Good' Pantheon in Norse religion.

I continue as his hands explore me, "The one that looks like a letter P is Thorn or Thauris. It's a Rune for protection and luck, but also reminds me to pay attention and be cautious. I need to know my strengths and weaknesses." I take a breath to think about my answer… "To consider what I can do to change any circumstance, even if it means walking away from a situation because if I continue living in it, the problem could destroy me."

I feel like this is the most adept Rune that symbolises my life. It gives me some kind of spiritual protection. I did exactly that, I gained strength from somewhere to change my circumstances and be brave and strong. Start over.

"That's all you're getting today. I haven't had my morning coffee yet," I say, and laugh to lighten the mood.

Jarrod laughs. "I did notice you're not a morning person, Brooklyn... Maybe we could change that?" I feel him lean in kissing my back, his hands sweeping up my arms to grip my hands.

"Never, but good luck trying," I breathe, and feel my heart beat faster: I'm getting hot.

Jarrod is not talking now; he is covering me with his whole body, I feel his erection on my naked arse, firm and warm and ready. Oh god. I clench my legs together to stop the sudden tingling happening there.

"Are you sore Angel? I'll be gentle this morning," he tells me as he grips my right thigh and pushes my leg up, bending from the knee. "I want you just like this. I want to come on this beautiful back, Brooklyn," he whispers into my hair. And fucking hell, my body just responds to him like melted marshmallow over flames.

I don't answer with words. He can tell by the response my body is giving that I'm right there with him. I move my arms up to grip the wrought iron of my vintage bed frame as his fingers start to explore, he barely touches me and I'm already open and wet.

"Oh god," I whisper into the pillow; this is not how I usually wake up in the mornings, I think, with a hot, hard, blue-eyed stunner pushing his fingers into me, smothering me with his body in the best way. I feel him leave me for a moment and then I hear the tear of foil, and a few seconds later he is back, gripping my hands on the bed frame, holding me while I hold myself ready for him.

He flexes his hard body and enters me in a smooth full thrust, I gasp, my back arching as he fills me. It's so deep in this position, my knee bent up, opening me to him. "Fuck, Brooklyn, you feel so good," he says, holding himself in me fully, grinding into me without withdrawing, trying to push as much of himself in me as he can.

I close my eyes and concentrate on feeling and breathing. My body pushes back into his and I hear him growl into my hair... he likes that. I just feel like I have to push against him, and the friction is driving me mad. Jarrod starts to thrust now, slow and measured long strokes, in and out, driving me crazy. I'm not sure how long we do this for, slowly, sensually, and I moan; it's creeping up on me, that feeling he gives me, and I push my body harder against his, my grip firm on the bed frame gives me leverage.

One hand leaves mine as he takes my bent leg, holding my thigh and pushes it up even higher, his strokes and thrusts getting faster now and hitting that spot — fuck, that perfect spot — and I let go. I combust, my hands white-knuckled on the frame, my arse pushing up to get as much of his hardness as possible, and I bite down on my pillow as the orgasm takes me over the edge. I feel so free; it's never been so good for me before, this trust.

I hear his breathing change; he is holding me so tight now, but I don't care, I'm not scared or fearful at all: I trust him to know what I can take. My body gripping his from the inside, throbbing and squeezing him, I had no idea it could feel like this. He gives me a couple of hard pumps and then he pulls out, leaning over me; the hand on my thigh is gone, and I feel wet, liquid spreading over my lower back in hot spurts.

"Fuuuuckkk," he breathes out, his hand moving up and down his length, spilling every last drop onto my back.

I try to breathe in slowly and control my body because it was not mine in the moment, it was his.

Jarrod slumps down next to me, his heavy weight gone, but he keeps one leg over my spread thighs, one hand on my backside, stroking up and down. We lay like this for a few minutes, just the sound of our slow panting filling the room.

When I can speak again, I say, "Well, maybe if we do that more, I might be persuaded to wake up earlier." And he lets out the biggest belly laugh I've heard him give so far, which makes me smile.

Jarrod kisses my head as he gets up. "That can be arranged," he says with a breathy chuckle.

"I'm going to shower with you now, then make you that coffee you so badly need," and suddenly I'm lifted into strong arms and carried into the bathroom. Yes, I think, I could get used to mornings like this.

Jarrod leaves me around three p.m. to head home, kissing me senseless at my door, telling me that he'd see me soon. I believe him. I don't think any of what is happening between us is 'casual' or uncertain at all. I think he does want something more. It scares me, I won't lie to myself, but I need to see where this goes. I'm ready for my life to open up and let him in.

I take a nana nap in the afternoon because, well, I'm fucking exhausted: late-night Karaoke, singing, drinking, dancing, then the best sex of my life with Mr Blue-eyed Rock Star himself. He performs like he was made for the stage, and I'll never get that visual out of my mind: on stage, his eyes penetrating me from across the room, singing to me with his husky, gritty, sexy voice.

He could get a band together tomorrow and tour the world with that face and those vocals, his ocean eyes mesmerising every single person in the room... Then it hits me!

I grab my phone off the bedside table. I have the perfect song to set as his ringtone. It's a little personal, and revealing, but it's perfect. I smile to myself. I'll sing it to him one day.

I drag myself out of bed, dress in some comfortable clothes and head into the kitchen to make food. It's Margarita Monday bitches.

I arrive at Anton's door with a plateful of goodies. Vegetable frittata I whipped up because it's pretty much a veggie omelette and shit easy to make. I cut some fruit I had left over that needed to be used: bananas, apples, strawberries, and pears. My hands are full, so I tap his door with my Ugg boot. Anton answers in his basketball shorts and a tank top.

"Honey Bee!" he says, smiling. "Oh, that smells good; you're the best mistress a man could ask for," he takes a plate from my hands.

"Thanks, I'm not even wife material," I say, pouting with fake agitation.

"A straight man's wife, but a gay man's mistress... Meaning the other love of my life, but without the fucking," he says, cracking up, and I can't help it, I do, too.

"Shut up and get me my margarita, bitch," I give him a nudge into the kitchen.

Anton comes back to meet me on the couch, and hands me a fresh frozen limey sweet margarita. "Mmmm, I needed this," I say, as I take a nice cool sip. Anton taps on his phone and the light haunting sounds of an orchestra float over the speakers.

I recognise this one, it's 'The Dance of the Sugar Plum Fairy' from *The Nutcracker*. I saw Anton dance this show a couple of years ago. The song is constantly crescendo and decrescendo, a combination of a homophonic and polyphonic piece. So beautiful and magical. I listen for a minute with my eyes closed.

"So, Honey Bee... give it up. I've been waiting patiently."

I open my eyes and Anton is giving me his full attention, perfect eyebrow arched, waiting. I know what he means... he is talking about Jarrod.

"It's been two years since you got some action, I need details, and for the love of god, don't skimp baby," he takes a sip of his drink and gives me the megawatt perfect smile.

I roll my eyes, but I know I'll have to give him something. "Ahh…" I say in frustration. Where to start?

"He is…" — I take a deep breath — "not human Anton… I don't know what to do with all this chemistry, magnetic attraction… I can't describe it in words. He rocks my world."

"I bet he does, Honey, it's obvious how much he's into you; just seeing you together last night was freaking adorable," he gives me a gentle squeeze on the shoulder. "And that song, that voice, that body," he closes his eyes and makes kissy lips. I just giggle.

"Actually, he told me he doesn't usually do this, like date. I think he has casual sex and leaves it at that. He said he wanted more with me," I'm almost to the bottom of my drink. I lean over and take a piece of the still-warm frittata, nibbling my way through.

Anton takes one as well. "Oh, so good Bee, delicious," he says with his hand over his mouth, and I nod, because it's perfect.

"Now get to the sex; how good was it? No! Wait, I bet it was amazing! How big is his English sausage? Like eight, nine inches of prime British…"

"ANTON!" I cut him off, laughing. "You pervert," I say, and throw a pillow at his face. I try to smother him with one hand, the other holding onto my now-empty margarita glass.

Anton is killing himself laughing. "Honey, you have to give me something, the man's a dish!" he throws the pillow over the couch. He takes my glass and stands up to get refills. I blow my hair off my face with a puff.

"OK, OK... You know how nervous I can be, well, especially the first time with someone."

Anton nods at me; he knows my past, I opened up to him years ago over one of our first Margarita Monday sessions. "He better have been considerate and tender with you, or I'll have to kick his arse into next week. I don't care how fucking hot the guy is, I'll rip his balls off," he tells me seriously, and I take the drink he offers me as he sits down again.

"No need for arse kicking, I promise," I say, smiling as I take a sip. Anton appointed himself one of my protectors long ago, especially seeing we live next door to each other. Mel, Will and Anton are my self-appointed guardians.

"He was absolutely perfect. I mean, I was nervous, but he made me feel... beautiful and special. So gentle, well, mostly," I blush because I am feeling a tad sore tonight in all the right places.

Anton grins at me, wide-toothed and eyes sparkling. "Oh, I can imagine!" he says, fanning himself.

I grin back. "And... yes, he is fucking huge. He knows exactly what to do with that beast and hell, Anton, I had multiple orgasms, like earth-shattering, never-felt-before, volcanic eruptions. I think I cried the first time," I breathe heavily now, still in shock that I slept with the hottest guy on the planet; me, Brooklyn, I did that, and I'm definitely going to do that again, soon!

"Aww, Honey, that's beautiful; you deserve to be treated like a princess," he leans over to kiss me on the forehead. "And every princess deserves a massive dick to pleasure her for the rest of eternity..." he says, cracking up again. I just put my hands over my face to hide my telling eyes and pink cheeks.

I hear the speakers begin to play the theme from *Dirty Dancing*, 'Time Of My Life', and Anton stands up, holding out his hand to me. "Well, Honey, it's that time again; we need to get dirty," I stand up, kick off my Ugg boots and smile.

"I'd love nothing more, my Caribbean Prince," I say, as I take his hand and we dance all night. This has to count for cardio; between sex and dancing, surely I've reached my quota for the week.

I sleep like the dead Monday night, waking up Tuesday to check my emails and messages over my morning coffee ritual. I find one from Mel.

Hi, Little Bee,

Your turn to host family dinner night this Wednesday. I'll bring dessert because, seriously, I'm fucking over ice-cream.

Love your guts, Mel xx

I laugh, but we seriously need to talk; no one bags ice-cream on my watch, and I text back:

Hey, you can't bag the one true love of my life and get away with it. Revenge is a dish best served cold! [Devil face emojis]
Do you mind if I invite a couple of extras to dinner? Love, Bee

She replies immediately, the ever-efficient person she is.

Oh... This is interesting, and if it's who I think it is, then NO! I don't.. Will has tried to lock that vault, but he's no match for my prying ways. I hear a certain hotel mogul has been very attentive. I'll be the judge of that. Now I'm even more excited to come over, for more than your cooking.
See you Wednesday night, Bee. [Wink-wink and kiss emojis] *xx*

Oh god, this is all I need. Mel giving Jarrod the full inquisition. I send her one last reply.

Don't you dare! Be on your best behaviour PLEASE. [Praying hands emoji]
Don't bring dessert, I'll make apple crumble — to have WITH ICE-CREAM. [Middle finger emoji]

Hopefully, she behaves, but not likely, knowing Mel.

I send off a group text message to Mel and Simon, Will, Anton, Trey, Vivian, Christopher and Jarrod.

Hi, Everyone,
Family dinner night is @ my place this month. For the regulars, you know how it goes.
To the newcomers, I cordially invite you to our Inner Sanctum, the family dinner night. I'll cook, and you will eat, drink and enjoy the hospitality, telling me abundantly how great my cooking is!
Wednesday night, 7pm. RSVP when you can.
Love, Bee x

I press send. I'm kind of nervous: is it too much too soon for Jarrod? I'm not sure what he is comfortable with, how much time does he want with me during the week…? All these questions go through my head, making me rethink the invitation. 'Shut up, Brooklyn,' I tell myself, 'this inner monologue is not helping.'

I write myself a list, thinking about what to cook for dinner tomorrow night, and then I head out to do the grocery shopping. That way, I can be prepared to start cooking after rehearsal with Will in the afternoon.

I return home two hours later, loaded with grocery bags containing everything I need for my 'Hey, I may have a boyfriend now' family dinner party. Maybe I should have waited a couple of weeks before inviting Jarrod and Christopher. I can't take it back now, it's out in the universe.

I put the food away and sit down with a glass of fresh orange juice to check my phone. I haven't looked at it once since I sent the text message invite, too nervous and embarrassed. I have to bite the bullet.

I have replies from everyone except Jarrod. My heart flips a little in my chest.

Hi, Honey,
You know I'm in. Can't wait.
Will

Hi, Bee,
LOVE TO ATTEND, BABY GIRL.
See you then.
Viv

Little Bee,
I make no promises to behave. This is going to be such fun. Love your guts,
Mel

Hi, Bee,
Are you kidding?
I haven't had a home-cooked meal in MONTHS, or maybe all year, I'm a Fuck YES!
Chris

Honey Bee
Trey and I are a Yes. I'll bring a salad
A

It's almost midnight and I've spent the afternoon planning my dinner party food. I forced myself to do Yoga and Pilates to expel some nervous energy, then I took a nice hot relaxing mineral bath. Still nothing from Jarrod since the invite. I'm so stupid, I don't know what I was thinking. It's too soon.

I hit the bed with a sigh and realise I can't escape him. My whole bed smells like him. I put my face into the pillow and breathe in; he wears something beautiful, It is citrusy, maybe bergamot, pepper, sandalwood, so earthy yet warm. Like the outdoors under a starry sky. 'Bee… stop it,' I tell myself. I have to change the sheets tomorrow, as much as I love sex bed sheets; well, I never did before, but I do now. I need to clean my room just in case a certain someone does attend.

I pick up my Kindle and try to find a new book to read before I fall into a mindless slumber.

My phone chirps with a text message and I pause… Just check the phone, Brooklyn… You know you want to. I lean over to pick up my phone, and sure enough, It's a message from Jarrod.

Brooklyn
Sorry for the late reply
I had a few issues at work
I'd love to taste you…
I mean your cooking, that is.
See you tomorrow night.

Sleep well, Angel.

Oh god, how can a girl sleep after that? Even his text messages ignite a flame. I believe he is telling the truth. I hope he doesn't feel pressured, but I'm still cautious. I respond:

Jarrod
I hope everything is sorted at work now.
Honestly, no pressure if you can't make this one. I know how busy you are. Bee [Kiss emoji]

Two minutes later, my phone starts ringing with the sound of his new ringtone, haunting my quiet bedroom, and I pick up.

"Hi," I say, a little shyly, because I'm still embarrassed that I jumped into a 'Meet the Family' scenario so fast.

"Angel," he breathes into the phone, "are you okay?"

"Yes, I promise, I just…" I take a breath, trying not to sound like a dick. "I just don't want you to feel pressured or anything. I know we have only just started seeing each other and…"

"Brooklyn, stop." His tone is low but firm, making me pause.

"Yes," I wait.

"I want this, too. I got held up with some issues here and didn't have time to check my phone," he says in a quiet voice. "I'm sorry if the delay made you think I didn't want to attend, because I do. I want to spend time with you and get to know you, your life, your music, your body, everything…"

Wow, how do I respond to that? He keeps surprising me.

"Jarrod, you just have to be patient with me. I haven't been in a relationship for a long time, and it… Well, the last one wasn't the best. I'm not sure how to navigate this ship," I say in a quiet tone.

"To be honest, I don't, either," he laughs, all breathy, into the phone. "I have zero relationship experience, Brooklyn, but I do know I want to have it with you."

Wow, way to blow my brain tonight. "Zero, huh?" I ask him, smiling. "I would have guessed otherwise based on the outstanding performance I was privileged to receive Sunday and Monday." I think I blush right through the phone.

"Ahh… Angel, I may have no relationship experience, but I have more than enough practice in physical activities to steer this ship. I'm sure I can share my expert knowledge with you, repeatedly, frequently." Now I'm all hot and bothered, literally.

"And Brooklyn, you were spectacular, in case you were wondering, sublime. I can't stop thinking about pushing into your tight hot body… Fuck…" I can hear the change in his voice, husky and deep.

I suck in a quick breath, he is making me so hot. I'm mesmerised by his tone, his words, "Jarrod," I breathe out.

"Sleep well, Angel, I'll see you tomorrow night." He ends the call, leaving me breathless. No way I'm going to sleep after that. I might need some ice-cream to cool off.

Chapter Thirteen

DINNER PARTY PART 1

I spend mid-morning preparing food for tonight's dinner party. My nerves are getting the better of me: having Jarrod, Christopher and Vivian over with my tight-knit circle is a huge step. I never had my last partner included in family dinner nights. Oliver and Will didn't exactly like each other, so it was difficult. Besides, two years have flown by, and even though it sounds like a long time between boyfriends, it really wasn't for me.

I've been busy working, creating music, living life, and being true to myself. Men, or partners for that matter, were not my main priority. I guess I shied away from too much intimacy because of my history. It made it hard to trust, and I needed that trust to feel completely safe.

This is different. I have to be honest with myself because the feelings I am developing for Jarrod are nothing I've ever experienced before. I want to see where it will go, but I am cautious, too. Was I just a fun distraction? Was I a bit of sparkling arm candy? I don't think so by the way he is behaving, but I can't read men well; at least, I don't think I can. My instincts are warped, and distorted. I didn't have that father figure example. Hell, I didn't have a mother figure either, and it set the precedent for my adult years.

I do a quick clean-up of my flat, wipe over the surfaces, mop the floors and set the table ready for tonight. I lock up and head out to meet Will for our weekly rehearsal.

"Hi, Honey." Will gives me a bear hug when I arrive in the afternoon.

"Hi, hot stuff, how are you? Did you have fun at Karaoke night?" I ask, and give him a cup of hot tea. "I haven't chatted to you since then," I mention while taking a sip of warm tea with blossom honey.

"I did, you know. It was a nice distraction. I've been busy lately working on new material, studio sessions." He runs his hand through those chestnut locks and takes a deep breath. I think he is about to say something else, but he averts his eyes and looks down at his tea.

"Will, is everything all right? Are you burning the midnight oil or something?" I place my hand on his forearm, trying to catch his eye.

"No, Honey. I'm just a little knackered, that's all," he answers sombrely and looks at my face. Something is different, but I don't know what.

"Well, if you're sure. You know you can tell me anything, right? I squeeze his arm and smile.

"I know, it's nothing," he gives me a bright smile in return and leans over to pick up his guitar.

"How about we get this rehearsal over with and you can head back home to prepare for dinner? Can I bring you anything?"

"Bring only your amazing self, I'll do the rest," I give him a wink; our easy camaraderie is back.

Besides, Will is a terrible cook! He orders in from the best traditional Indian tapas house in London for our family dinner nights at his place. It probably costs a bomb, but the aroma and spice explosion is more than worth it.

"Let's shred some tunes, Bee," he begins playing. I grab my mic, ready to sing my heart out.

I arrived home in the early afternoon, the rehearsal went well, and we finished early so I could prepare. I have a couple of hours before everyone arrives. I picked up some beautiful flowers on the way home, a cottage garden bouquet with sweet pea, hollyhocks, roses, marigolds and the most beautiful blush peonies. I am adding a few extra touches than I normally would if it was just a regular family dinner night. I light a few fragrant candles around the room; not only will they give off a perfume, but my flat will have a lovely glow.

I place a few candles in the centre of my dining table; it's an informal provincial-style round cedarwood table that seats ten. There is no head of the table at my place: everyone gets seated equally, and we can all chat easily. I like the relaxed vibe, nothing overly formal or stuffy.

I preheat the oven, take all the dishes out of my refrigerator and leave them on the counter until the oven is hot. I should get myself ready, giving myself a pep talk to calm the nerves, "Suck it up, Brooklyn, it's going to be fine," I whisper, as I head into my wardrobe. Now, what clothing says 'I'm casually hot for you, Jarrod', but with 'It's just a regular family dinner night' style? Yeah, right, Brooklyn... This is more than a bloody family dinner and you know it! This is the first time I'm letting a man into my world, fully.

Two hours later, I'm dressed in a pale sage-coloured sleeveless dress, V-neck fitted bodice and flowing pleated A-line skirt, pulled in at the waist with a silk belt. It's dinner party elegant, falling just above my knees.

I have enough time to paint my nails in a dusty rose pink, matching toes sliding into my pink open-toe heels. I'm wearing a cute lace pink bra and matching panty set underneath the dress — a girl has to be prepared, after all.

I keep my hair out, adding in some hair oil to give it a nice glow, a touch of pink gloss on the lips and some volumising mascara does the trick. I spray my favourite perfume around me and head into the kitchen to check on the food baking nicely in my oven. My flat smells enticing; the citrusy scent of lemon herb chicken baking in the oven is delicious, and I realise I am hungry. I was so busy preparing food today that I forgot to eat lunch.

The lit candles in the dining and sitting room give off a heavenly scent called Amalfi Coast with notes of lemon and lime; wild freesia, and base notes of sandalwood and amber. It's fresh and warm and delightful. I check on the food in the oven, turning it off and letting the residual heat keep everything warm. I take out the apple crumble dessert

I made earlier and sit it on the bench, ready for the oven when the time comes. I place a pot on the gas and add fragrant white rice and water — it goes perfectly with the lemon-baked chicken.

I'm just wiping my hands when I hear the sound of my front door buzzer. I pick up my phone and open Spotify to play some dinner party music... hmm... I settle on Harry Styles' new album: which just dropped recently, a nice collection of shimmering mood melodies, a pastiche of nineties-style pop with an intimate feel. Probably his best album to date. Perfect for a dinner party. I head over to press the buzzer and let my guests up.

Mel and Simon are the first to arrive. Simon is average in height, probably around five foot nine inches, but next to Mel's teeny frame, he looks positively stalk-like. He is handsomely dressed in a grey shirt and dark charcoal trousers. The sleek black frames of his glasses give him a mature intellectual look. His dark blond hair is a little longer than he usually wears it, combed back in his usual smart clean-cut style. Simon is holding a very adorable package; this package is currently squealing at me with chubby hands outstretched like she can't believe she sees me, and wants to grip me before I disappear.

"Well hello, Missy," I say with a huge smile, and pluck her from Simon's arms, sniffing her fuzzy head and kissing her pudgy pink cheeks. Katie is smiling and laughing as I nuzzle her little neck and chin.

"Are we invisible?" Mel asks me, as she puts the baby bag over by the bookshelf.

Mel looks tidy as usual, in her signature fitted slacks and a lovely plum-coloured blouse. She has on flat slip-ons tonight, making her appear even smaller than usual. But I know she is going for comfort — she will be chasing Kate around my flat for the majority of the evening, at eighteen months, she is a curious wonder to behold, touching everything she can get those sticky hands on.

I give her and Simon a peck on the cheek. "Hello, beautiful people, welcome. Help yourself to wine or beer, it's in the fridge. I'm going to cuddle this one while she lets me," I say, as I pretend to nibble on the fingers she is currently trying to shove in my mouth. Katie lets out a belly laugh that makes us all laugh.

"Simon, doesn't Bee look sensational tonight? Wonder why she got all dressed up; it's just family dinner, right?" Mel comments with a smirk on her face, giving me arched eyebrows.

"Bee always looks sensational, my darling," he says to Mel, as he pours them both a glass of chilled wine.

"Mel, I swear, you better behave or I'm pulling the pin on babysitting duty next date night." I give her a smirk back. I have hope she will be on her best behaviour, but let's be honest, Mel is a tornado on a good day; when she is vetting potential 'Boyfriend Material' for me, she goes the extra mile. No one is good enough.

The buzzer goes again and I head over with my wriggling package to let them up. "Katie, press the button," I tell her, and she lets out another ear-piercing squeal of excitement as she pushes the button.

We open the door and Will walks through with a big smile for me and Katie. He looks gorgeous in black denim jeans and a dark button-up shirt, sleeves rolled up to mid-forearm, his leather wristbands on. His hair is tied back in a messy knot at the nape of his neck, a few strands framing his face and eyes. He hands me a box as he snatches Katie from my arms, giving her a big smacking kiss on the cheek. She just melts.

"How's my best girl?" he asks her, then swings her above his head as she screams in delight. Yes, she loves Will, her little eyes shining with so much affection and happiness.

"Hi, Honey, you look stunning," he gives me a soft kiss on the cheek. "I stopped and got your favourite honey cakes on the way over." Will is always so thoughtful, and yes, these Greek honey cakes are next-level addictive. I'll have to hide a couple for breakfast tomorrow; if the others get to them, there will be none left by the end of the night.

"Thank you, always spoiling me," I say with a smile, and take the cake box over to the kitchen.

I grab him a beer from the fridge and leave it on the counter till he is ready to let Katie go. I check on the rice and turn off the gas, leaving the lid on to continue steaming. Everything is ready to serve; we are just waiting for the rest of my guests to arrive.

The table is set, and the flat looks clean and smells amazing. My nerves are stirring up butterflies in my stomach, so I pour myself a glass of wine. We all stand around the kitchen island, laughing at Katie making faces at Will, and Will making funny faces back, Katie practically peeing her pants laughing. He whirls her around to the music.

I hear a knock, and Anton and Trey let themselves in. "The guest of honour has arrived, bitches," Anton announces, holding a huge wooden platter filled with a colourful fresh-looking salad.

"Anton, you are not the guest of honour tonight. Sorry, babe, Bee has that box checked for someone else," Mel chirps in, smiling behind her glass of sauvignon blanc.

"You are always my special guest, Anton," I tell him and give him and Trey a kiss each. "Thank you for this, it looks amazing!" I exclaim, looking at the masterpiece he created with all kinds of healthy delicious vegetables: snow peas, nuts, tomatoes, cucumbers, roasted corn, spiced cauliflower, and a mix of green salad. I place it on the bench. Anton looks like his usual chic self, in dark-fitted trousers and a red shirt, with open buttons showing his gleaming smooth skin. He is wearing jewellery tonight, rings on his slim fingers. Trey looks immaculate in casual slacks with a black belt, a blue shirt tucked in, and his signature Tom Ford specs.

Katie is doing the rounds of each guest, beguiling everyone with her cheery face and enthusiastic laugh. I make sure everyone has a drink in hand, and then I check the oven when the door buzzer sounds.

"I'll get it," I call, at the same time Mel makes a run for the door. I knew she wore those flats for a reason!

She beats me and presses the buzzer, eyes shining with a wicked gleam.

"Mel," I say into her face.

"Brooklyn," she gives it back to me, while she puts her hand on the doorknob. The attitude!

A minute later, I hear a knock at the door, and Mel swings it open without allowing me even a single breath. Standing there looking like a dark lord dressed in black Armani head to toe is Jarrod, shirt open at the top, sleeves rolled up, fitted black trousers and belt, casual elegance dripping off him while he observes us, his blue eyes shining like sapphires in the night, taking me in: my shoes, my dress, my face. I can't take my eyes off him.

I force myself to, and I see Christopher looking smashing in a charcoal-fitted long-sleeve soft jumper and trousers. His expensive watch glints on his wrist, and he is holding a huge basket of goodies. Vivian is next to him, dressed in a baby blue tight dress and matching heels. Her hair, all silky and soft, is out tonight, and gold rings and earrings adorn her tanned skin. She never looks less than amazing every time I see her.

"Jesus, Brooklyn, did you call Elite London Models as our dinner guests tonight?" Mel asks with her mouth open, her face tilted up, eyes scanning the three tall, striking humans in front of us.

Jarrod smirks at me, those lips giving me tingles. Christopher laughs and gives Mel his best 'I know I'm beautiful' blinding smile. Vivian stretches her hand out to

Mel. "You must be Mel. Bee has told me so much about you." Mel takes her hand and gives it a gutsy shake.

"Mel, this is Christopher, whom you met earlier, and his brother Jarrod. Their family owns the Houston; and this tall goddess is Vivian, the stylist at the hotel. Everyone, this is Mel, my manager and surrogate mother.

"Hey, don't make me sound old, Bee. I'm totally in the 'hot older sister category'," she says, smiling. Mel shakes hands with the guys, and Vivian moves over to hug me; her perfume smells divine, lingering between us.

"Thank you for having us, Bee, your place is lush," she says, taking it all in.

Christopher leans over to kiss me; he is holding a massive gift basket.

"Bee, this is a small gift from the three of us, a thank you for having us for dinner. I'm fucking starving mind you" He hands me the basket as Jarrod smacks him on the shoulder. I laugh at their brotherly antics.

I can see lots of epicurean items: chocolates, bottles of Hendrix Lunar gin, Bloom dry gin, grapefruit and lime segments, citrus-flavoured tonic water — wow, a plethora of ingredients to make my favourite G&T. I look up, smiling at them.

"You didn't have to bring anything, let alone such an extravagant gift," I say in awe.

"Yes, we did," Jarrod answers, leaning over to give me a soft, gentle kiss on the mouth, eyes shining at me.

"Yes, I agree, Bee, even if Jarrod took a portion of my inheritance to arrange this for you," Christopher says, laughing at me.

I roll my eyes at him. "I'm sure your piggy bank can handle the loss, Christopher," I smirk.

"Well, barely in the door and we have a score on the board. Fifteen love," Mel whispers to me in amusement. She looks at Jarrod and they share a little silent repartee.

"Come in, please," I tell them, and we head into my flat. I get everyone settled at the dining table with drinks and nibbles. Music is playing in the background, wall lamps are on, and candles give the room a beguiling glow.

"I forgot to ask about food allergies or such. I know these guys eat just about anything," I say, gesturing to Will, Mel, Simon, Anton and Trey.

Vivian barely hears me: she is absorbed in watching Will and Katie blowing raspberries at each other. He has her sitting on the table, facing him, and she is probably splattering him with baby drool, but he doesn't even care. His eyes are alight with laughter. He hasn't put her down yet, but I'm sure soon enough she will want to explore and touch all my shit. She does that. One time I found a half-eaten lump of banana behind my TV unit.

"Brooklyn, I'm sure we will love everything," Jarrod murmurs, watching me with those blues.

"Bee, no allergies, we eat anything and everything," Christopher pipes in. "Well, except sprouts; those fuckers are disgusting," he pulls a face like he just ate dog shit; but strangely, he still looks cute pulling that face.

No brussels sprouts tonight, I promise," I laugh, and head into the kitchen. I'm just getting all the trays out of the oven as Jarrod slides up next to me.

"Brooklyn, you look beautiful tonight," he whispers in my ear as he takes my hand in his large one. God, he doesn't give me any space. He kisses the back of my hand, his eyes on mine the whole time. Always so intense, so direct.

"Thank you. So do you," We share a moment, and I remember the hungry people ten feet away are probably going to be gnawing at the table soon. I put the oven on low heat and place the covered apple crumble in, leaving it to slowly warm for dessert.

"It smells amazing," Jarrod tells me, as I hand him a platter of roasted sage and butter potatoes. I carry the tray of baked lemon herb chicken and we walk back to the dining room. It takes a couple of trips, but we manage to carry all the food and place them in the centre for everyone to share.

I have the salad Anton made in the centre, the baked lemon chicken and roast potatoes on one side, steamed green beans, fragrant rice, and roasted pumpkin with honey drizzle on the other. The smells, the colour, it all looks delicious and I give myself a mental pat on the back for pulling off this dinner, with enough food to feed a small army. Anton opens another bottle of wine and hands it around the table.

"Please, help yourselves," I gesture to the waiting food.

The table erupts in oohhs and ahhhs. "Bee, this looks delicious," Vivian remarks, giving me a huge smile, like cooking is a superpower or something.

"Honey, you have outdone yourself tonight," Will smiles over at me, Katie on his lap already nibbling on a green bean.

"Bee, please teach my wife how to cook someday; she is perfect in every other way, mind you," Simon says, giving Mel a wink. She just rolls her eyes: she has heard it before many times. Mel burns water.

"Honey Bee, you know what they say, Madonna in the bedroom, Nigella in the kitchen — every man's dream." Anton gives his thoughts to the table and I almost spit out my wine. Christopher laughs while loading up his plate with mountains of chicken and rice. I try not to look at Jarrod because my face will be as pink as my underwear if I do.

"Well, if that's the case, I need to work on my Nigella game," Vivian states, while she takes a sip of wine. Will finally takes his eyes off Katie and gives Vivian an appraising look. I wonder if they have taken this infatuation further yet. I know Vivian is very interested.

I stand up and head over to Will with my arms out. "Give me the beastie, you can eat," I put Katie on my hip. Will thanks me and starts to fill his plate with steaming hot food.

"Oh god, Bee, this is so good," Mel moans, stuffing her face with a huge forkful of roast potatoes. "Almost tastier than those delicious Aussie Hemsworth brothers," she exclaims. Simon just shakes his head with a smile, enjoying his own meal.

That starts Anton and Trey in a discussion about which Hemsworth brother is hotter. I sit back down next to Jarrod, holding a soft moving bundle of fuzz on my lap. I give Katie a warm potato and she holds it in her chunky little hands and slowly nibbles on it while I place some food on my plate.

Jarrod knocks Christopher on the shoulder and I look over to see him basically shovelling food into his face. "Chris, the hounds of hell are not after you, slow down, bro," Jarrod tells him, shaking his head.

"What? I haven't had a home-cooked meal for months, years even! I'm sick of hotel food," he exclaims. "Brooklyn, can I move in? I'll pay for all the food, and utilities, just cook for me, please? I beg you!" He closes his eyes like he is offering up a silent prayer. "This is beyond... the best food I've eaten in ages."

I just laugh. I'm so glad that everyone seems to like my cooking. Jarrod is making good headway on his plate of food, too. I hold Kate with my left hand and eat with my right hand, as best I can with just a fork. I want to give Mel and Simon a break, they don't usually get time to themselves; Kate is at that age, and she rarely sits still like this.

"Here, give her to me," Jarrod asks quietly. "You eat, and I'll hold her." I turn to look at him, a little shocked. He has only just met her, and he is comfortable to hold her for me?

"It's OK, really," I say, a little unsure.

"Brooklyn, you have been cooking for hours; give her to me," he reaches up to push a lock of hair behind my ear. Jesus, I just melt. What have I done to deserve this amazing man sitting next to me?

"OK, if you're sure." I move Katie over to his knee, and she doesn't even bat an eyelash. Jarrod's big hands hold onto her little body like she's a precious doll. He mimics what I did earlier, holding her with one arm and using his free hand to keep eating like he is doing something so mundane, it's no big deal.

My brain is frazzled and I look over at Mel. She has stopped eating and is watching Jarrod casually keep up a conversation with Chris and Trey, while multi-tasking like a bad arse, eating his food and holding her baby so I can eat my dinner.

We share a look, and she says over the table, "Thirty love."

I take a deep breath. I know what she means: he just scored a major point. Mel isn't looking for him to fail her test, but she isn't expecting him to ace it, either. I wonder what she is thinking in that busy mind of hers.

We get through dinner, and Mel takes Kate from Jarrod. She lets out a little noise, a sulky pout on her face as she's taken away to my guest room, to be changed and cleaned up for bed. Mel will give her a bottle and put her down to sleep.

A chorus of "That was amazing" and "I'm stuffed" comes from around the table; most of the food is gone, a few leftovers lingering, but I think we did a stellar job of working through the mountain I cooked today. I enjoy more wine, happily watching everyone chatting, Anton holding everyone in hysterics telling us about catching his stage manager in a compromising position in the bathroom with a dancer.

Jarrod holds my hand under the table, giving it a little squeeze. I look over and feel my heart flutter. He takes my breath away; even sitting next to him now, our arms brushing, his signature scent, warm and earthy, I can't stop my eyes from needing to look at him all the damn time. *Brooklyn, you are well and truly fucked*, I tell myself, as I melt under the heat of his twin blue flames.

Chapter Fourteen

DINNER PARTY PART 2

Anton rises from his seat and walks over, tapping something on his phone, and my background music stops. "Honey Bee, it's time to get dirty, show everyone what we've been working on," he holds his hand out to me.

"Anton! What… No!" I say, giving him the sternest look I can. I look around and everyone is watching us.

Jarrod tilts his head, curiosity shining in his eyes.

"Honey, yes, it's time," smiling, he grabs my hand to left me from the chair. I let go of Jarrod's hand and smooth my dress down with nervous hands. I'm miffed he is doing this to me now.

"What's going on?" Christopher asks, sitting up straight, his full attention on us.

"Bee and I have been working on a little number, *mon cher*, and it's show time," Anton moves over to the couch and pushes it back, giving us a dance floor space. Everyone is watching with rapt attention. I glance at Jarrod; I'm so nervous, this was not supposed to be performed with an audience.

Mel walks in, takes in the scene and asks, "Why do you look like you just swallowed a turd, Bee?"

"Because Anton is being a twat," I say, crossing my arms over my chest.

"Come on, Honey, you are amazing. Let's do this," he kisses me on the forehead. "Please," batting his eyelashes at me. How can I refuse now? I trust him, he knows how to lead.

"Aghh… fine." I huff out a breath and push my hair back over my shoulders. Anton taps on his phone, and the *Dirty Dancing* theme song starts to play. Everyone now realises what the hell is going on, and I look over my shoulder, giving the table a little smile. Jarrod's eyes are sparkling with interest.

Anton steps up and holds me in his tight frame, exactly as we have done countless times before.

We start the dance as the beat kicks in, and I'm lost. I dance with Anton like I'm really Baby and he is Johnny, my skirt flicking up around my legs like hers does in the movie. God, I realise too late that my dress is perfect for this dance, flowing out every time I spin, but my underwear was supposed to be for a singular set of eyes, not the whole table. Oh well, too late now.

As we dance, I can hear clapping and I'm sure they are all enjoying the show. Anton is giving me his eyes to concentrate on; looking at him as I go, it feels so right to dance with him, he is so talented, and he makes me look awesome when I'm really just following his expert lead. We don't do the lift, but we finish the song with Anton's own choreography, and I'm breathing like I ran a marathon as we end the dance, bowing and taking in the applause from everyone.

I'm smiling as I find Jarrod's eyes: they are locked on me in awe, and lust, his face not hiding the fact that he wants me. I think everyone can see it, and a blush rises to my cheeks.

I look over and Vivian is clapping with glee. "Anton, can I please hire you for dance lessons? That was amazing, and Bee, you were perfect, just like the movie!" she tells us excitedly.

Will is smiling at me; he gives me a wink and I smile back. His cheeks are flushed, probably from the wine.

Simon, Mel and Trey give us compliments.

"Thank you, everyone," Anton announces. "But all the credit goes to Bee, the perfect dance partner." He gives me a smacking kiss on my cheek, then lifts me in a sky-high hug.

"I need a drink after that," I state and sit down, still calming my breathing. Jarrod pours me another glass of wine, and I take it from him. He still hasn't said anything, but his eyes are hot blue flames all over me.

"Bee, that was amazing; truly, is there nothing you can't do?" Christopher asks me, and I just chuckle, because it's not like I'm doing anything special. Anyone can do it with practice and a dance teacher like Anton.

"It's all Anton, the master dance instructor. Mind you, we are usually three or four Margaritas in when we practice," I admit.

"Well, that was the bee's knees," he says, then leans over to me in a quiet voice, "And did you know my brother loves the colour pink?" He gives me a wink and I feel my cheeks heat again, just to match my knickers, of course.

"Ouch," Christopher yelps and Jarrod removes his hand from his brother's leg.

"Shut up," he says to Chris, but he's smiling. "Don't mind him, Brooklyn, you danced beautifully, Angel" — and in front of the whole table, he leans over and kisses me, a direct hit on the lips.

"Jarrod, I heard you are a bit of a talent yourself," Mel chimes in from the other side of the table.

He looks over at her and puts his arm around the back of my chair.

"My brother and I studied music, secondary to business studies, of course, it's a passion. I guess you could say we do all right," he comments.

Christopher pipes in then. "Mel, if you have room on your books, my bro would sell out every show. Trust me, he is wasting his life in the family business," he tells her, which gains him an arched brow in return.

"Really?" she asks, taking a sip of wine and looking at Jarrod with interest.

"It's just a bit of fun," Jarrod responds, under-selling himself immensely.

"Come on, man," Anton speaks up, "own that shit, mate. Did you see the crowd in that bar? They were hypnotised, a multi-orgasm-inducing performance, my friend," he raises his glass towards Jarrod.

"I wasn't looking at the crowd," Jarrod answers looking at me, and I look down into my wine. I feel like the whole table can feel my heart beating a staccato.

"Forty love," Mel says, and raises her drink to me with a smile. I have no idea if Jarrod realises she is keeping score. Will laughs into his wine. He is more than familiar with Mel's ways.

"In that case, I need to sample this talent. Jarrod, would you do me the honour?" she asks, and I wonder if he knows this is probably part of the game for her.

"You want me to perform now?" he asks. They are locked in an intense eye duel.

"Yes, unless you're not comfortable, of course," but her tone is goading — she wants to see how he does under pressure.

"Sure." That singular answer garners clapping from everyone around the table.

Jarrod looks at me, and I give him my best 'I'm sorry' look. "Brooklyn, do you have a guitar?" he asks, and I nod. I head into my small studio room and fetch the acoustic guitar from the rack.

We all get up and move to the sitting room, everyone taking seats on the couch and chairs, wine glasses in hand. I sit next to Mel as Jarrod takes a seat in front of me on the coffee table.

The room is perfect for this, dimly lit, candles flickering, we are sipping the wine, waiting for him to check the guitar is in tune. My heart beats faster in anticipation. Mel leans back waiting, her hand moving to my hair, playing with the ends, keeping her hands busy, she doesn't realise she is doing it. Usually, she does this to Katie when she is thinking about something important.

After a few strums of the guitar, Jarrod starts the song; it's slow and mellow and sounds like a love song. Then he starts singing, his husky voice with perfect pitch commanding the room.

He is singing James Bay's 'Wild Love', and he is singing it to me. If he is not looking at the guitar as he plays, then his eyes are on me; no one else in the room exists. He takes my breath away.

Jarrod is a gorgeous baritone, fearlessly navigating sudden transitions from low humming to husky growls, hitting the wispy high notes easily. He conquers all octaves of the song, my heart desperately wants to sing with him. This is a bold choice. You can't hide playing it acoustically. Mel should give him a point for that.

He sings about wild love. It's a song about a man falling in love, love that knows no distance, yearning for that one special person.

Jarrod is only a few feet from me, making it feel so intimate, yet the room is full of friends watching his every move, listening to his every note. He does it with such confidence in his own talent, something I feel myself when I sing, but I have been performing for many years.

He is a natural, that's obvious. Will would be impressed with this guitar playing no doubt, I think as I look over at him, but Will is not watching Jarrod — he is looking at me. Something in his face gives me pause. Just for a second. Why is he looking at me like that? I return my eyes to Jarrod as he finishes the song. I have no words, it was so beautiful.

Jarrod gives me his intense blue gaze for a few heartbeats, then looks down. I think the raw openness of his song just hit. Black hair falling over his face, he runs his hand through those dark locks.

"Well, that was something, Jarrod," Mel tells him. "Game, set, match," she mumbles to me. She sits straighter on the couch next to me, looking from me to Jarrod in astonishment. She is not usually lost for words, but I think she is gobsmacked for once in her life!

"Honey, I think you just got pregnant," Anton announces to the room, and everyone bursts out laughing. I have to cover my face, because, well, Jarrod is right there, looking at me smiling, and not even embarrassed in the slightest by that comment.

"I'm putting pepper in your Margarita next week," I tell Anton through my fingers. "Hot fucking Carolina Reaper!" Which makes everyone laugh again.

He leans over and kisses my head "That was hot, Honey, I couldn't help myself."

"Jarrod, honestly, I'm not usually lost for words," Mel says, and Simon coughs into his hand as if to say his wife is NEVER lost for words... Cheeky.

"But that was incredible. If you want to put yourself out there, I can arrange a meeting with producers, songwriters, that kind of thing. I think you should take the next step; your voice is studio-ready," she admits.

He gives it a moment to digest, looking at her before he answers. "Thank you, Mel, I appreciate it, but my place is at the Houston." He hands the guitar over to Christopher and stands up to put some distance between him and me. Or him and Mel? I'm not sure. Chris makes an annoyed sound, shaking his head as he plays with the guitar.

"That's a shame, Jarrod, you would be a catch for any agent to sign. You know where to find me if you change your mind," she leaves it at that. He gives her a nod and looks out the window, breaking the spell.

"Bollocks, I forgot dessert!" I announce, leaping up from the couch "Who's in for hot apple crumble and ice-cream?" I ask the room.

"Heck, yes!" and "Bring it on" come the replies as I head into the kitchen to take the dish from the warm oven.

"Are you trying to kill me, Bee?" Christopher moans. "You made all that food, and know how to make a delicious pud as well? I should have left more room," he says while rubbing his flat, toned stomach.

"Please, I don't know where you put it, but you have to finish the night at least tasting some of my homemade apple crumble," I say, smiling over at him.

Mel comes over to help me dish up the pudding. The kitchen smells like hot cinnamon and baked apples — it's like walking into a bakery: sweet, spicy and fruity goodness. "My god, that smells fucking amazing," her eyes are closed as she inhales the aroma. "Can I just shove my face in the whole dish?"

I laugh. "You could, but you'd get that pretty face burnt. It's hot," I reply.

I take out a tub of creamy vanilla bean ice-cream and we hand out the bowls, choosing to stay in the sitting room rather than sit at the dining table. I make sure to top up the drinks, then take a bowl over to Jarrod, who is sitting on a chair by the window.

I move to hand him the bowl, but he takes my hips and pulls me towards him, I end up sitting in his lap holding the apple crumble. "If we were alone, I'd be enjoying this with you naked," he whispers into my ear, his arms wrapping around my hips. God, one line from him and I'm all hot and bothered. "And I've been thinking about those pink panties ever since you danced earlier. You're killing me here."

I try so hard to look normal; the others are pretending not to watch our every move, but it's hard to escape with such close confines. They are intrigued: it's been a long time since they have seen me with a man. But this man is breaking all my walls down, rendering me breathless.

I take a nice big spoonful of his dessert while it's still warm, closing my eyes and enjoying my masterful creation. "Do I get a taste Brooklyn?" he asks me, ocean eyes up close, watching me lick the ice-cream from my lips; that wolf-like smile is back.

I dip the spoon in and collect a good amount of pudding, then bring it to his mouth, that perfect lush mouth that holds me captive. He takes the spoonful into his mouth and moans, closing his eyes. I watch his face, because who knew dessert could be so sexy; until Jarrod.

"Bee, this is divine; seriously, you are one talented woman," Vivian comments, devouring her dessert. "If I could bake like you, I'd be three hundred pounds," she says, laughing.

"No kidding, Viv. I'm going to hit the gym for an extra two hours tomorrow," Christopher says dramatically, sticking out his washboard-trim stomach.

"Honey, you know the way to a man's heart, that's for sure," Anton says, licking his lips, but I know he will only eat a small portion. Anton is fierce when it comes to his diet: he won't overdo it.

"Spectacular, Bee." Trey gives me a big grin and a thumbs-up.

"Nothing short of heavenly, Honey; thank you for everything tonight," Will says next, so heartfelt as always.

I smile at the praise, slightly embarrassed because it's nothing amazing, it's just food. "I'll pack you some to take home," I tell Will, and make a move to stand up. Jarrod kisses my cheek and lets me up, and I hand him the bowl to finish as I head back into the kitchen. Will lives alone, so I like to give him leftovers to take home.

Vivian comes over to help me pack the dishwasher with the dinner dishes, and clear the table.

"Brooklyn, it was so nice of you to invite us over, it's been a great night." She hugs me as we stand in the kitchen.

"You are now part of the inner sanctum; anything you see or hear can't be repeated, or we'll have to kill you," I kiss her smooth cheek.

Jarrod comes in and helps us clean up the mess, rinsing dishes in the sink before we load up the dishwasher. Thank god I had that installed with the kitchen renovation; when it's just me it doesn't matter, but hosting a dinner party creates more mess than I'd usually have. I'm glad I don't have to hand-wash everything.

Mel and Simon do the rounds and say goodbye to everyone. Mel is holding a sleeping Katie in her arms, while Simon holds the baby bag and hugs me. "Thank you, Bee, it was perfect." He kisses me on the forehead.

"Call me tomorrow. Love your guts," Mel says with that sparkle in her eyes. She kisses me, and I lean in for a sniff and kiss on Katie's fluffy head. God, she smells good; sleeping baby, that has to be the best smell ever.

"I just want to eat her," I whisper to Mel, giving Katie another kiss on her baby head.

"I know; me, too," pride and love shining in her eyes as she looks down.

I look up and Jarrod is watching me, again, with those midnight blues. Vivian has everything put away now, and I thank her for the help.

I pack Will's take-home food into a bag and walk over to him. "Did you have a good time tonight?" I ask as I hand him the container. He has been a little quiet tonight.

"I did, Honey, thank you," he says and pulls me in for a tight hug, his arms wrapped around me.

"Is everything all right?" I ask, looking into his eyes, trying to read his face.

"Yes, I'm fine. I'll see you Friday night," he kisses the top of my head and releases me.

Will says goodbye to everyone, shaking hands, then heads over to my door. I walk with him and notice he takes a lingering look over his shoulder at Vivian, who's still at my kitchen bench chatting with Jarrod.

"Why don't you share a taxi with Viv?" I ask as he walks out the door.

"Another time, Honey. I have to be in the studio early tomorrow," he gives me his rock-star smile and leaves.

Anton and Trey are next to leave. I clean the platter they brought the salad on, and hand it to Anton at my door.

"Thank you for the salad, it was super," I kiss them both. "How'd I do tonight?" I whisper.

Anton gives me a look that says 'Are you serious?'

"Honey Bee, you nailed it, and you are going to nail that stud muffin in black over there who hasn't taken his eyes off you all night." He makes kissing noises and I laugh, pushing him out the door.

Christopher comes back from the hallway, probably using the bathroom. "Bee, Viv and I are going to take off. Thank you for an amazing night. Pencil me in for any future dinners here; I will be dreaming about your cooking for weeks." He leans down and gives me a hug, my shoes leaving the floor as he lifts me.

"Get your hands off my girl, Chris." Jarrod materialises at our side and Christopher laughs, kissing me on the cheek, winding his brother up.

"I would, but Bee is hard to top," he tells him.

"I know," Jarrod replies, wrapping his arms around me from behind, his chin on the top of my head, because he is tall as shit and I'm over here in heels and still barely clear his shoulders.

Vivian hugs me again and tells me she will see me Friday night. They leave and suddenly we are alone. I turn around in his arms and look up, my heart beating that fast rhythm that seems to only happen around Jarrod. "You have the most amazing eyes, Brooklyn. Have I told you that?" he says quietly, ardently.

I stare at him for a moment, because, hell, my eyes are nothing compared to his blue depths.

"Call me," I whisper to him.

"What?" he asks, searching my eyes for understanding.

"Call my phone, Jarrod," I say, my hands moving up his tight stomach and stopping at his chest.

One hand lets me go, and he feels in his pocket for his mobile phone. I look down as he taps a few buttons, and I see he has my name saved as 'Angel'. I smile: I like that he calls me that.

He looks back up and our eyes lock, then my phone starts crooning the haunting voice of Billie Eilish: 'Ocean Eyes'.

Her radiant celestial voice breaks the silence in the room, singing about his ocean eyes, how they scare her, make her cry, make her fall from so high. This is how Jarrod makes me feel. It's like this song was written for us.

We stare, eyes locked for the full forty-five seconds my phone rings, singing to him from the table nearby. Forty-five seconds I hold my breath because this song gives him everything I'm feeling inside.

"Brooklyn, you fucking wreck me," he breathes before he kisses me senseless. He throws everything into the kiss, passion, reverence, and adoration. I feel it seeping into my bones as his mouth worships mine.

Jarrod slowly stops kissing me, touching his forehead to mine. He glides his fingers across my face like I'm precious, killing me softly, like the song I sang to him that first night at The Wave. So very softly.

His hands slide down my body and I feel my dress moving before they cup my arse, lifting me. I wrap my legs around his trim waist; he kisses me again as he carries me down the hallway to my bedroom.

"I can't wait any longer, Brooklyn, I want the rest of my dessert now," he whispers, smiling through the kiss; and holy fuck, he devours me like I'm the best apple crumble and ice-cream he's ever tasted.

Chapter Fifteen

COCKTAILS

I'm sitting in Vivian's chair, being made up like a magical princess fairy unicorn. I don't know how she does it, but she makes me look like a Hollywood movie star every time.

"And of course, I told him to bugger off. I swear, Bee, some men are so disgusting." She huffs out a breath as she adds the final touches to my face. "Do they think those kind of lines really work?" She rolls her eyes at me, smiling. Vivian has been regaling me with stories of the men who hit on her at the bar. The line he used was, "If I flip a coin, what do you reckon my chances are of getting head?" We both cracked up laughing so hard, that I had to run for a pee.

"Wait, this one is good… I had a guy hit on me after a show; do you know what his line was?" I ask her.

"Oh god, what?" she answers, already shaking her head, dabbing my cheeks with blush.

"Baby, that dress would look great in a crumpled heap next to my bed" — we laugh so hard.

"Bee, we have to stop! Your make-up will be ruined!" She is trying not to laugh, and make me laugh more.

"OK." I take a deep breath to try and smooth my face for her, doing my meditation breathing steps.

"I'm done. Take a look, baby girl." She steps back and gestures to the full-length mirror on the wall.

I walk over and take a good look. "Viv, you are freaking amazing, truly!" I say, turning around and inspecting my outfit, the hair, the make-up. Wow, just wow.

Tonight I'm wearing a stunning gold and silver beaded strapless mini dress that falls to mid-thigh, fitted, sparkly, and beautiful. I wear gold peep-toe mega-heels, making my legs look miles long. My hair is up off my shoulders in an artfully styled messy bun. A few strands are floating around my face. Gold dangle earrings shimmer in my ears.

"It's Zuhair Murad. Taylor Swift wore this dress to an Oscars after-party years ago. Isn't it glorious?" she asks me.

"Taylor Swift? It's just exquisite," I say in awe, running my palms gently over the dress. We hear a knock at the door, and Vivian opens for Will to pop his head in.

"Ten-minute call, Honey," he says, smiling at us.

"Just about ready," I answer.

"You look dazzling tonight, Bee," he tells me with a wink. "You, too, Vivian," then he heads back outside.

"Aghh... every time," Vivian huffs, and drops onto the couch.

She looks model perfect as usual, wearing a beautiful tropical print dress with a ruffled hem, and a cut-out back giving it a sexy edge. Her hair is swept back on one side with a stylish gold pin.

"Every time what?" I ask as I adjust my cleavage in the dress, making sure the girls are contained nicely.

"Every time I see Will, my stupid heart races. I can't help it, Bee," she says with a sorrowful expression.

"Ah... yes, I know exactly what you mean," I give her a knowing look. Boys... they can mess us up so hard. "Give him time, Viv," I gently pull her up from the seat. "He hasn't been himself lately," I tell her because it's true. I have to talk to him soon.

"I know, he's a gentle giant. I'll wait him out," she smiles. "Now, Honey, you go out there and enthral the patrons like you do every week."

We open the door and I'm stopped in my tracks: gorgeous eyes are holding me captive again. Jarrod is waiting for me, leaning casually on the opposite wall, his usual attire making him look like a creature of the night: black shirt, black fitted trousers, black luscious hair and those eyelashes that seem to frame his eyes like charcoal. He looks like a beautiful villain.

"Jarrod, if you mess up Bee's face, I'll kill you," Vivian warns as she walks off, his answering smirk telling me he'd love to do just that. Bad, bad boy.

He gives me a once-over, very slowly, not hiding the heat in his eyes. He likes what he sees. "Brooklyn, you take my breath away," he whispers, gently putting his big warm hands on my face and leaning in for a soft kiss on my lips. "Stay here tonight, after the show," he states, our eyes inches apart. It's not a question.

"Yes," No other words enter my brain. He captivates me. I drag myself away and head out into The Wave to do what I do best.

Will escorts me to the microphone and I switch my brain to work mode. Tonight's set we have prepared includes some originals Will and I wrote together, and some classic sultry tunes, starting with one of my favourite female singers, Helen Folasade Adu, otherwise known as Sade.

Sade is a modest contralto, who vocally resembles a young Nina Simone and Billie Holiday. She sings about raw naked passion, love, loss, a little bit jazz, a little bit soul, and a little bit pop. The song I chose to open with is 'No Ordinary Love'. Not easy to play with just a guitar, but Will is exceptionally talented and adapted it well for us.

"Welcome to The Wave. I'm Brooklyn, and this talented man next to me is Will." I look over, giving him a nod to start the song. I sway my hips as he begins to play, and the room quiets down. The music takes me to my happy place, my zone.

I sing to the audience, expressing to them that this is no ordinary love, slowly, sensually, and seductively. This style of music just embodies a rawness that can't be hidden. I find my blue-eyed prince by the bar, drink in hand, watching my every move.

He doesn't notice the eyes he draws, the women who watch him while he watches me. I can see everything from my elevated position; the lights are dimmed, but still allow me to see faces in the crowd.

During the set tonight I spot Christopher, Vivian and Daniel in the back, enjoying drinks and swaying to the music. I add in the classic George Michael 'Careless Whisper' and finish with a Lana Del Ray song. Will is amazing as usual, and after our final bow, we walk off stage. Two hours flew by so fast tonight.

"You were flawless tonight, Honey," Will tells me, as we walk over to the VIP seating Daniel has sectioned off for us. Many people stop us on the way, congratulating us on a beautiful show tonight. I graciously thank them as I go, making sure to be polite, Will artfully manoeuvring me away from a handful of men who seem to want to get closer to me. It's just part and parcel of show business, but I'm glad to have some help, otherwise, it can be a little overwhelming.

"You were the flawless one tonight, rock star. What would I do without you?" I ask, and smile up into his lovely face.

I see a pained expression flick into his eyes, fleetingly, and then it's gone. He plasters on a big smile and I wonder if I misread him for a second. "Come and enjoy the rest of the night; let's get a drink," I say as we join the others. He lets me go and I walk over to receive the complimentary hugs I have now become accustomed to from Christopher and Vivian.

"Smashing show once again, Bee," Christopher tells me.

Daniel arrives with a waiter in tow, holding a tray of cocktails for us. "Brooklyn, in honour of your stay at the Houston, The Wave staff have designed a cocktail named after you… Honey Bee," he hands me a glass.

"It contains Hendrick's Gin, with notes of cucumber and rose, honey syrup, fresh lemon juice, aromatic bitters, and it's garnished with lemon zest." It's a beautiful crystal cocktail glass full of sunshine.

My face splits with a huge grin. "Oh my god, Daniel! You made me a cocktail?" I ask in awe. I take a sip, and wow, it's to-die-for good: perfect, crisp, sweet and sour at the same time.

"Mmm… Goddam, this is good," I tell him, squeezing his arm. "This delectable creation is going to fuck me up good and proper," I exclaim, and everyone laughs. They are taking sips and moaning, eyes closed, because, seriously, this is an orgasm in a glass. It's happiness and deliciousness combined.

"I need to taste that, too," I hear whispered in my ear, as warm hands slide over my waist, I shiver. Jarrod spins me around and claims my mouth with a hot warm kiss, plunging his tongue into my honey and lemon-flavoured mouth. I don't even care if people are watching us; this is beyond hot, I'm melting.

"Christ, Brooklyn," Jarrod puts his forehead to mine, holding me so close. His eyes are sparkling at me, firm hands gripping my waist a little too tight, like he can't let me go. "One hour. Then you're all mine," he's so intense, so raw, I know he is hanging on by a thread.

I nod, because my words have melted away with that kiss, that stare.

The others are laughing and chatting, I drag my eyes away from my dark prince to join them, partaking in the delicious cocktails and just enjoying myself. Everything feels so right, so real. For the first time in my life, I feel revived, and free.

An hour later, to the second, Jarrod drags me away from our cosy plush seats in The Wave, taking my hands into his. "Time to go, Angel." He gives me that smirk, the one that I now realise means all kinds of hot and steamy.

We do a round of goodbyes, and I leave the others to carry on with a continuous flow of cocktails and beautiful finger-food platters Daniel had the chef prepare for our late-night dinner.

It was superb, with a tasty array of gourmet nibbles to help soak up all the alcohol. I am feeling full and very, very happy. Am I drunk? Hmm… no, but warm, and slightly giggly after four sublime cocktails created in my name.

Of course, I had to enjoy such a wonderful surprise.

Jarrod leads me to a private lift, separate from the main ones. As we wait for it to arrive, he starts nuzzling my neck, then I feel his warm lips travelling from my neck to my ear.

"Brooklyn," he whispers.

I try to answer him, but I'm suddenly having trouble… I grip his arms to hold myself up. "Hmm," I answer eventually because he is distracting my foggy brain right now.

The lift pings and he steps back, giving me a second to shake myself out of the dream. I look up into his chiselled face, those intense eyes — did he ask me something?

"Angel, are you drunk?" He smiles at me, then leads me into the lift and scans his card and the doors close.

"Being sober on a bus is, like, totally different than being drunk on a bus… or a lift," I muse, smiling.

"OK, definitely drunk," he says, pulling me in, watching my face closely. "Not making sense is an obvious clue. Angel, what do we do with you?" The humour in his eyes makes me smile; I can't help it.

"What? I am totally making sense Jarrod; that was a quote by the great man himself," I say with assurance.

"Umm… hate to break it to you, but that is not Shakespeare, baby," he tells me, trying hard not to crack up laughing as we ride the lift to his floor.

I roll my eyes. "Shakespeare? What…? No, it was Ozzy Osbourne," I punctuate that with a quick kiss on those luscious lips. That makes Jarrod bark out a laugh, holding me tight and laughing so freely with me, at me… who cares, but his face lights up like a billboard in Times Square, all sparkly and gorgeous.

"Come on. I'll get you some water and give you the tour." He is still smiling his beautiful wolfy teeth at me as we disembark the lift and arrive at a massive smooth walnut timber door, with no lock or key, just a digital panel that lights up as Jarrod presses some numbers onto the screen.

When the door opens, it's like I've been transported into a new world, completely soundproof, with no outside noise, no hotel noise, no cars on the street at night, just a silent and still apartment. It has marble floors, timber accents, and classic art deco lights that glow down the long hall, like an airport runway lit up at night.

"Wow..." I breathe. "Jarrod, this is amazing," I say, as he leads me into an open-plan sunken lounge with windows along one wall. It leads into a massive chef's kitchen: stainless steel, black granite benches, sleek modern cabinetry. He walks me over to a bar stool at the massive island bench.

"Sit here, I'll get you a cold drink," he makes sure I'm sitting comfortably before he walks around the island to pour us chilled glasses of water.

"You live here with Christopher?" I ask — surely it's way too big for just the two of them.

"It's the family apartment, four bedrooms; my parents have the primary suite down the back when they reside in London, Chris and I occupy the other two on this side, and the spare room is our music room. It's not a conventional brick home, but it works for us. We need to be accessible at all times. Hotels never close," he leans on his side of the bench, watching me take it all in.

"It's lovely Jarrod. You guys said I had a nice home— mine is a row boat compared to this stunning yacht," I smile, sipping my cool water.

"Angel, your place is perfect. Not many people in their twenties could afford your front door in that location, let alone a historical Victorian flat. You should be proud of your accomplishments," Jarrod watches me with something like admiration shining from his blue depths.

"I am…" I answer sombrely, because I made a lot of money when I was younger.

"But?" he questions me seriously… sensing something has shifted.

"It came at a price," I say truthfully, the alcohol making my inhibitions fuzzy.

Before he can question me further, I change the subject. I want the light-hearted laughing we had earlier back. "So, are you going to give me the grand tour or what?" I ask, as I slide my shimmering body off the stool. I'm still in my gold beaded dress and heels. I'm ready to kick them off and get comfortable.

"Of course, Angel, starting with the main rooms, and ending with my private bedroom suite," and the wolf is back, those lips lifting into a smirk as he takes my hand, walking backwards while his eyes give me heated blue flames. Still feeling warm and tingly, I've sobered up a little, and I follow him down the runway-lit hallway — wherever he wants to lead, I will follow.

The music room he shows me is awesome, the walls and ceiling are covered with acoustic black noise-cancelling foam, ensuring that the rest of the hotel can't hear them belting out heavy drum and guitar sounds. A sparkling black and gold drum kit is set up in the corner, which Jarrod tells me is Christopher's. Racks of guitars line the walls: acoustics, two vintage Strats, four Gibson Les Pauls, including one Jarrod calls his Black Beauty.

"It's a 1975 Gibson Les Paul Custom, with ebony fingerboard, mother of pearl inlays, mahogany body with a maple top. Three-piece maple neck with original waffle-back tuners, twin gold-covered humbucker pick-ups with original electronics." I haven't seen him this animated before.

His eyes are glowing, telling me about this guitar, like it is one of his precious babies, the way a parent would talk about their child. He loves this instrument, I can tell. It is beautiful indeed. A perfect match for him.

"Wow, she's a beauty, Jarrod, you must love playing her," I say. "I love the sound of a vintage Les Paul, that classic rock sound with a pronounced bite through the amp, yet they can have a warm mellow tone, too."

He smiles as he puts his Black Beauty back on the rack. "I'll play her for you one day Brooklyn," he leads me out of the room, holding my hand, not letting me escape. I sense the connection we have: it's beyond words, it's music, it's a feeling, a pull that drags me under when I'm with him. Jarrod is like the ocean: calm and soothing one minute, then strong, fierce and hypnotic the next. With depths I'm yet to reach.

Chapter Sixteen

PLEASURE AND PAIN

I walk into Jarrod's private suite, his bedroom. He gives me a moment to look around, check out his space, see where he sleeps, rests, and is himself without the mask of professionalism he puts in place when he works. This is the real Jarrod.

A huge low timber king bed is the centrepiece of the room, with a black leather headboard and charcoal sheets that cover the massive expanse. Music and guitar magazines are stacked on the bedside table, wall lamps give an inviting glow to the room. A huge wardrobe is to the left, walnut timber cabinets are visible, and another door, which I assume is his bathroom, is to the right. I walk over to a cabinet that has a few personal items on it. A couple of men's watches, some pens in a stylish black marble holder, and a bottle of men's cologne. I pick it up to smell it; yes this is the scent that holds me captive whenever he is close.

I look down to see it's a bottle of Dior Sauvage for men; it smells incredible, a scent I will only ever attribute to Jarrod now. Like his very own signature, a blend of him and this fragrance together — it creates some kind of kinky magic that gets me high.

"Do you want to get changed, Angel?" he asks, as I feel his arms fold around my middle, his chest to my back.

"I wasn't expecting to stay over, I don't have any clothes," I turn around in his arms. Jarrod gives me a peck on the lips, smiling, watching me so intensely.

"I'll get you something," he walks off towards his wardrobe.

I take off my shoes and leave them by the door. I sit down on the bed and feel the plush warm fabric under my bare legs, it feels so soft, and the whole room is thick with the smell of clean linen and that magic Jarrod smell; it's all him, and I'm getting drunk on it.

"Here you go." He hands me a clean black T-shirt and some hotel products: toothbrush and paste, facial cleanser, moisturiser, body wash, all with the Houston Hotel logo on the packages. "Take your time," he tells me, and starts to take off his shirt while I'm standing there unapologetically eyeing his slow strip. He gives me that knowing smirk, lips curving up, and I shake my head to clear the brain fog and walk into the bathroom.

I take my dress off, careful to hang it on the clothes hook in his modern black marble bathroom. I wash my face and freshen up using the beautiful hotel pamper products. They smell so beautiful, like grapefruit and mint.

I walk out in Jarrod's soft black cotton top and just my underwear, face clean and glowing with the moisturiser he gave me. It's warm in here, no doubt temperature-controlled throughout the whole apartment. I can see he also changed, wearing nothing but black sweat pants, hung low on those cut hips, his smooth chest and hard abs on full display. If he wanted to distract me, it's working. He is sitting on the bed with the remote to a very large TV screen on the wall.

The screen comes to life and he makes a selection. The 1975 live at the O2 London starts playing. I love this band. They are a British Indie pop rock band formed in 2002 in Cheshire, now based in Manchester. I've seen them live and they are cool cats for sure.

Jarrod turns his head, his gaze sweeping me from head to toe, radiating that heat and electricity he gives out every time his eyes hit me. "You didn't give me pants," I say, standing there, bare legs, hair still up in a messy bun.

"That was intentional, Brooklyn. Come here," he holds out his hand. I walk over and take it, the sounds of the crowd cheering from the TV, music starting, lights glowing from the stage. The sound is low, but creates a nice ambiance in the dimly lit room. Jarrod has the moves, I realise — I wonder how many women have been in this room, in this bed, music playing, watching him half-naked just like I am now. It makes me feel a little jealous. I hate that feeling, I've never felt that before.

He lies down on the bed, so comfortable and free in his own space, pulling me on top of him, my legs intertwining with his. I put my arms under my chin, his warm naked chest beneath me as I stare into his eyes. "Can we talk for a bit?" I ask. I'm still feeling the cocktail buzz, making me bolder than usual.

"Of course. What do you want to talk about?" he asks, sliding his hands behind his head, bulging biceps in front of my nose, his perfect face smirking at me with those kissable lips right there, just an inch away.

I'm trying hard to not let him distract me because we haven't had much of a chance to really talk, I want to find out more about him. I take full advantage tonight. "Twenty questions. I'll go first," I tap his nose with my finger. He smiles wide, teeth gleaming, then he bites his bottom lip and I can tell I'm in for some fun tonight.

"Fire away, Angel; what do you want to know?"

"Number one," I say, and move my hand to touch his inky black hair, trace his black brows. "Where did you get the black hair and blue eyes from?"

He takes a minute to enjoy my touch, then answers. "My mother is French; she has the hair, and my father has the blue eyes." Those eyes in question never leave mine, so close I can see my reflection.

"Do you speak French?" I ask the next question while still exploring his face with my finger.

"Oui, mon ange, je parle français," he answers fluently while grinning at me.

"Ahh... Seriously, Jarrod?" I huff at him. "You play guitar, you sing, you look like this" — I wave at his face — "and you speak French! You're killing me!" I whine, covering my face with my hands, my skin flushed from one line of his deep voice speaking French, giving me butterflies in my stomach. Why is he so perfect? It's disgusting.

"Tu me fais rire, mon ange." He laughs, peeling my hands away from my face as he lands a kiss on the corner of my mouth. "Next question."

"I have no idea what you just said, but I need a minute to think," I try to get my wits back.

"I said you make me laugh," his hands distract me further, landing on my arse. He gives me a cheeky smile, and I know exactly what he is doing: trying to distract my train of thought, touching me, making me forget my questions.

"Favourite band?" I ask next.

Jarrod thinks about it before answering. "That's a tough one. I don't have a favourite. I like a lot of different bands, different styles, metal, old school heavy stuff, alternative metal, progressive rock, grunge," he tells me.

"Like?" I ask.

He looks up to the ceiling, thinking for a second. "Bullet For My Valentine, The Raven Age, Breaking Benjamin, Alter Bridge, Soundgarden, Sleep Token, Five Finger Death Punch, Avenged Sevenfold." He likes it heavy, and I do know most of those bands.

"Nice," I reply. "Favourite concert you have ever been to?"

I feel those hands moving up and down on my butt, his fingers playing with the edge of my underwear.

"Foo Fighters two years ago. They rocked hard," I smile. I heard they put on a good show.

"What University did you attend?" I ask, not for any other reason than to know more about him; the small details intrigue me.

"Cambridge, post-grad business, finance and economics. I added an extra nine months of music studies," he tells me, pushing some hair behind my ear. I decide to throw in a curve-ball question while I have him at my attention.

"When you first saw me on the street, what did you think?" I ask with a nervous laugh. I'm not fishing for compliments, I just want to figure out what was going on in his head, because he blew me away that day.

Jarrod takes a minute to watch me, looking over my face like he has something to tell me but needs time to process first. "That wasn't the first time I saw you, Brooklyn," he admits, his eyes watching me closely.

I cock my head to the side, not understanding what he means. "I don't understand? You picked up my folder, remember?" I remind him.

"I know, but that wasn't the first time Angel," he states in a quiet tone. Background music fills the silence for a second as I stare at him.

"What do you mean?" because now I'm really interested to hear what he has to say.

Those hands move up under my top, smoothing over my back, leaving a warm trail all over me.

"I saw you sing at the Cavendish a couple of times, Daniel and I." He pauses, and I wait for him to continue. "I wanted you here, to sing, so we made it happen." I'm stunned, because I had no idea that Jarrod saw me perform, knew who I was before that day I came to work at the Houston Hotel.

He can see I'm speechless, taken by surprise. "I wanted you, Brooklyn, from the first time I saw you on that stage, singing like you do, so beautiful, so passionate," he tells me. I have no words; I'm astonished.

"No more questions, Angel. I can't wait any more," he leans in to kiss me, one hand sliding into my panties, squeezing my arse, the other hand on the back of my neck, bringing my face to his. I can feel his need; he isn't holding back. I'm instantly hot all over. I will have to think about his confession tomorrow when I have my brain back, because right now I'm lost. I give him what he wants.

He rolls us over so I'm beneath his long lean body, those hard muscles, his firmness surrounding me, kissing me, touching me. Jarrod leans back, giving me a chance to catch my breath, and removes my top, leaving me in my white lace underwear, but not for long.

He takes those off next, and I help him by lifting my hips.

No more talking now; his face is determined, fierce and fixated on me.

He kisses me everywhere. My neck, my chest, sucking first one nipple, then the other into his hot wet mouth and I moan; he is just too good at this. He keeps moving down my body, leaving kisses all over me, and I can't hold still, my body moving without my control.

"You are so beautiful," he whispers, before he puts his mouth on me, sucking and licking me with relentless energy. I grip his hair in both hands, pulling it hard, because that's what he does to me, makes me lose control.

I hear him growl a response then his teeth graze my clit, biting that little bud, the sting mixing with the pleasure he is giving me, my breath hitches. "Fuck!" I say, as my back arches into him. I'm going to come. Jarrod holds my hips with a firm grip, sucking me so hard, harder than he has previously like he wants to devour all of me.

"Give it to me, Angel," he demands, and I do, I let go, my nails clawing at his shoulders as I come like a fucking fireworks display.

My eyes are closed, my breathing ragged as I hear him move, the sound of plastic being torn open, and when I open my eyes he is over me, watching me with those ocean eyes, shades of blue I've never seen before. He enters me with a smooth hard thrust. I again close my eyes; the feeling, the fullness of him inside me is ecstasy.

"Look at me, Brooklyn," Jarrod whispers, I open my eyes. I watch him watching me, he looks down, seeing himself stroking in and out, pushing all the way into me like he can't get enough. He is so beautiful in this moment, so strong, his body flexing. He watches my face again, his arms on either side of my head, I grip his wrists to hold on, my body starting that climb, the sound of the music in the background muting the sounds of our bodies colliding together.

Jarrod picks up the pace, thrusting harder, making me feel all of him and I can't hold on, my orgasm sending fire through my body, my toes curling, I explode again, arching into the headboard as I let go. He thrusts so hard into me he has to put one arm on the headboard to stop us from hitting it, and he comes, releasing his warmth into me, I feel it through the condom, my body pulsing around him as he does. I love to see him lose control.

"Fuck, Brooklyn." He breathes hard, a little shiver going through his body as he lays on top of me, his chest and my chest hitting each other with every deep breath. "Are you all right, Angel?" he asks, leaning back to kiss me gently, his hand pushing the damp hair back from my face, looking at me like I'm a precious diamond.

"No," I answer, smiling. "I think you fucked me to oblivion." I kiss him back; his warm mouth opens for me and I take what he has on offer. It's never been like this for me.

Jarrod cleans me up with a warm washcloth and tucks me in wearing his soft cotton T-shirt. He holds me tight against his bare chest, and I fall asleep with his body holding mine, his nose in my hair, his hand moving gently up and down my spine.

I wake up to the sound of buzzing some time later. I don't know what time it is, but I think it's still dark. I don't want to wake up from this deliciously soft comfortable bed. I vaguely hear Jarrod murmur to me, his hand on my face, touching me.

"Wake up, baby," he whispers, as he tries to coax me from a deep sleep. "Brooklyn, Mel is on the phone; you need to wake up, Angel," he tells me, and that sparks something in me to open my eyes.

"What?" I ask, sitting up slowly. He looks at me with concern, holding the phone out; it's his mobile phone, not mine: I must have left mine in the downstairs change room.

I take the phone, dread seeping into my body, my throat constricting, because there is only one reason that Mel would call me in the middle of the night, to chase me using Jarrod's number must be important.

"Mel, what is it? Is it Katie?" I ask, panicked, rubbing my eyes, trying to wake the fuck up now.

"Bee, I'm sorry to call you. Katie is fine" she tells me, and I take the first real breath in what feels like minutes.

"What is it?" I ask, still needing an explanation.

"Bee, I had a call from the coroner's office. They are trying to locate any family members for Samantha Barrett... Honey, your mother is dead. They found her hours ago. They wouldn't tell me much as I'm not related, but it sounds like an overdose."

I sit there, shocked. I don't answer her immediately, because I don't know what to say, but I'm relieved to know that my family — the family I have now — are well; no one is hurt, and I'm alleviated from the weight that was sitting on my chest a second ago. Should I feel guilty for that? I don't know. But it's how I feel.

"Bee...? You still there?" Mel asks softly through the phone.

"Yes, sorry, I just needed a second. I thought something else when you called," Mel understands what I mean.

"They need you to go and sign some paperwork, and speak to the authorities. Can you do that?"

"I'm not sure. Can I think about it?" I ask, because I need time to process this.

"Yes. I will send you the details when you are ready. They may ask you to identify the body, but you absolutely don't have to do anything you don't want to, Bee. I'll be with you every step," there is more concern in her voice than I've ever heard before.

"I'll call you in the morning," I say, and she murmurs a goodbye, telling me she loves me.

I hand Jarrod the phone and he places it back on the bedside table. I know he heard every word, the quiet room allowing everything she said to be projected out of the device like a megaphone.

"What can I do, Brooklyn?" he whispers to me, touching my face reverently.

"I haven't seen her in ten years," I admit, then it hits. The finality of it, the ending of our pathetic mother-daughter relationship, the anger I still hold in my heart that will never get the chance to be released. As the tears silently fall down my cheeks, I wonder why I'm crying for her, he holds me.

Jarrod holds me the rest of the night, till I can't cry any more. I fall asleep with my head on his chest, the sound of his steady heartbeat firm and strong, comforting me. This is where I feel safe. This is where I belong now.

Chapter Seventeen

OLD GHOSTS

My head the next morning feels heavy, not a hangover pain, but the heaviness of long-time hurt. A pain that I'll never get to tell her about. I'll never get to express how much I despised what she put me through. I will never hear an apology; she will never see how I survived and created a life for myself. *Never* is so ultimate, so final. I hate her more now, for dying without having it out, letting me speak the words I always wanted to speak. I feel emptiness towards her. Hate got me through; now I'm angry I'll have to let that hatred go. I wasn't ready.

I don't want to remember that little girl who begged for a real mother, like the other children, someone who cared enough to feed, to hug, to protect. I haven't seen Samantha Barrett since the court case ten years ago. After she delivered me to the man who took my innocence, my body, crushed and humiliated that teenage girl forever.

She evaporated. Sam looked like an apparition during the case, she wouldn't look at me, stone-cold eyes never looking my way once. I wanted her to see me, in that courtroom. I wanted to see remorse or sadness in her eyes, but she wouldn't give me that. She never gave me anything, and that was the ultimate pain for a child... For me.

Jarrod is not in the room. I'm alone this morning. I take a moment to just breathe, deep and long. After a few minutes, I look over to see a glass of fresh juice on the side table and a note from Jarrod.

Angel,
I didn't want to wake you.
I'm in the music room when you are ready,
J

I sit on the edge of the bed and drink the whole glass of fresh orange juice. I'm only wearing Jarrod's cotton T-shirt, so I wander around looking for something to put on. I find his black sweat pants from last night. They are way too big, but I roll up the waistband and cuffs till they fit. I tie a knot in the T-shirt so it doesn't hang down my legs so far. I must look like a kid in adult's clothing, but they are comfortable, soft, and smell like Jarrod, so I'm fine with that.

I wander down the hall, bare feet warm on the marble floor; it's not as cold as I expected. The door is shut to the music room, but I can hear the muffled sounds of music, drums and guitar coming from inside. I push open the door and close it behind me. The sound hits me: loud, aggressive, yet melodic at the same time. Christopher is slamming the drums, wearing only sports shorts, sweat glistening on his chest. Pounding the drums is a workout in itself, and I wonder how long they have been playing this morning.

Jarrod is playing his Black Beauty Les Paul, wearing only black jeans and nothing else, bare chest, rock-hard abs flexing as he slays his guitar and sings into the microphone in front of him. He watches me, but doesn't miss a note; his voice is rough and yet polished at the same time. I don't know the song, but it's heavy, with lyrics I can understand as Jarrod sings with clear delivery and diction.

I walk over to the black leather couch along the wall and lie down, curling my legs up, my arm under my head, relaxing while I watch these two talented blue-eyed gods rock out like they are playing a world-class arena. I tap my fingers on my leg to the beat as I listen to the song. Jarrod is singing about angels falling, not giving up, there is darkness and he won't give in. He is singing to me, about broken wings, wounded souls never saying goodbye.

When the song ends, the room is silent. He puts his guitar on the rack and comes over to me. Kneeling by the couch, he gently pushes my hair back from my face, watching me closely with those deep blue depths. "Morning, Angel, how are you?" concern written all over his face.

"I'm OK. I think," I answer, because I am, when I'm near him. But I know the rest of the day will be shit, so I want to linger with him that little bit more. He stands and pulls me up, giving me a warm all-encompassing embrace, so that my face is squished to his naked chest and all I feel and smell is Jarrod. I just breathe him in for a minute.

When he finally releases me, I'm pulled into another hug, as Christopher gives me a kiss on the top of my head. "Bee, I'm sorry," he says, giving me an extra firm squeeze, his sweaty body soaking into my top, but he doesn't care. I don't think they know their own strength. I feel so cared for in this moment, albeit squeezed like a trapped kitten in the clutches of a toddler, Chris petting me a little too hard. It makes me smile.

As I disengage from giant number two's arms, I ask, "What were you playing?" I'd love to listen to that song some time.

"It's 'Angels Fall', by Breaking Benjamin," Jarrod answers. "Too loud for you, baby?" he asks me.

"No, I loved it. I want to listen to it again," he smiles. I do like some heavy metal when in the mood. Jarrod leans in and gives me a gentle kiss on the mouth. I run my hand through his hair, scraping my nails along his scalp.

"Brooklyn, if you keep doing that you won't get your morning coffee," he says, eyes closed, that smirk is back.

"Fuck no, I do not need to see or hear you two humping around our home. Have mercy on me, please," Christopher begs with a sour look on his face, while he wipes a towel over his sweaty chest and face.

"Fuck off!" Jarrod swipes the towel and whips him with it, the two of them exploding into some post-teenage wrestling match, half-naked bodies grabbing at each other and grunting. Is this what brothers do?

Men! They revert to acting like little kids at any given moment. I laugh, because it's so ridiculous seeing these grown men who run a grand five-star hotel on the floor, wrestling like a college locker room brawl. They are not doing any damage really, just fucking around, seeing who can get the upper hand.

Jarrod ends up on top of Christopher, just barely taking him because he is a little bigger in size, and has five years on his younger brother. "Give up, Chris," he demands, and Christopher stops fighting, laying limp on the dark carpet, both of them breathing like they just went five rounds in a boxing ring.

"Fine, get off me, you big Neanderthal," Christopher says, then he smirks. "I'll take you down, brother; it's just a matter of time," he tells Jarrod.

Jarrod leaps up and steps over his brother, a winning smile on his face, because besting Chris is obviously a thing he enjoys. "You wish, pussy," he replies, and looks over at me, eyes alight.

"Well, that was a shot of testosterone-fuelled madness I wasn't expecting so early," I say, not holding back my smirk. These two could be walking down a runway at Paris Fashion Week, and yet they have no clue how striking and genetically gifted they are… even acting like tools rolling around on the floor. Well, what girl would complain? They are half-naked, after all.

"Take a shower, bro, you reek," he tells Christopher as he takes my hand. "I'll get you some coffee, then drive you home. Mel is waiting for you to call her," he reminds me, which drags me back to my current reality real fast.

"Sure," I answer, just as the towel comes flying past us, missing Jarrod's head by an inch. He spins around and rapid-fire French flies out of his mouth. I have no idea what he said, but it definitely contained some rude words. Christopher gives his brother the middle finger, a big grin on his face. Jarrod just rolls his eyes and leads me to the kitchen, shaking his head. God, even angry French is hot coming from his mouth.

If I ever needed a dark brew it was now. I need a double-shot thick and strong black coffee before I can face what the day will bring me.

An hour later, I'm back in my flat. After a shower, Jarrod got dressed and drove me home. I'm just out of the shower myself, sitting on my bed in a towel. I need to call Mel, and get this over with. I make the call.

"Brooklyn, are you all right, honey?" she enquires gently with so much care.

"Hi, I'm fine," I take a much-needed calming breath. "I'm glad I wasn't alone last night; that news took me by surprise," I tell her honestly.

"I can imagine. Look, they need you to go down and sign some paperwork, as the last surviving family member I guess; just a formality. I will meet you down at the station, and we can go from there. Say, three p.m.? Do you need me to send a car?"

"No, Jarrod is here, he will drive me over," I let her know.

"OK, honey, I will text you the address now. See you soon," but before I can reply she continues, "Brooklyn, I love you, you know that, right, more than anything; you mean just as much to me as Kate does."

And that, right there, kills me. Mel, my surrogate mother, my white knight, my saviour shreds me. Because they are the words that a daughter should hear from her mother, but I never did. Yet somehow this woman who doesn't even share my blood gave me back my life, mother, sister, and unconditional love. I realise at this moment all the years I worked hard to fix myself, sing, be successful, be a good person, and finish my education, wasn't to prove to Samantha that I could do it without her, it was to show Mel that I was worth it. She would never regret taking me in. All along it was for Mel, not my biological mother.

I'm still reeling from that epiphany when she asks me, "You still there, Bee?"

"Yes, I just… Fuck!" I take a breath. "I know, Mel, and I will never be able to put into words everything in my heart for you. You, Simon and Katie."

"And you don't have to; just know we are here for you. And Bee, I haven't said this yet, but I'm so happy you have Jarrod; he seems to really care about you," she says, and if that's not the Mel official seal of approval, I don't know what is.

"I think he does," I agree. "See you soon. Love your guts," I end the call.

I get dressed in some casual jeans and an off-the-shoulder emerald jumper. I put my hair up in a high ponytail and add some mascara and lip gloss; nothing over the top, but I don't want to go out looking like a puffy-faced disaster, either. Jarrod is tapping on his phone at the kitchen island when I walk in.

"You ready, baby?" He takes my hand and pulls me in between his black denim-clad legs.

"As ready as I'll ever be. Let's get this over with," I answer putting my phone in my back pocket.

"Brooklyn, when you are ready... can we talk?" he asks, looking very serious, watching my face and my expression. "It doesn't have to be today, I know you didn't have an easy time when you were younger." He is cautious in his tone, but I can see the determination on his face. I knew this time would come.

"You want to play twenty questions again?" I ask, kind of pretending I don't know what he means.

"No, not a game, Angel. I just need to know, from you. I need to know everything," I knew he would want to hear the whole sordid truth. I exhale a deep breath and look up into that perfect face, waiting for me to answer. This is not going to be easy. Sharing my pain with him.

"I know, Jarrod... Shit!" I close my eyes for a second. "You should know, though, it's not something you can unhear once it's out, and I don't want your pity or sadness. I need you to be the same Jarrod you've been the past month with me, deal?" I need that from him. I don't want him to look at me like I'm a broken baby bird who needs fixing.

"Yes, Angel," he pulls me closer, kissing me with his whole body around mine, telling me without words how much he feels, he wants me to understand and feel it too.

Once we slow down, and break the kiss, I give him an answer. "We can talk after dinner tonight. I want to get it over with and move on. I don't want all this old crap to haunt me any more." I want it gone, once and for all.

He nods in agreement and we head off to meet Mel at the police station. We walk through the doors, and Mel is sitting in the public waiting room. She gets up and heads over to me, engulfing me in a massive hug despite her tiny frame — she has a deceiving strength. We don't say anything else; she just holds my hand because she knows that fluffy words don't work with me. That's not Mel's style anyway. She talks when she has something to say, not to fill the silence.

She gives Jarrod a quick hug hello, and I wonder how things moved so fast. She isn't normally affectionate with outsiders; she is very protective of me. But clearly Jarrod impressed her enough for her to let him in. He murmurs a hello but lets us do what we have to do. He remains quietly by my side.

Mel signals to a gentleman on the other side of the room, who must have been waiting for me to arrive. I turn around and he heads over. He is probably about six feet, wearing a dark navy suit, not the usual police uniform. He is handsome, with dark brown hair clipped short, olive skin, and maybe a European background. He's fit, and good-looking enough to garner some head turns in the busy room as he walks through with purpose.

"Brooklyn, this is Detective Rossi. He asked for you to come in today." Mel waves her hand towards him and I smile in greeting.

"Hello, Detective," I hold my hand out. He takes it and doesn't immediately answer, and I wonder if he heard me. He is still holding my hand, but his eyes are fixated on my face, my eyes, and I hear Jarrod clear his throat next to me.

His eyes break contact with mine and slide over to Jarrod for a second, before coming back to me. "Brooklyn, thank you for coming in on such short notice," he says, letting go of my hand. "I'm sorry for your loss." He conveys genuine sympathy in those words and I feel a little awkward, because I don't deserve condolences when I hadn't had a relationship with her for some time.

"Thank you. I'll do what I can to help, but it's been many years since I last saw her," I confess.

"It's Just a formal procedure to sign paperwork and such," he tells me. "I need to take you to my desk out back, if that works for you?" he asks, motioning his hand towards the door on the other side of the room.

"Sure, I can do that," we start walking.

"Just immediate family to the deceased; you can both wait here, we won't be long," he tells Mel and Jarrod, who both look like they want to argue.

I don't know who looks more indignant, Jarrod or Mel. They share a look between them.

"I'll be fine," I tell them, and step away. As we walk, I feel a light touch on my lower back: Detective Rossi is guiding me with his hand towards the door. He presses some buttons on the security panel and the door swings open.

"Just through here," we arrive in a large room, desks and people everywhere, the rush and noise of a busy city police station surprising me. I haven't stepped foot in one for many years. He leads me to a desk at the back; it's a little quieter here. "Take a seat, Brooklyn. Can I get you a tea or coffee?" he asks me.

"No, thank you, I'm good," he nods and takes a file from the pile on top of his desk.

"You're a singer?" he asks from across the desk, and I'm surprised for a second; he must see it in my face. "I read the file…" he explains. "On Samantha Barrett… We have to look into everything to determine the cause of death," It makes sense, I nod. I guess it's all there in black and white.

"As you probably gathered from our history, I haven't seen her in many years, not since the court case," I explain, and he takes a minute to look at me, in that way that comes naturally to a detective; it's not a leering creepy look, rather one of a person who can determine so much about someone in a short time. He knows how to get the answers he wants, I have no doubt.

"Will I have to view her?" I ask because that's something I don't want to do.

"No, Brooklyn, that's not necessary; we have dental records and photos to confirm it's her. But if you want to see her, to say goodbye, then I can arrange that for you?"

"No, thank you," I answer. Relieved now, I can take a breath. That would be too much for me.

He takes some paperwork from his file and stands up, coming around the desk to stand next to me. He places the paperwork on the desk and leans over to explain what I'm looking at.

"If you can read through and sign here; it just confirms that you came in to acknowledge Samantha Barrett, your mother, forty years old, date of birth and so on, was found deceased, confirmed by the medical practitioner, cause of death as it states here — it was a heroin overdose, with traces of MDMA and alcohol found in her system."

"Sure," After reading through the statement, I sign my name. "Is that all, Detective?" I ask, looking up.

He takes a moment, looking into my eyes again as I wait for an answer. He suddenly looks away and moves to sit back around the other side of the desk.

"There is also the matter of her final wishes. Will you be taking care of the arrangements? We have no further contact or next of kin to ask. Your mother's body needs to be transported soon," he explains gently to me.

I think about that for a second. What am I going to say? Just dump her body in the Thames. I'm angry with her, maybe I will be forever, but I am not cold enough to let her rot in an unmarked grave, either.

"Can you send the information to my manager? We can arrange for her to be moved to a funeral home, probably cremated or something like that. I'll take care of the financial side. I gather she didn't have any assets?" I ask.

"Not that I'm aware of. That reminds me, we have a few belongings found with her; you can take them with you," he gives me a large yellow envelope across the desk. I don't open it, just hold it in my hands. "Come on, I'll escort you back outside," he stands up and I do the same.

We exit through the security door, Mel and Jarrod stand as soon as they see us walking over.

As we walk back to my two sentinels, the detective stops me, gently holding my arm. "Brooklyn, if you need anything, please don't hesitate to call; you know, if anyone from your past gives you any trouble." As I look down, he hands me his card, 'Detective David Rossi' written in bold black letters. I look back up into his brown eyes.

He doesn't elaborate, but I know what he is insinuating. I know the monster who hurt me is free out there somewhere. I don't want to think for a second that he would be stupid enough to come near me, even with an indefinite life-long restraining order. "Thank you, Detective Rossi, I hope that won't be necessary," I say with a smile.

"I'd love to hear you sing one day, Brooklyn," he tells me. "Where can I find you?" he looks directly into my eyes, smiling, and now I get the feeling he is interested in more than police work.

"At my hotel, the Houston." Jarrod is suddenly right next to me, taking my hand, his blue eyes firing daggers at Detective Rossi. "Isn't that right, Angel?" he murmurs to me in that smooth voice I love, and my cheeks flush pink.

"You can catch her set on a Friday night, Detective. Bee is one of this country's best singer/songwriters," Mel chirps in now, the two of them doing some kind of tag team action. I just roll my eyes, because it's not like I don't get hit on, especially in my line of work.

"Maybe I'll take a night off and stop in," Detective Rossi says, then he gives me a smile that says he probably will, just to piss off these two next to me. "Take care, Brooklyn, it was nice to meet you." He gives Mel and Jarrod a nod and takes off, heading back to the security door, before he disappears through it.

"Wanker," Jarrod mumbles under his breath, and I turn around, smiling.

"Are you jealous?" I ask, putting my arms around his middle, and grabbing hold of his soft cotton T-shirt.

"No." The one-word answer is a total bogus lie, I can see it written all over his face.

Mel snorts like she thinks his answer is total shit as well. "Let's get out of this madhouse," she says, and we do. I need a whole tub of cherry ice-cream and maybe even a G&T or two.

We drop Mel home, and I instruct her to engage a funeral home and cremation service to take care of Samantha, to pay whatever needs to be paid from my account, making sure it gets done. Mel is so much better at that stuff than I am; she organises my life, and I'd be a hot mess without her. I appreciate her for it.

"Of course, Honey, leave it to me. Now go home and get some rest. It's been a rough day for you." She kisses me, thanks Jarrod for the lift and we head back to my apartment. The traffic is not too bad, but by the time we arrive, it's late afternoon.

"Do you want to stay tonight? Unless you have to work?" I ask, as Jarrod and I walk up to my front door.

"Of course I can stay. Chris took care of work this weekend, so I'm all yours," he replies as we walk into my flat. The silence bothers me, so I tap my music App and scroll through some tunes. I need something to distract me from my thoughts because soon I'm going to unleash all my junk on Jarrod.

I find an easy-listening jazz album to play. I take off my shoes and we take a seat. Jarrod lifts me to sit in his lap, touching me, caressing my hair, my face. I just close my eyes and enjoy it.

"How about I order some food? We can have an early dinner and wine," he speaks into my ear, kissing me there, his hands smoothing down my back, softly, soothingly.

"Sounds good, but I have one condition," I say, opening my eyes, and looking right into his blue diamonds.

"What's that?" He smiles with those lips I love, kissing me on the mouth, while his hands explore my back underneath my jumper.

"Ice-cream. There has to be ice-cream, like a whole fucking tub," he laughs, eyes crinkling at the edges, full lips and white teeth visible. He lifts me and I wrap my legs around his waist, wondering where this is going as he stands up and starts walking towards the kitchen.

"There will be ice-cream, lots of ice-cream, I promise. I know just how you like it, Angel," and he absolutely kept that promise, because while the early dinner plans went awry, I got my tub of Cherry Berry ice-cream and a naked Jarrod in my bed, making me forget all the bad in my past, the sourness of my mother's early death, the pain of unfinished business between us.

He takes it all away and reminds me how much he loves having me for dessert.

Chapter Eighteen

THROUGH THE DARKNESS

I wake up with a start. My heart beating through my chest like a jackhammer, I try to focus on shaking the fog away. It's dark in the room, and I am covered by a big warm body. Jarrod is sleeping next to me, his arms and legs hanging over me like heavy ropes. He likes to sleep touching me, holding me close, and I relax. I turn my head and squint in the darkness to take in his sleeping form. His face looks so peaceful, so young in sleep; even though he is thirty, a few years older than me, he still appears so youthful.

It's those bloody Disney prince genes, mixed with his mother's French heritage. He got lucky, barely a wrinkle on his perfect face. I sigh... Will I ever get used to looking at him? It's hard not to stare when I'm with him. I met plenty of famous people when I was a child star — movie stars, musicians — yet none of them affected me the way this man does. I'm star-struck every second I'm around Jarrod.

I must have had a nightmare, but I don't remember anything other than feeling frightened and trying to catch my breath, like I was being strangled. I take a few minutes to calm myself. Looking at Jarrod helps; I want so badly to touch his face and run my hands through his hair, but I don't want to wake him. I look over to my side table and see the envelope Detective Rossi handed me at the station this afternoon. Something is gnawing at my insides, telling me to open it. I very slowly remove Jarrod's limbs from my body, making sure not to wake him while I leave the bed.

I pick up the envelope and head into my sitting room, taking a seat on the couch, holding the personal items of my mother, my deceased mother. The one who drove me to be assaulted by the man who started my music career. The two adults who were supposed to look after me, and protect me, treated me the worst.

I take a few moments to breathe and then rip open the sealed envelope. I tip the contents out: a wallet, some change, a thin gold bracelet, a pack of gum, mobile phone and a pamphlet for a church. I don't remember her being very religious, but maybe that changed in the past decade.

I pick up the gold chain — it's a delicate thin bracelet with little charms — I look closer and realise what they are. A treble clef, a musical note, a little piano, and a heart: four little gold charms on a beautiful fragile band. I don't remember her having this when I was younger.

I place it on the couch and pick up her wallet. It looks like a man's wallet, not a typical purse. It holds about sixty pounds in notes, a bank card, driver's licence with a

Newham address, and as I search behind the cards, I find a thick stack of photographs.

They appear to be old, but as I look through them I realise what they are. They are me. All me. Photos of my first time singing on stage in a local musical, my smiling face holding up my first album, backstage at shows, me singing to an audience, paparazzi photos, all images of me performing, working, doing the only thing I was good at. A stab of pain hits me because there are no photos of me doing mundane things, none eating ice-cream, playing with other children, none of us together; just me, working my young arse off.

The pain hits right in my chest. The regret of unspoken words, the disappointment of not having the mother I deserved, the childhood I deserved, and I realise I will never get over what she did. Why did she have these? I can't reconcile the mother I remember with the woman who kept these photos of me with her every day, like cherished family photos regular parents keep in their wallets. Like the photos Mel keeps in her purse of Simon, Kate and me. Her most loved possessions.

This doesn't make sense, and my brain is hurting trying to figure out why she kept them. I don't want to go digging into her life, the past ten years, it's too painful. I don't think I'm ready to face whatever she felt for me. I want to close the door on that part of my life for good. Somehow, I need to accept this ending and move on.

"Brooklyn?" Jarrod murmurs, walking into the room, just wearing his boxer shorts and nothing else, his hair pushed off his face, like he ran his hands through it just now. My dark prince. I look over as he approaches, so sculptured, so pretty, yet with an unyielding firmness to him as well.

He takes a seat next to me, his eyes wandering over my face, then down at my hands holding the photographs. He takes them and slowly looks through the pile. I watch his face as he witnesses the young me, the one who just wanted to please, perform, and sing. The innocent me before the pain. He takes his time, and when he is done, he places them on the coffee table next to the couch. Jarrod takes my hands in his big warm ones and waits. I know what he wants, a silent appeal for me to open up.

"My life wasn't typical," I start with quiet strength, because I know I need to get it out, and when it's over I can burrow into Jarrod, I can put it behind me and move on with my life. This life I've built for myself, and now I desperately want him in it. I want him so badly, more than I've wanted anything before.

"My mother, Samantha, got pregnant very young; she was barely fifteen when she had me. I believe she left an abusive family. I don't know for sure, but some things that were mentioned in the court case, and her defence lawyers said that she had a terrible childhood. Like that's some kind of explanation for why she was the way she was." I take a breath. Jarrod is silent, waiting for me to take my time.

"I don't know who my father is; she lived on the streets for two years before she had me. Whenever I asked where he was, she just clammed up, like ice. I assume she didn't actually know who my father was. Either that, or it wasn't something she wanted to re-live." I look at his strong hands holding mine as I talk.

"We lived in some pretty shady places; social workers could barely check in because we kept moving around so much. I attended many schools, nothing regular, but by the age of ten I was performing on stage, musicals mostly, the West End, London theatre. When I started to get regular work, we finally had a stable place to live.

"A nice flat, food, heating." I look out the window: the night sky looks so peaceful as I talk about my past, it's like another lifetime ago. He just listens, patiently.

"I had my own bedroom for the first time. I remember I was so happy, I put posters up on the walls." I smile as I remember how excited I was at having my very own room. "Amy Winehouse, Pink, Avril Lavigne," He gives my hands a little squeeze in acknowledgement.

"I'll never forget the song by Avril Lavigne, 'Keep Holding On'… it got me through some dark days. I must have sung that song in my room a thousand times over," My eyes prick with tears thinking about the lyrics. "Her words gave me hope, like I could make it through. She knew exactly what I was going through."

"Music is powerful, Angel. I'm glad you had that to keep you going," he tells me, touching my face gently.

"The more I worked, the more I got noticed. Then, one day, I was being introduced to record producers, and offered large sums of money, and it all just happened. One minute I was singing in musical theatre, decorating my bedroom, meeting friends, going to school, and bam! it just exploded. I was given songs to sing, a new wardrobe, stylists, music videos, live performances, touring, and for almost three years I had no life other than making everyone money. Do what I was told, perform when they told me to, wear what they told me to, eat what they told me to. My life was a circus, literally — I was the main act."

I look down at our joined hands and take a minute to gather myself before I go on. I can't look into his eyes for this one; the disgust I feel is palpable.

"They usually had meetings with my mother. I was a child, so she handled everything. But one afternoon she insisted I attend a meeting on my own. She told me I was old enough, a teenager and had to step up, take on more responsibility." I can feel my heart beating now, my chest getting tighter.

"My producer raped me when I was fourteen," I whisper, not wanting to say it any louder in the quiet room. "He offered me a drink. I didn't know I was drugged, but it was enough to ensure I couldn't fight him."

"Fuck!"

My head snaps up at Jarrod's harsh exclamation. He stands up, his chest rising and falling with every deep breath he takes, his hands running through his soft black hair roughly. I don't think he knows he is doing it so brutally.

"Brooklyn, fuck!" He is looking at me with such a pained expression, anger and sadness rolling off him in waves. "I knew something happened, I knew you left the music industry," he tells me, pacing my sitting room like a caged tiger, back and forth.

"I don't know what would have happened if Mel hadn't found me. Jarrod, she saved me." I stand up and take his hands to still them. "She was working late that night. No one was supposed to be there, but she was a new talent agent, putting in the long hours to get ahead. I made it to the bathroom when my legs could move again.

"He thought I was just going to fix myself up and come back, like it was no big deal." I'm still looking down; it's so hard to see the pain in his eyes. Pain for me. "He told me this was part and parcel of being a star."

"Angel, look at me." Jarrod gently tilts my head up, our eyes meeting at last, mine like burning fires and his like cooling oceans. He calms me down, pulling me into his warm chest, kissing my hair, holding me so tight, like I could float away from him at any second.

"I'm so sorry, Brooklyn." His voice is solemn, emotive, and raw.

"I know you are," I tell him, because I can see it in his eyes, and it's written all over his face. "I can't forgive her for that, Jarrod. I can move on from the assault, from the court case, from my past, but I don't think I can ever get over her. What she did to me," I let the tears fall. I cry into his chest, his heart beating a fast rhythm under my cheek.

Jarrod lifts me, cradling me like I'm breakable, and carries me to my room. He places me under the covers and moves in next to me as I cry, not giving me an inch of space, his body telling me he will never let go, never leave me.

"You are so brave, Brooklyn, you are so strong and beautiful, despite what happened," he whispers into my hair as his hands roam over me, soothing me, consoling me.

"If he ever comes near you again, I'll kill him," he murmurs so quietly I barely hear... But I do...

I turn around in his arms, my eyes finding his in the darkness. "Make me forget. Give me something beautiful, Jarrod," I beg. He knows what I want, as he leans in, taking my mouth with a lush soft kiss, I taste him, mixed with my salty tears, and I know I'm done. I have fallen in love with him, this gorgeous, talented, dark-haired prince who rocked my world with his song and his ocean blue eyes.

The next day Jarrod insists on taking me for a ride on his motorcycle. This will be my first time.

I'm waiting at the front of my building when he arrives. He left my warm, cosy bed to drive home and bring his bike back. It's loud as fuck and I can hear him coming from a mile away. I'm dressed in warm clothes, black skinny jeans, boots, a wool jumper and a leather jacket. Apparently, it gets cold out of the city, with the wind whipping at us.

He shuts the engine off as he parks; it's loud, and there is no chance I will hear anything he says to me if it's running. "Are you ready, Angel?" Jarrod has that bad boy smirk on his face as he takes his black helmet off and runs his hands through his dark mass of hair. I could stand here and watch him all day, just like this. I take my phone out and snap a picture, to keep a visual of this moment for myself.

"Wow, it's a beautiful bike, Jarrod," I tell him, not knowing much about bikes at all. I have no idea what it is, but it's sleek, muscular and blisteringly loud. He dismounts the beast and takes the spare helmet from the back of the bike, placing it over my head, pushing the hair from my eyes.

"It's a Triumph Speedmaster Gold Line Edition," he explains while fixing the chin strap for me. I watch his eyes as they light up, talking about his bike.

"It's a British classic. 1200cc high torque parallel twin engine, two twin-skin exhaust system with chromed stainless silencers, and she comes with lustrous silver ice and sapphire black paintwork." He smiles at me with that full glorious mouth, and I just have to kiss it, because I have no fucking idea what the hell he just said, but it got him excited, and now I'm more than excited seeing him happy.

Jarrod pulls me off him and laughs. "Brooklyn, if we start that, we are never going to enjoy our ride," I huff out an annoyed sound. He puts his own helmet on and gets back on his baby. "I won't hear you on the ride, so just hold on tight, and tap my leg if you need me to pull over. Let's get out of this city, just for a few hours?"

I nod, swing my leg over the beast and hold onto my motorcycle god, the same one who took my breath away on the street six weeks ago. I hold him tight as we take off and I finally understand the freedom and exhilaration Jarrod feels when he rides. It's like I can breathe for the first time in days.

Margarita Monday arrives and I'm more than ready to suck down a few chilled glasses. I knock on Anton's door, holding a tray of mini pear Waldorf salad pita wraps and my yummy wholemeal banana muffins still warm from the oven.

"Honey Bee, I could French kiss you right now," Anton announces, as he eyes the food in my hands. He looks his customary stunning lean self, in casual singlet top and long athletic shorts. I'm in my usual Yoga attire, after pushing myself to work out this afternoon, still a little sore from hours sitting on the back of Jarrod's beast yesterday. I'm not complaining, though: it was a day I won't soon forget.

"Hello, my beloved, you look well," I comment, as I enter his flat. Music is already on, sounds like Drake. I know Anton is a huge fan, and we both agree Drake is totally bangable. The beat gets me and I dance my way over to the couch, placing the food on the coffee table.

As we sit, Anton hands me a glass of sweetness and I suck down half before I come up for air. God, I needed this tonight.

"Yes, Gurl, we in di lime tonight!" Anton yells, making me laugh. I love it when he speaks using his Caribbean accent. He is giving me his full-wattage smile, moving to the music while he sits on the couch. He has been in the UK for years now, but he never forgets his roots.

"What exactly does that translate to?" I ask, grinning.

"Honey, it means we are going to get our party on tonight," and he clinks glasses with me, before we alternate between munching on the tasty food and blitzing up more chilled drinks. By the third drink, Anton has filled me in on his new work schedule, behind-the-scenes antics at rehearsals and his mother's weekly phone call blistering his eardrums, asking if he is eating enough.

"Food is so important, it's a way of life where I come from, but she doesn't understand that my body is my livelihood. I can't perform with excess baggage, am I right, Honey Bee?" he asks.

"I know, babe, we are performers, it's the whole package that counts," I agree, because I do know what he means. The pressure to look a certain way can be tough at times. I unload all my junk from the past week on Anton, sucking down a fourth drink to get through the hurt and anguish of speaking about my mother's passing.

"Oh, Honey, I'm so sorry," he pulls me in for a big hug, kissing my head, and he just holds me for a while.

We don't need words because Anton knows my past, he knows everything, and there is nothing else to say. What's done is done. "I'm ready to move on now," I tell him. "Put on my big girl pants and live the life I always wanted. Great friends, singing my guts out, and hello, a hot boyfriend that I'm totally crazy about," my cheeks bloom pink as I think of Jarrod.

"In that case, we need to celebrate; it's bad bitch o'clock, Honey!" Anton gets up and taps his phone. Next thing I know, I'm being yanked up from the couch and Lizzo's 'About Damn Time' starts playing and we dance, Anton throwing me around in a mix of *Dirty Dancing* style and basic samba. God, I love this man.

This is what you call a bitching Margarita Monday.

I wake on Wednesday to the haunting sounds of Billie Eilish's 'Ocean Eyes' and I smile. My man is calling and I'm not even angry he woke me up. Isn't that a new feeling?

"Mmm... hello," I answer, my voice still sleep croaky, I run my hands over my face. I'm paying for the plethora of cocktails Anton and I smashed on Monday night. I don't regret it, but boy, do I still feel a little green. We haven't hit them that hard in a while. I need to drink copious amounts of water today, I make a mental note for myself.

"Brooklyn, are you still in bed?" he asks in that seductive voice I love.

"Yes," I breathe, shaking the cobwebs of sleep as I begin to wake up fully.

"Christ, how am I meant to work thinking about you in bed?" he asks, and I laugh, because it pleases me that I affect him just as much as he does me.

"I'm wearing those pink lace…" I start to say, and he interrupts me immediately.

"Fuck… Stop, please." He takes a breath, I can hear him inhaling deeply on the other end of the phone. "If you start that, I'm going to drive over right now," I think about pushing him to do it because I really want him to, but I know he has obligations; his work is important, and I don't think it's fair to distract him. Feeling a little guilty, I give in.

"OK, I'll stop for now, but no promises tonight," I hear him exhale; he was holding his breath.

"I'll pick you up after rehearsal. Text me the address, Angel," I kick my legs under the covers, because when would I turn down an offer to spend more time with this blue-eyed prince? Never. I'm in too deep now.

"Yes, see you tonight, Jarrod," I end the call. I don't wait for him to answer, because I am about to send him a very naughty photo of me in my pink lace underwear and the Metallica T-shirt I slept in.

I wait, and it doesn't take long to get a response back. It just reads 'YOU. WRECK. ME', I laugh. About an hour later, I get another one: 'Still can't concentrate, you are my fantasy come true'; and I send him one back: 'You are MINE', I add hearts because I'm a dork like that.

I turn up to rehearsal later with my guitar slung over my shoulder. I have a list of songs I want to play this Friday night and I think adding a second one in will work. Will is waiting for me as I enter, I hold the cardboard tray with our hot tea, careful not to spill it as I walk in.

"Hi, Honey, how are you?" He takes the tea and places it on the bench. I am engulfed in his big bear hug, Will kisses my head as he squeezes me tight. "Mel told me; are you all right?" he asks, and I look up into his face, so much care and concern for me on display.

"Yes, I'm good now. I got it out of my system. Let's just say lots of tears and lots of alcohol fixed me." I smile and pat his chest.

"Honestly?" he asks, double-checking, his eyes roaming my face.

"Yes, I promise," he kisses me on the forehead, holding me a little longer, and I wonder if this is more about him feeling sad right now, rather than me. After a while, he takes a deep breath and releases me.

"Let's get started, Honey," he says but he sounds reluctant, I nod, patting his arm before I move away.

A couple of hours later, we have run through the whole set list, and it sounds amazing. I'm so happy with the arrangements we came up with. I'm just packing my acoustic guitar away when Will speaks.

"Honey, I have something to tell you," the sound of his voice immediately makes me pause. I put the guitar down and when I turn around to look at him, my heart lurches. Will is looking at me with such pain in his eyes I can't breathe for a second. My brain is in all kinds of panic mode.

"Will... what is it?" I whisper, because my voice is suddenly gone. His face has lost all colour now.

"Brooklyn, I'm leaving, going on tour for a while," I frown, not understanding what he is saying.

"What do you mean, leaving?" Because I know what leaving means, but in the context of Will, it doesn't make sense; he never leaves me.

"I mean, I've been offered a job, touring the UK and Europe with an Indie band, and I'm going to take it. I leave this weekend. Friday is my last show with you." He steps forward and I put my hand up to stop him. I can't think when he is so close.

"You're leaving me?" I ask shocked. "Did I do something wrong?" I can already feel the tears pricking my eyes.

Will's eyes look glassy as he watches my face. I'm breathing faster now, so confused.

"Fuck, no, you have done nothing wrong, Honey. It's me; I need some time away, that's all," we are in some kind of stand-off, him looking pained and me looking gutted. I don't know what to do with this.

"What about us, singing together?" I ask stupidly, because I have no idea what else to say to his revelation.

"Mel has it all worked out; she has a replacement organised. You don't need me, Bee; any musician can take my place — it's you they come to see," I start to cry. He is wrong... So, so wrong. It's us together. That's the real magic.

"You both did this behind my back? You didn't even come to speak with me first?" I raise my voice. I'm hurt. This has all been done, not giving me a say, not giving me a chance to talk it over with him first.

"I couldn't do it. I knew you would change my mind. The flight is booked, it's done," his voice breaking on that last word. It breaks me, and I feel the tears streaming down my face. I can't hold in my sobs. This man, my friend, my protector, my musical partner, is leaving me for the first time in ten years.

"Why? Why do this now Will?" I scream at him. I can't take it, I can't believe this is happening right now.

"Because I LOVE YOU," he screams back, and I stare at him, my lungs struggling to suck in enough air. "Brooklyn, I'm in love with you," he whispers, grabbing me by the arms and holding me in place, my face a mask of shock and pain. "I can't stay watching you fall in love with someone else, someone not me. Let me go," he begs, his eyes on mine, imploring me to hear what he is saying.

"Will..." I breathe. I touch his face, watching a single tear slide down his cheek, and my heart shatters in two. His eyes hold mine, and we are frozen like that for endless seconds. Neither of us knows what to say, then suddenly he is kissing me, Will holds my face in his hands and kisses me with everything he has, all the love, history, and music we share — it's a kiss loaded with all that and more.

I am stunned and confused by what just happened, what is happening now. I kiss him back. I know I love him, and a big part of me is angst at the thought of him leaving. This may be the last time we get together. I don't want to hurt him more by refusing his love. I hold his hands on my face and gently break the kiss, we are both breathing hard, and my emotions are raw.

I hear a loud noise across the room, I turn to see Jarrod in the doorway, his face a mask of fury, his angry gaze flaming at us, his hands balled into fists at his sides, and I shake my head, the magnitude of what he just witnessed hitting me like a tsunami.

"Jarrod…" I beg, my face imploring him to understand. I feel sick, my stomach suddenly in my throat.

"FUCK!" he growls, slamming his fist into the wall, leaving a huge hole in the plaster, then he's gone, his angry steps fading down the hallway of the rehearsal studio. I move to run after him, but Will holds my arm and I turn around, my face soaked with more tears.

"I'm sorry," he whispers to me. "I'm so fucking sorry."

I fall to the ground. I kneel on the dirty studio floor, gasping as sobs are ripped from my throat. Will kneels down, holding me while I cry, and I mean ugly cry, tears streaming down my face, snot, the works. I cry like I've just messed up my life. I've managed to lose not one, but two amazing men. One I love with all my heart, with years of history, and one I'm in love with, who came crashing into my world like a raging sea, unpredictable and profound. Now they are both gone.

What the fuck have I done?

Chapter Nineteen

THE SHOW MUST GO ON

I'm numb as I head home to my flat. I don't even have the energy to call Mel and rip her a new one. I'm so broken inside. Today, I was amazing. Today, I woke up feeling so free and happy for the first time in years; and now, a few hours later, I feel like my body just crash-landed from five thousand feet without a parachute.

I walk into my building after leaving Will at the rehearsal studio. I need space to process everything that just happened. I can't even remember what songs we decided on for our set. Thankfully, I wrote them all down in my folder.

"Honey?" Anton's worried voice floats down to me as I climb the stairs to my door. I look up, and he gets a full-frontal view of my face: blotchy, puffy, mascara in streaks down my cheeks.

"What the fuck happened, Brooklyn?" He grabs my arms, his concerned eyes scouring my face, my body, looking for any physical hurt. I'm hurt all right, but nothing that can be seen from the outside.

I look up at his worried face. "Anton, I fucked up," my voice breaks. "Will is leaving me, and he… he kissed me, and Jarrod walked in," I can't get the rest out, because the tears are clogging my throat again.

"Oh shit, Bee," he drags me into a big hug, gliding his hand up and down my back in a nurturing manner, holding me while I get my voice back.

"It's all a mess, I'm a mess," I pull back, trying not to get his T-shirt dirty with my messy face.

"Honey, I'm here. How about you go and get cleaned up, then come over and we can talk. Whatever it is, we can fix this, Brooklyn, OK?" he kisses the top of my head and steps back.

I nod and take a deep breath. Anton helps me open my door, my hands so shaky that I can't get the key in the lock myself.

"I'll leave the door unlocked; just come in when you're ready."

"Thank you," and that's all I can say right now.

I almost scald myself in a hot shower, trying to wash off the hurt and pain that I'm feeling. I don't know if I want to push the limits of physical hurt to punish myself, I know this mess is all my fault. How did I miss that Will was in love with me? We've been friends for so long, I have no idea when it changed for him. When did he see me as a woman and not just the kid who sang with him? Why did he never mention it before? These are questions that I need to ask him, but right now it's too painful.

As I get dressed in comfortable loose clothing, I recall Jarrod's face, the shock and pain etched over that captivating face I've fallen for, it hurts all over again. I don't know what to say to him, it all happened so fast. He probably doesn't want to talk to me right now anyway. I need to get some clarity before I can explain things; that's if he is willing to listen.

Anton is cooking as I walk in. He hands me a glass of white wine as I take a seat at his kitchen bench. I look marginally better than I did when he saw me on the steps.

"Take your time, Honey, tell me what happened," and his calm, smooth voice settles me as I take an unladylike gulp of chilled wine.

"Everything was great, Anton; things seemed so fucking amazing, spectacular for the first time in my life." I take another big swallow of wine. "My work is on point; singing at the Houston is a dream. Mel, Simon, Kate, Will, you guys, everyone is healthy and happy. Then I meet a guy who turns me inside out." I take a deep breath and close my eyes, thinking of Jarrod, of everything that's been growing between us.

"We have something real, Jarrod and I… We have something intense," Anton nods, stirring his chicken coconut curry. It smells amazing, those aromatic spices, but my stomach is in knots. I'm not hungry.

"I had no idea… Will, he told me he loves me, Anton; he said he is '*in love*' with me. How is that possible? I missed it. He never said anything, and now he's leaving. He's taking a tour — Friday is our last show together," I can feel the tears prick my eyes again, threatening to fall over my still-damp lashes.

"How is it possible, you ask? It's possible because you are an amazing person. Talented, beautiful, yes, but you have a heart as big as the Atlantic Ocean, that's why. You love your friends passionately, you overcame such a fucked-up childhood, baby, and yet you still open your heart. how can he not love you?"

Anton walks around to my side of the bench and takes my face in his hands.

"He has no choice; no one does with you, Bee, you draw people in like a moth to a flame," my tears spill over at his words.

"I didn't mean for it to happen. I love him, I do. Maybe things would have been different if I had known earlier, but now… Jarrod," My heart hurts, getting pulled in two different directions. "Will said he needs time away; he can't be here right now."

"I understand Will's decision, Bee. He needs time; it will do him some good. He's been with you for such a long time, you need to let him go, let him find his own way." Anton wipes my eyes gently, and I nod.

It hurts like hell that I have to let him go. It's a pain I wasn't expecting to feel, a loss holding more weight than that of my mother passing. Sad to think, but Will going away is more painful than Samantha's death. It speaks volumes of how important he is to me.

"You need to think about things, turn the phone off, and be true to your heart. Don't drag it out; these guys are both hurting, honey, pretty fucking hard, I'd imagine," he hands me a bowl of his mother's coconut curry with steamed cauliflower rice. I take the bowl, but I know it will be a struggle to get any food down tonight.

"I know... Fuck!" I curse. "I love Will, I do, and part of me wants to give him all of me; he deserves it, he deserves to be loved fully," I know that's the honest truth. Will is the kind of person who would give you his whole heart; he would never make you question his loyalty or love. "I knew he loved me, but I didn't realise it changed for him, turned into a romantic love."

Anton is eating and stops to take a sip of his wine. "We suspected it, Bee, to be honest. Will looks at you like the sun rises in those gemstone eyes of yours," I feel even worse now, for not seeing it earlier, for hurting him.

"I've messed up royally, haven't I?" I try to take a mouthful of food, but my stomach has other ideas. "And now, I know it's new, but... Jarrod... I've fallen hard, Anton. I'm in love with him," I cry again. I can't stop the deluge of salty water leaking from my eyes, my emotions everywhere, like a hormonal teenager. My period has arrived and is most likely contributing to my distress.

"It's not your fault, baby, you can't determine other people's hearts; you can only decide what's best for your heart," I nod. Anton is right. I have to make a decision, it's going to hurt one of them, which hurts me in return.

I sleep at Anton's on Wednesday night. He holds me as I cry myself to sleep in his big bed; he comforts me and strokes my hair till I fall into sleep oblivion, where I can't feel my shattered heart.

I turn my phone on Thursday mid-morning to a deluge of missed calls, one from Will and the rest from Mel. I decide to call her; she will keep ringing me otherwise. I'm still in Anton's bed. He left for rehearsals a while ago, and I'll make sure to tidy up before I leave today.

Mel answers on the first ring. "Bee, I've been calling for hours," she says in a rush of breath.

"Yeah, well, I didn't want to talk to anyone," I say in a snippy tone. "I can't believe you knew and didn't say anything." She knows exactly what I'm referring to.

"Honey, please, he made me promise. I was between a rock and a hard place. You have to believe me, I tried everything I could to work this out so neither of you got hurt." She exhales on the phone, I can hear the emotion in her voice.

"Fucking hell!" she lets out the expletive. I do know she didn't do this deliberately, so I give her a break; she is not only my family but our band manager. She needed to do what was best for Will on a professional level, too.

"Mel, I didn't know… that he… You know," I say in a quiet tone; I'm still so shocked by Will's declaration.

"I know you didn't, honey, it's not your fault," she uses that motherly tone when I'm upset, when I'm hurting.

"Did you know before this? Did you know how he felt?" I'm trying to work out when it all came about.

"Yes, sort of. Not officially, but I could see it, I guess. He loves you, Bee, and as much as he is happy for you, to see you happy with Jarrod, it also hurts him. You have to let him go, just for a while, OK? Give him some time," she continues after a pause. "But Bee, if you have feelings for him, if you can see a future with Will, then you need to say something now," she speaks with a soft tone.

"Fuck!" I breathe into the phone. Closing my eyes, I rub my temples, my head is beginning to hurt, and I can feel the start of a headache coming on.

"Let me get through tomorrow night. I just need to get through that before I can think clearly about any of this," I tell her. I need a bucket-load of coffee today, like a whole mother-fucking jug.

"Call me if you need anything... And Bee, just follow your heart." Then she ends the call. Is that so easy? Just follow your heart? Because my heart is currently in pieces, and I have no idea how to put it back together.

Friday arrives, and after some meditation and yoga, I try to calm my mind. I need to be in the zone tonight for work. Getting through this last show with Will is going to be difficult; then Jarrod: what do I even say to him right now? I have given him space since the Wednesday nuclear bomb blast, and I haven't heard a word from him at all. I decide to text him. I know he will be there tonight, and I want to speak to him after the show. I need to see him. It's killing me inside thinking about him.

Jarrod,
I'm so sorry.
Can we talk after the show? Bee x

I spent all afternoon with a knot in my stomach: no answer from Jarrod. I even tried to call, and it just went to voicemail. I forgot I had a doctor's appointment booked today; lucky my phone calendar reminded me. I was about to call and cancel, but decided to go; it got me out of the flat, and forced me to do something mundane and regular, despite my current torment.

I had booked in a couple of weeks ago for a contraceptive implant. I had to wait for a certain time in my cycle, and if I missed this I would need to wait another month. Does it even matter now? I've never taken birth control before. My past two partners used condoms, but with Jarrod, I wanted to take the next step. This implant lasts for three years, effective after seven days. Was it a total waste of time now?

My heart is pounding as I walk into The Wave cocktail bar. People are mingling at the bar, or sitting at the tables enjoying an early-bird drink. I still have time before I take the stage as I arrived early today. I don't see Jarrod, or Christopher for that matter. Daniel spots me across the room and gives me a wave. I nod and head over to the private dressing room. He looks busy talking to a bunch of corporates.

Vivian is setting up as I enter. I put my guitar case down near the door. When she turns around, I can see she isn't her usual vibrant self, either. Her eyes are slightly puffy and red-rimmed, despite the beautiful make-up she has masterfully painted on her own face.

"You look just as miserable as me," I comment, my face conveying my current predicament, no doubt. "It's all a mess, Viv," Her face softens at my words. She comes over to me, holds my arms and gives me a soft hug.

"I know, honey. I had drinks with Will last night; he filled me in." She pulls back and takes my face in her hands. She is so comforting, and such a great friend that I really appreciate her right now; especially knowing how she feels about Will, it can't be easy for her.

"It's not your fault, Brooklyn, don't you dare blame yourself," she says, and my eyes start to tear up; I can feel the salty water pooling on my lashes. "There is no rhyme or reason when it comes to matters of the heart, honey. You can't make someone fall in love with you, and you can't stop someone from falling in love with you… if that's what their heart desires." She moves some hair off my face with a supportive, caring touch.

"I know, but it doesn't stop me from feeling like shit. Like I've messed up all our lives," I tell her.

Vivian guides me over to the racks of stunning dresses. "Bee, it will work out. I believe in fate; things happen for a reason, your destiny is around the corner, and mine… Well, whatever that is will reveal itself soon… Shit! Now I sound like my grandmother reading the tea leaves," she laughs, and I crack up with her.

"You mean all I had to do was have my tea leaves read to know all the answers?" I question with wide eyes.

"Honey, in the words of my fortune-telling grandmother, 'The magic can guide you, but the soul will decide what it wants in the end'," she wiggles her fingers like the woo-woo magic is in the air around us.

"So that's how you have the gift of magically turning me into a princess every week? You inherited special abilities, my fairy godmother," I kiss her on the cheek. I'm feeling much better now. Vivian laughs and just moves over to the glorious array of dresses we have to choose from.

I'm ready to get into work mode and put on a show for the patrons of the Houston Hotel. "Oh, before we start, I need a dress with sleeve coverage tonight. I just got a contraceptive implant in my arm today and I'm a little bruised." I take off my blazer and show her my inner arm; the implant is not visible, but I have swelling and bruises starting to show.

"No worries, Honey, I have just the thing!" She runs her hands over the rack before pulling out a beautiful dress: a pink floral off-the-shoulder tiered mini dress with small sleeves, chiffon fabric in a floral print with ruffle trim, elastic waistband and A-line silhouette. It's a little bohemian and a little romantic, I love it.

"It's Zimmerman, spring collection from Australia. So floaty and feminine," she tells me, as she rummages through the boxes of shoes. "Ah -ha! Found them," she holds up a pair of stunning tan leather point-toe, high-heeled pumps to go with it. "Now, get dressed so I can make you look like a goddess already."

So, I do. Then I sit and clear my mind from all the hurt and pain of the last week, while Vivian works her magic on me. This is showbiz, folks; no matter what happens in your personal life, the show must go on.

As we put the finishing touches on my hair, Vivian insists on some cute flowers to pin one side of my hair back from my face, when there is a knock at the door. Vivian calls out to enter and Will walks in, his eyes glancing between us, and as much as he tries to hide it, the pain is still evident in the set of his jaw, the furrow of his brow.

"Vivian, can you give me a minute with Bee?" he asks.

"Sure," she nods and touches his arm on the way out, before closing the door quietly. I'm ready, but those damn butterflies are back in my stomach. Lucky I didn't eat earlier, I think, as I walk over to Will, who is waiting just inside the door for me.

"You look beautiful, honey" his eyes roam over me in sadness, and my heart breaks seeing him like this. "Are you all right?" He asks.

"As well as I can be, but you know how it goes; we have a commitment, I'll make it work," he nods. Will takes my hands in his strong ones with calluses on his fingers from years and years of plucking strings.

"I'm sorry for what happened, and especially for leaving you," he tells me, his eyes imploring me to understand everything.

I take a deep breath. I have to choose my next words carefully, as I don't want to hurt anyone in this situation, least of all Will. "I know, and I'm sorry for hurting you, Will. I had no idea; why didn't you talk to me earlier, tell me how you felt?" I ask, my eyes searching his face for any sign of what he is thinking right now, and I wish I could read him like those damn tea leaves Vivian talked about.

He lets out a big gust of air, looking up to the ceiling, and then back at me. "I guess I wanted to give you time. You were just getting your life together, I didn't want to wreck our friendship," he rubs his fingers over my hands, touching me softly. "Would it have made a difference?" he asks, his eyes boring into mine now, so deeply. "If I told you earlier, would it have changed anything?" I hold my breath because that is the million-dollar question I've been playing on repeat in my head for two days.

I think about it for a second, looking between his caramel eyes, and I tell him the truth — he deserves that. "Yes, probably. I'm not comfortable with many men, you know that. But with you, I trust you, I would have given you a chance. I love you, Will and friendship can be a great start to a relationship," I see the pain in his eyes.

I know I haven't had a lot of time to think about what that means, really means, moving from a friendship to a romantic relationship, but I would have explored it if things were different. Before I fell into the deepest blue depths of my dark-haired prince.

"But now... Jarrod," I whisper, he nods his head, his eyes not hiding the ache and hurt. Will smiles and touches my face so lightly, looking at me like he is taking in his last sunset.

"Don't feel bad, Honey. I just want you to be happy, and if he makes you happy, then it's the right choice. I need some time to do my own thing for a while," I nod in agreement. I have to let him go for the both of us.

I reach up and take his face in my hands, because ten years of love for this man is running through my veins, and I'll forever be grateful for his support, friendship, and music, no matter what happens. I give him a chaste kiss on the lips, just a small press of my lips to his. "I'll always love you, Will. I'm here for you no matter what," No more words are necessary, it's done.

"Come on, Honey, the crowd is waiting for your magic," he picks up my guitar and opens the door. For a second, I hold my breath, and when I don't see anyone waiting on the other side, I'm momentarily gutted.

Jarrod is not there waiting for me. I shake it off and smile at Will, as fake as it feels. "You mean OUR magic," I tell him, because it's true. Finding that special bond with another musician is like striking gold.

We take the stage, Will places my acoustic guitar on the stand next to me and takes his seat, ready. "Good evening, I'm Brooklyn and this amazingly talented guy is Will Stanton. We hope you enjoy tonight's performance," Will begins to play, his fingers strumming the guitar as we start the first song. As I sing and look into the crowd, I see Daniel, Christopher and Vivian in the back, drinks in their hands. The room is full, barely standing room, faces smiling, people singing, but I can't find the one face I really want to see.

We finish the first song and I plaster on a showbiz smile, looking like the perfect musician they see on the outside, yet inside I'm crushed. I pick up my guitar and Will and I start the next song, Fleetwood Mac's 'Rhiannon'. The minute the first chords are played, the crowd claps: they know the familiar notes.

Will plays lead guitar and I play rhythm, playing the chords with perfect timing. We slowed down this arrangement, the sound of both guitars together is enchanting. Rhiannon, a girl's name, is of Welsh origin meaning 'great queen' or 'goddess', and Stevie Nicks wrote the song about a bewitched woman from a fantasy novel, inspired by an ancient kind of magic.

I don't know what kind of magic the song holds, but in that moment my blue-eyed prince appears. I watch him walk towards the bar, behind a sea of people, dressed in his customary black shirt, open at the neck, sleek black hair pushed off his face, those eyes locked on me, I can feel them burning me as I sing the words into the microphone.

His ocean gaze, dark and stormy, is holding me captive again, like the first time I saw him at the bar, watching me sing, yet this time with more fervour and seriousness in those blue depths.

I watch him for the whole set, take in every sip of his drink, every movement he makes, watch his lips as he replies to anyone who speaks to him, yet his eyes always find their way back to mine. Every time.

After singing for almost two hours, contemporary and classic songs, we end our performance with a final song which Will added in at rehearsal. One of his favourites, he moves over to the piano for this arrangement.

It's 'Wicked Game' by Chris Isaak, but we have used a cover version by American artist Daisy Gray for inspiration. Her version is geared toward a female singer: slower, more sensual, and haunting on the piano.

"This is our last song tonight," I say, and the crowd of people sigh their disappointment, showing me how much they enjoyed tonight's performance. "This is Will's last night here at The Wave, so let's make it special," I nod to Will to begin the song. The piano notes float around the silent room like the tide rolling on a deserted beach. No other sound; even the bar staff have stilled. The whole room seems to be holding their breath.

I sing, my voice, clear and strong, rings out in the room, singing about losing someone, about not wanting to fall in love, desire, dreams, wicked games. I look at Jarrod, my body, my eyes, my voice singing to him. Everyone else disappears and I put all the passion I have into this song. For him.

He watches me, mesmerised, his gaze penetrating right to my soul. As I finish the song, the room is frozen in silent appreciation, before they all start applauding, a standing ovation like we've never seen. Will stands and whispers in my ear and I nod, trying to hold back the emotion, the tears that have pricked my eyes again. They threaten to fall for my last night with Will, for the pain I can see in Jarrod's eyes, the torment I see on his perfect face.

"Thank you. I'm going to leave you with Will to perform a classical piece on the piano before he finishes tonight," I walk off stage, my legs carrying me across the room, and I lean on the wall near the hallway to my private change room. I can't hold myself up any longer. Not one second longer.

Will starts to play, his classical background coming out to show everyone just how talented he is. Sure, playing originals and covers is what we do, but Will is a stunning pianist, with roots in Beethoven, Bach and Mozart.

Tonight he is playing a beautiful piece called 'Mariage d'Amour' by Paul de Senneville, a French composer from the seventies. It translates to 'Marriage of Love'. It's passionate, eerie, and nostalgic, the title would have you believe it's a love song, but the chord progression and timing give you the impression it's about lost love.

As Will's fingers fly over the keys like a bird in flight, my eyes find Jarrod's ocean-blue depths of their own accord.

I'm drawn to him, lured like a bee to honey. We stare at each other over the crowd, our eyes meeting in fire and ice, and I crack. I can't hold my pain in any longer, my face crumbles, the tears finally spilling over to the sound of Will's passionate piano playing.

Jarrod watches me as I disintegrate before him. My face is open for all to see, streaked with tears rolling over my lips, and onto the floor. But he doesn't move. He doesn't take a step; he just holds me there with his stare.

As the music comes to its completion, and the crowd stands for Will, clapping him for such a flawless magical performance, I run, I turn and run back to my dressing room, collapsing on the couch in floods of tears. Tears for my friend who loves me, is leaving me, and tears for the man I'm in love with, who won't even speak to me.

I feel someone sit next to me, hold me, gentle hands stroking my hair. "Baby girl... don't cry," Vivian murmurs. Her voice is rough, like she is holding back her own tears. She must feel it, too. I stay like that for what seems like hours, Vivian consoling me, holding me. Eventually, I have to get myself together and go home, because it's clear now that I'll be waiting all night. My dark and stormy prince is not coming.

Chapter Twenty

STRINGS

The weekend is a mixture of tears and pain, Anton forcing me to the gym for a punishing couple of sessions. I think he is trying to kill me; either that or chastise me in the physical sense for my self-appointed loathing.

In the words of my fitness drill sergeant, "You don't get an arse like that by sitting on it! Now squat, baby!"

And I sure did. My legs are now so rubbery and sore, I can barely stand up.

I still haven't been able to contact Jarrod, so I cave and call Christopher on Sunday afternoon. "Hello," he answers on the third ring.

"Chris, it's Bee," I speak sombrely into the phone.

"Hello, Bee, is everything all right?" he asks me in a similar tone.

"Not really. Look, I'm sorry to have to call you like this, but I need to speak to Jarrod," I wait to see what his reaction will be. He would know everything by now, I'm sure.

He lets out a puff of air into the phone, almost like he was expecting me to ask that. "Bee, just give him some time; he's kind of crushed right now," he tells me, no animosity in his voice, just a matter-of-fact tone.

"I know, Chris. Fuck, this whole situation is a mess," he can surely hear the emotion in my voice over the phone without having to see my face in person.

"Look, he's never let this happen before, you know, get close to someone. Give him more time. He'll come around, honey," I nod to myself, hopeful yet still a little dejected at not being able to just talk to him.

"OK, thank you. And Chris… Just tell him I'm here when he is ready."

"Will do, Bee; take care," and he ends the call.

I need to keep myself busy, so I tap the music app on my phone and the speakers pound out the epic shreds of Metallica's 'Master of Puppets'. I need some angry heavy metal while I clean my flat and endeavour to stop thinking about Jarrod, at least for a couple of hours.

On Monday, I decided to get out for a while; as sore as I am, I need some inspiration, I need to do something we girls are good at… something to make me feel better — and nothing lifts the spirits like a little retail therapy!

After two hours of hitting the shops down Oxford Street, I've made a good dent in my bank account. New dresses, new shoes, some stunning new perfume by Jo Malone London, and of course, the scented candles to match. I went a little over the top with the perfumes, but I couldn't help it: the Beauty of the British Isles collection was too breathtaking. The Salty Amber and Aqua Lemon cologne especially made me think of Jarrod, like diving into crystal-clear water at sunrise.

I wave for a taxi when a thought hits me, and I tell the driver to take me to Denmark Street.

Hanks Guitar Shop is an institution in London, a quarter of a century in this old building, selling not only to enthusiasts but some of the UK's most famous musicians. It's not a large shop, but it contains some of the best custom guitars on the market. As I walk in the door, hands full with my shopping, I hear a booming male voice.

"Well, ain't ya a sight for sore eyes… It's the one and only Brooklyn Grace Barrett, people," he shouts, using my full name. He has a wrinkled face, an unlit cigarette in his mouth and skinny tattooed arms holding his lean hips. This is Mick. Mick is a retired muso with years of experience, and he has been at Hanks for as long as I can remember. I haven't been in for a while, but Will and I made regular visits to check out the stock and say hello in the past.

"It's been far too long, Mick," I put my bags behind his register as I lean in for a bony hug.

His skinny arms welcome me in with a surprisingly firm grip. "You must be a hundred by now?" I comment, laughing as he pulls away, his eyes sparkling at me with humour. He reminds me of Keith Richards from the Rolling Stones, only with longer hair but no less wrinkles. The years of booze and partying have weathered his skin like the creased pages of a well-read book.

"What brings ya by our fine establishment today, Milady," his southeast cockney accent is still prevalent when he speaks.

"Mick, I need a guitar today. Something special for a true metal head — it's a gift," He nods and rubs his jaw for a moment.

"Come upstairs, lovey, I 'ave a few ideas," he says and I follow him up.

Wow, I never get sick of seeing so many pretty instruments all at once. I usually play acoustic guitar myself as my music calls for that style, but if I was a rock guitarist, this would be heaven.

We spend almost forty minutes looking around the shop, everything from Gibson Les Pauls to Vintage Fender Stratocasters, Paul Reed Smiths, and more. He shows me a Veleno Aluminium guitar owned and signed by Ace Frehley from KISS for a whopping £55,000. "Ah, a little over-budget, Mick, but it's a hot number for sure," I hand it back gently.

As I turn around to keep looking, something catches my eye on the back wall. I take a minute to look it over, then it hits me right in the chest. This is it. I have no idea how much it costs, but this guitar screams Jarrod to me.

"Mick, what the fuck is that?" I ask, and point to the beautiful instrument taking my breath away.

"Ah… good eye, lovey." He walks over and carefully takes it off the rack, bringing it over to me to view up close. "This is a 2011 Paul Reed Smith 305 HSS private stock. Just look at this blue fade paintwork, would ya." He looks at the guitar like it's a rare sapphire. "Maple top, mahogany back and solid East Indian Rosewood neck. It's a beauty, all right."

I take the guitar and hold it in my hands. The ombre fade from dark to light blue reminds me of a beach, the lighter blue water in the shallows and the darker blue ocean depths. Just like his eyes. It's superb. PRS guitars are made for rock music. I think it's perfect. Impeccable condition, too.

"How much, Mick, and don't rob me blind, old man," I tell him, smiling.

"It comes with all the certifications, papers, and original case. It's advertised for seven thousand quid, but I can take some off the top for ya, darlin'. Best I can do is…" — he scratches his head, then looks back at me — "£5,950."

That's about fifteen percent, so a decent discount considering the value. "Done. Clean her up pretty for me, and can you have it delivered tomorrow?" I ask.

"Anything for Milady," he gives me a little bow, tipping his imaginary top hat at me with a wink.

I give him a smacking kiss on the cheek and follow him downstairs to pay. My bank balance is getting a mega-hit today, but of course, what fun is making money if you can't spend it on the people you love? And my heart flips in my chest. I do love him; I want to show him that, and I hope this gift voices that. No! *Screams* that to him when he opens the case tomorrow. I hope this blows his freaking mind. Whatever Jarrod's decision, I want him to have a special something to keep, just from me.

I tell Anton all about my indecent spending spree for Margarita Monday, and he even forces me into a mock runway parade, modelling my new purchases.

"Hot! Hot! Hot, Honey! I'd bang you wearing those heels, for sure," he exclaims while admiring my new olive green stiletto four-inch sandals, with soft fabric ties that secure at the back of my ankles.

"I know, right, I think I will take them this Friday and see if Viv has a dress to go with them. I just had to have them, Anton," and I kick my new heels up with a little happy dance. Anton appreciates my excitement over new shoes more than anyone else I know. As much fun as I'm having playing dress-ups for Anton, my mind can't seem to stop drifting far from a certain motorcycle-riding, guitar-playing, blue-eyed prince.

I've just woken up from my Margarita-induced coma Tuesday morning when my phone starts playing 'I Can't Get No Satisfaction' by the Rolling Stones, and I know that's Mick from Hank Guitar Shop calling.

"Hi, Mick," I answer.

"'Ello, darlin', I just wanted to let ya know the PRS Custom shop was delivered this morning. I've emailed ya the delivery docket and paperwork," he tells me.

"Oh, awesome, Mick. I can't thank you enough for organising that," I say, my excitement bubbling at the thought of Jarrod getting his stunning new guitar today. I wonder what he is thinking right now. I even left a handwritten card in the box for him to open. It reads:

Dear Jarrod,

Please accept this gift as a token of my thanks for all you have done to make my stay at the Houston Hotel so extraordinary.

I saw this stunning guitar and immediately thought of you. No metaphorical strings attached. Just enjoy playing this glamour.

I miss you,

Bee xx

"Just to let ya know, ya gave us the name Jarrod Houston to take delivery, but when my boy arrived, some lass called Elizabeth Burton answered. She said Mr Houston was in the shower, and that she could sign for the delivery. We have 'er signature on the docket I emailed ya. Just wanted to let ya know, these expensive guitars can go missin' what…" And with that sentence from Mick, all the air is suddenly gone. My stomach rolls like it's about to unload last night's Margaritas all over my bedroom floor.

"Brooklyn, darlin', ya still there?" Mick asks.

"Yes, sorry," I answer in a weak voice. "Got it. Thank you again for everything, and for following up about the delivery. I appreciate you taking care of me, Mick." I somehow get the words out, trying to remain calm after the bomb he just unknowingly dropped.

"Any time, Brooklyn, ya always welcome at Hanks. And I'll make sure to take the old bird out one night soon to watch ya sing. That'll be a corker, darlin'," he chuckles his Smokey cackle into the phone.

"You do that, and make sure you splurge to get Di a nice new dress, you hear? Don't be stingy, old man," I tell him.

"Well, I'll have ta now, won't I, with ya playing a fancy place like that? Take care, lovey," and he ends the call. I'm left with a sinking feeling in the pit of my stomach and have no idea what the fuck to do now, but that doesn't stop me from breaking my mid-week ice-cream ban, consuming more than my usual weekend quota in one night. Actually, I may have consumed my own body weight in ice-cream this week to get over the movie my head is playing on repeat with Jarrod and Elizabeth, in bed, in the shower, him and her, him in her...

I don't know if it was the ice-cream, the new contraceptive implant, or my own heartbreak, but I threw up all that ice-cream in my toilet. What a fucking mess, literally and metaphorically.

The rest of the week goes by in silence: no text message, no phone call, not even a bloody email, and my heart is about to literally explode out of my chest. I keep busy busting my arse with Anton at the gym, and rehearsals Wednesday with my new musical partner, Leo. He's on a break from touring with his band and happily took over from Will for the remainder of the contract at the Houston Hotel. This is why I work with professional musicians: they can adjust quickly, they know how to change up arrangements to suit the singer and the key, and they are always on time with minimal fuss.

Leo, like Will, provides great harmonies, and we click pretty fast. I think this is a personal favour to Will, seeing as Leo was supposed to be on a break, but I let him know how appreciative I am anyway. We nailed the set list, and I'm comfortable that Friday night's gig will go smoothly. Well, musically, that is. The rest is up for debate.

I arrive at The Wave early and find Vivian in her zone, placing her make-up brushes and styling items on the vanity table. She smiles when she sees me tonight, coming over to hold my shoulders and give me a once-over.

"How are you, baby girl? Holding in there?" she asks me, like a slightly older sister.

"Just perky, Viv," but I give her a face that disputes my comment. "How are you?" I ask, because she has to be mourning the loss of Will, too. I don't know how close they got in the past few weeks, but I know she was invested.

"I'll live. But don't worry about me, I have time to plan a hostile takeover," she winks at me. Hmm, interesting, maybe Vivian is planning to chase him down, and I smile at her enthusiasm. I wish I had some of that right now.

"I need a shot of whatever you've had; my plan failed miserably," I tell her about the whole guitar/Elizabeth situation.

"Well, let's use a little old-fashioned female creativity tonight, Honey," she says with a knowing look. I pull out my new smoking hot heels and the diamond choker necklace Jarrod purchased for me for his birthday party weeks ago. Vivian eyes them with appreciation and smirks.

"Can we work these babies in?" I ask with a sparkle in my eyes, because tonight I'm pulling out all the stops.

"Trust me, I have just the dress to go with those, and when he sees you tonight, there will be fireworks," she replies, and I manage a real smile.

I'm ready to take charge. It's been ten days of silence from Jarrod, ten days of agony being away from him, wanting to see him, talk to him, touch him, and now I'm at my limit. Tonight, I'll make him come to me.

Ninety minutes later, I'm ready, and wow, holy shit, I'm a work of art. Vivian has used every single trick at her disposal to create this look tonight… and I can't imagine I'll be ignored looking like this. I'm wearing my new green sky-high stilettos, soft fabric wrapped around my ankles and tied up into neat bows, and a red fitted mini dress that clings to every curve my body has. It has long sleeves, and a high round neckline, but my legs are on display as this hot little number is shorter than hell. Anton's arse-burning squats were worth the effort this week.

It's totally backless except for thin criss-cross rhinestone straps that barely hold the dress together. My whole back and legs are bare; you can see the tattoos running down my spine, and I know that is a weakness for Jarrod.

Good, let him look. This outfit screams attention, and although I will be in a room full of people, his are the only eyes I want on me.

The diamond choker looks stunning and complements the sparkling rhinestone chains on the back. Vivian has given me some green dangle earrings to match the shoes, and they bring out the green in my eyes perfectly. My hair is styled in a messy up-do. You can't have this stunning backless dress and cover it with hair, so she has artfully arranged my hair loosely but stylishly off my neck. My make-up is dark and smoky tonight, my eyes the feature; paired with a nude lip, the whole ensemble is striking.

We hear a knock at the door and Leo enters when Vivian calls out.

He is momentarily stunned, standing there in his sleek black trousers and black button-up shirt. His normal attire on stage would be more casual, but The Wave is an upmarket cocktail venue. Leo is a handsome guy, shaved hair cropped short, a couple of days of stubble giving him a rough edge, and tattoos from wrist to chest.

"Leo, this is Vivian," I say, giving the poor guy a reprieve from the stunned silence that hit him when he walked into the room and saw the two of us together. Tonight, Vivian is wearing a smoking hot black strapless dress, nude leather heels and fire-engine-red lips. She looks like a *Vogue* fashion model, and poor Leo just got hit with our female energy that's been building up for an hour and a half.

"Ah... Hi... Five-minute call, Bee," and he ducks back out the door like a guy who accidentally walked into a women's locker room. We both burst out laughing.

"Oh, poor guy," Vivian exclaims. "Not many men can handle the power we radiate; and baby girl, your goddess is out in all her glory tonight," she tells me, with one last sweep of her eyes over my outfit. "I'm betting on you tonight, Bee. Jarrod is toast," we laugh again. I hope she is right.

"Lead the way, pretty woman, I'm ready," I say, and kick my heels up as I walk the path to my microphone.

Leo and I are about three songs in when my dark prince makes his entrance. Daniel, Christopher and Vivian have been enjoying the performance from the back VIP section, I can tell they are loving the songs. I smile at them when I can. Vivian gives me a little conspiratorial wink when she sees Jarrod has arrived.

I keep my eyes on him the whole time, his dark hair and perfect face visible over the other patrons, not only due to his height and frame but because he walks with confidence, with an air of masculinity and authority. He does walk in like he owns the place — not in an arrogant way, but rather a commanding way. The same way he takes over my body when we are together — he is in control.

We mix our songs tonight, something a little edgier than what Will and I have done in the past. Leo is part of a hard rock band, and I wanted to spice it up. The arrangements are still suitable for The Wave and its patrons, but I've been singing here for weeks now, and the regulars need a change of pace to keep it interesting.

The last song of the night has arrived. I decided on 'False God' by Taylor Swift. It's probably her most personal love song to date. I'm a little nervous at being so revealing, so open and honest. I know he can read into my song choices, it feels as though he can read my very thoughts.

Leo plays the acoustic guitar perfectly, and the room falls to a hush as I sing.

I look into his ocean eyes as I sing about worshipping him, singing to him about love and sex and that feeling of all-consuming passion. He feels the same way; I can sense it as his eyes lock on me under the stage lights. It's impossible not to feel the emotion and power in this song with these lyrics.

Leo plays perfectly, harmonising with me during the chorus. The perfect pitch of our voices reaches the very edges of the packed room.

Jarrod is entranced, I can see it on his face, the way his eyes follow my every move, his body coiled tight, standing there, ignoring the rest of the room while he takes me in, the music almost hypnotising him. I sing to him: it's the only way I can really communicate, it's my siren song.

At the end of the set, Leo and I hold hands to take our bow, the packed room clapping their delight at our performance tonight. I smile at Leo and give him a pat on the arm. He isn't my Will, my rock, my protector, but he is one hell of a musician, and he saved my arse. "Let's get a drink," I tell him, and he gives me a big smile.

Christopher is first to greet me when we arrive at the VIP section. He hands me a cocktail, and yes, it's the Honey Bee cocktail named in my honour. "Thank you! I needed this tonight. Did you enjoy the music?" I ask him.

"Bee, you look bloody fabulous tonight, and the music was off the charts," Christopher grins at me, his eyes are a little glassy, because — why not? — he has a lifelong supply of top-shelf alcohol in this place.

"Thank you, Christopher, I kind of had someone to impress, you know?" I confess, and he smiles, all white teeth and sparkling pale crystal eyes.

"Brooklyn, I have to hand it to you, I've never seen anyone tie my brother in knots like you do; then, to top it off, send him the most exquisite gift — that PRS is fucking loaded. Seriously, you're mad!" he shakes his head. I know, that guitar is next level, and I'm about to answer him, when I feel a tingle up my spine.

Christopher looks over my shoulder and then back to me, and I know *he* is behind me. I can feel the heat radiating off him onto my bare back. My breathing increases, and I'm trying to stay calm on the outside, but his closeness affects me… it always does.

"Brooklyn." My name on his lips makes me melt. I take a second to inhale and then turn around.

Those eyes, those fucking blue, blue eyes get me every time. I can't look away; the ten days we've been apart have just confirmed that I'm in way over my head.

And as much as it pains me to think of Will, and what I should have given him, I can't regret my decision for a single second when I'm inches away from Jarrod. I realise I never really had a choice, after all.

We stare at each other, his eyes exploring my face like it's been years since he last saw me, his chest rising and falling faster than its usual steady rhythm. His eyes are flicking from my face to my neck, and the necklace he gave me. I can see the blue flames starting to ignite.

"Can we talk?" he asks, I can just hear him above the noise in the crowded room. I nod, not speaking, as my words fail me when I'm near him. He takes my hand and I barely get a chance to wave to the others as Jarrod strides towards the exit, towards the private lift he uses. We must be heading up to his apartment.

We walk into the lift in silence, both of us standing on opposite sides, just taking each other in. I haven't been this close to him for days, but it's still not close enough. His clear eyes observe me like he is trying to capture my image in his mind for all time. I let him look; I'll wait for him to speak first.

"Did you sleep with him?" The question is spoken so low in the confined space, I barely hear him. It is more like a rumble of sound from his chest.

"What?" My eyes fly to his in shock.

"Did you sleep with him, Brooklyn?" he asks me, louder now, not with anger but frustration, it sounds.

"No, of course not," I answer. "You know I'm not like that," My chin lifts a little at his blunt inquiry. Jarrod takes a breath for the first time since we entered the lift. He runs his hand through that inky black hair, releasing the tension.

"Did you fuck Elizabeth?" I ask him; turnabout is fair play, after all.

His gaze snaps to mine in confusion. I haven't seen him rattled before, he's usually so composed and intense, but just for a second he looks truly surprised.

"Why would you think that?" He steps closer to me now, just a foot away, so tall, so direct.

"She signed for you... the guitar," I tell him, and his face softens. He looks like he wants to smile, but I can't think of any reason to be happy right now, because the thought of him with another woman is making that cocktail swirl in my stomach, and not in a good way.

The lift arrives and the door opens, but we don't move just yet.

"Brooklyn, I haven't touched anyone else since I met you," he says, and I finally release my breath. "Chris, the tosser... Let's just say he took what was on offer. I think they had a few drinks Monday night."

Jarrod takes my hand and leads me out, my queasiness disappearing instantly. Bloody Christopher! I actually feel sorry for Elizabeth — she can't have Jarrod, so she moves on to his brother. She needs to get a life, I think to myself.

He leads me into the private apartment; no one else here, just the two of us. We head into his room, Coldplay playing on the large-screen TV, his signature scent hitting me like a smack to the face. I almost forgot what that was like. He takes a seat on the edge of the bed. I just stand and look around, like it's been forever since I was here.

"Why didn't you answer my calls?" I ask, as I look over at him calmly sitting on his giant bed, while I'm holding in butterflies that want to escape and take flight any moment.

Jarrod runs his hand through his hair again, thinking for a second before he answers me. "I needed to think. What I walked in on last week was fairly cutting, Brooklyn. I had that image of the two of you in my mind, and I needed a minute."

I nod. I understand that it would have been painful for him, to see another man kiss me. "I know, and I'm sorry. I wanted to tell you that I had no idea about Will's feelings for me," I answer honestly. "It kind of surprised the fuck out of me, too." I move closer to him: he needs to really hear me now.

"Jarrod, Will and I have been through a lot in the past decade. He will always be in my life, I want you to understand that." I take a breath and hope he accepts my truth.

"But what I feel for him is different, you and I are different. Do you know what I'm saying?" He looks up into my face, his eyes searching for the truth.

"Do you love him?" he gently asks me, those stormy eyes searching mine for the answer.

"Yes," I take a shallow breath. "But I'm not in love with him. I'm in love with you," and I put my hands on his face, run my fingers over his lips, his eyebrows, his jaw.

He closes his eyes for a moment, just letting me touch him. When he opens them again, I can see something has changed. A shift of emotions.

"Let me show you, let me love you, Jarrod," I whisper as I move to sit on his lap, getting as close as I can to him, his body, his warmth — he draws me in like a lighthouse calling lost ships at night.

"I want you so fucking much, Brooklyn; I want all of you forever," he tells me, and I give him my eyes, let him see that he has me. He had me from the first moment I looked into his blue depths.

"I'm yours Jarrod," I tell him, and then he moves, crashing his lips to mine in a feverish kiss, his control and caution gone now; he is all heat and fire. It consumes me.

I have no idea how it happens, but my dress and shoes end up on the floor, and Jarrod's clothing is suddenly ripped off, his actions so fast and aggressive, like he has been waiting for this moment for too long. I'm suddenly naked, in nothing but the diamond necklace he gave me. I'm back sitting on him, his strong body so heated and ready, his hard length jutting up from our seated position on the bed.

I break the kiss to let him know I want him, just him, no barriers now. "Jarrod, I'm on birth control," his eyes fly to mine, the raw passion on his face clear to me, his control held barely in check.

"I'm clean. I want this with you, only you… If you want to," I say looking into his eyes again.

"Christ!" He breathes out, his hands tightening on my waist, squeezing me. "You have no fucking idea how much I want that with you, Brooklyn. I'm clean, too," and there is a heartbeat of time as we both look at each other, barely two inches between our faces, and I can see it — the decision is made.

Jarrod's lips come crashing down on mine, his hands roaming my back, my waist, my arse, like he can't stop touching me everywhere. In this position, facing each other, it's so intimate, so heightened. I'm ready, I can't wait any more, I need the connection. I place my hands on his strong shoulders and raise my body enough for him to position himself under me.

As I slide down his hard length slowly, my body opening for him, I feel everything. I'll never get over this feeling, Jarrod and I together.

When he's all the way in, I suck in a breath. It's so much more this way, so much deeper. "Jesus, Brooklyn, you feel amazing. I can barely take it, Angel," he speaks into my neck, kissing me there, while his hands keep my hips steady on him.

"I love you, Jarrod," I tell him, and his eyes find mine, the connection between us so vivid, so exquisite, I can't help the lone tear that drops from my lashes. He kisses my swollen lips so tenderly, so delicately, then murmurs the words I've been waiting for, hoping for all this time.

"Je t'aime, mon ange… je t'aime tellement." And even though I don't speak French, I understand exactly what he says, because he shows me, all night; his body, his mouth, his eyes, they speak to me in the one language that matters most.

Chapter Twenty-one

THE BIG APPLE

I feel his fingers running over my back tattoos, down my spine, his mouth is on my neck, kissing me there as I float into consciousness.

Last night felt like a dream, Jarrod offered me everything I wanted. My heart is almost perfect. He revived me, but there will be a little piece that still won't heal till Will is back. Until I can see Will happy one day, that little piece will remain adrift.

"Angel, you bought me a guitar," he whispers into my neck, those hands still roaming over me slowly.

"Mmm, I did," I mumble sleepily. It feels like I've only had two hours' sleep; last night was incredible, but I'm wrecked today. "Do you like it?" I ask him, turning my face to see his disgustingly handsome one up close.

The smile he gives me is crazy beautiful. "Are you serious? I fucking love it, Brooklyn. A custom shop PRS?" he huffs a breath, falling back onto the bed, his eyes looking straight up to the high ceiling of his bedroom.

"John Mayer, Mark Tremonti, Dave Navarro, Carlos Santana... The sound these guitars produce is phenomenal. A dense weighty tone, full and fat, but lots of clarity, so sweet." He is talking and I'm just listening; he is totally buzzed about my gift, and that makes me so happy.

Jarrod looks over to me then, his face so open and clear. "You shouldn't have spent so much, Brooklyn. It's extravagant," he looks at me with a frown between his black brows.

I lift my hand to touch the frown and smooth it out for him gently.

"Jarrod, I have my own money, and I can spend whatever I like on the people I love. Besides, you can talk," I touch my neck, the neck currently still surrounded by diamonds. His eyes dip to my neck for a few seconds, then return to my eyes. There is a heartbeat where we just watch each other silently.

His smirk is a dead giveaway that he is thinking all kinds of dirty things. "Brooklyn, that necklace was for me. I'm going to give you your present now," and he does. My morning coffee fix is delayed indefinitely because Jarrod spends the rest of the morning thanking me for the guitar personally, and I accept his thanks, many times over.

The next few weeks fly by in a haze of absolute bliss. My little heart is going to burst with happiness, even though a small piece is off touring with Will. I try to give him space, we text weekly, but I have to make sure he is doing well on his own. I have to keep a small connection with him, and I suspect I always will.

Anton hosts the next family dinner night, him and Trey cooking up a storm of Caribbean-inspired food that Anton's mum recommended they make. It all smells amazing and tastes just as incredible!

I'm helping Anton wash up in the kitchen when he tells me, "I'm thinking of asking Trey to move in," and I turn around, a huge smile on my face. We are whispering so the others don't hear us talking.

"OMG, Anton, I'm so happy for you!" I do a little silent shimmy dance in his kitchen. He gives me a quick hug, the excitement exuding from him is so great.

"I know, Honey, I'm elated… I just hope he says yes!"

"Are you kidding? You two are amazing together, babe. He loves you, Anton, it's the right time," I tell him honestly, because these two are perfect for each other. Hello, relationship goals!

"What are you two whispering about over here?"

I turn around and find Jarrod walking into the kitchen, his eyes laughing at our antics, which would have looked amusing from over the other side of the room, I'm sure.

"Bee was just telling me how big your equipment…" Anton starts, and I reach up to smother his mouth with both my hands, because the rest of that sentence was going to be seriously dirty… Anton-style.

"I was not!" I say, and I turn around, still holding Anton's mouth closed, to see Jarrod holding in a laugh, his shoulders shaking slightly, my face probably resembling a beetroot now.

"Angel, don't be embarrassed, I'm not," and he winks at Anton when he says, "She loves my massive…"

I let go of Anton's face and smash my mouth to Jarrod's, kissing him silent. He is trying to kiss me back, but his laughing is getting in the way.

"Fuckers, both of you," I breathe, when I detach my lips from Jarrod's face. They both crack up now.

Mel saves me and walks into the kitchen, a tiny fluffy head visible under the blanket. Little Katie had a ball tonight, dancing with Uncle Anton, her little body grooving to Dua Lipa's 'Don't Start Now'. It was adorable to watch. She is really growing up fast. Her second birthday party was a hoot. She was totally spoiled by us all.

"Bee, we are heading home. I'll see you Friday night. I booked a sitter so Simon and I could make your last show at the Houston," Mel says over Katie's head.

"Fabulous, I can't wait… But part of me is a little sad. The last few months have flown by, and I've loved singing at The Wave," I tell her. "I have no idea what I'm going to do next," I'm disappointed to be moving on from singing at such a stunning venue; but not only that, it's the end of performing at Jarrod's family's hotel.

Mel gives me a kiss on the cheek, her face softening at my sorrow. "Honey, I've been inundated with offers; that article in the entertainment rag a few weeks ago was great PR for you," she tells me, lifting my chin and looking into my eyes. "But something tells me there is an exceptional offer on the horizon; just wait and see," her eyes flick to Jarrod standing behind me. They share a look between them, and I look back to Jarrod, a question in my eyes.

"I'm sure something will come up, Angel," he tells me reassuringly, taking my hand and giving it a little squeeze.

"Just finish this last performance and take a couple of weeks to relax and recharge," Mel says, and I nod. I will definitely enjoy a break; maybe Jarrod can take a weekend off and we can go to Paris for a few days. I'll have to talk to him about it later. Listening to him speaking French all day is a ridiculously hot thought.

I have one final rehearsal with Leo and manage to make it to the gym with Anton for a couple of punishing sessions during the week, and all of a sudden my last night has arrived. I'm a bundle of nerves, excited because everyone is coming to see me sing: Jarrod, of course, Mel and Simon, Anton and Trey, Vivian, Daniel, Christopher and his mates. Even Mick and his partner of fifty years, Di, will be in attendance. Everyone except Will, and my heart breaks a little at the thought, but the show must go on, and I have to finish with a bang.

The last four months have been something special. Playing a couple of months with Will before the heartbreak situation was everything; his love and support were immeasurable. These last weeks have flown by, and playing with Leo has been eye-opening. I can do it, I can make music without Will; it's shown me that I can. Will is always in the back of my mind, but he was right: we needed to go our separate ways for a while at least. I found my wings; I just hope he finds his wings soon. I want that for him more than anything.

Jarrod and I have been inseparable, our love of music gives our relationship extra ties that bind us together. It's like our connection is more than just physical; it's like the perfect song, when the music and lyrics come together to make some kind of magic. Our own brand of magic.

It's said that music lifts dopamine in the brain, reducing stress, and it can even work miracles for people with injuries, helping them to heal faster. He healed me, that I know for certain.

My past, my mother, the assault, it's not gone, but it's less. Jarrod and his music have drowned it out; I can no longer remember the pain I carried for so long.

Making music with Jarrod is better than any high on the planet. He gives me everything I crave, and I know I'll be drawn to him for a long time, chasing that high he gives me with just one look.

Since Will left to go on tour, Jarrod has been my everything. We began writing songs together, and I was wondering how we would flow. I have been writing with Will for so long, but somehow the notes fell in perfect accord.

The past few weeks we have compiled almost a whole album of songs. A mix of his raw vocal talent, melodic guitar playing, and my uniquely soulful, other-worldly vocals have created some of the best work of my career.

There is a spark lit. I haven't mentioned anything to Jarrod, but these songs need to be heard. I'm considering re-entering the recording industry again, for the first time in a decade. With him by my side, together.

One of the songs I especially love is a song we wrote together called 'Stay' the lyrics being drawn from our own emotional ride. Jarrod sings lead and I come in with the harmonies.

"Angel stay
Don't go away"
Don't leave me for one more day,
Angel stay
Can't let you leave
Can't let you go and walk away"

His voice so deep in the lower register, just makes me melt when he sings. Christopher was right all those months ago on karaoke night, Jarrod's talent far surpasses his business skills. He may be more than capable of running a successful five star hotel, but he was made for the stage, he was made for something bigger.

I arrive at The Wave early Friday. Vivian is setting up her magic wands of beautification that she will be using on me shortly — for the last time, I brood. I've gotten used to this pampering extravagance and her lively feminine chatter. Spending this time with her every week for four months has cemented a life-long friendship.

"There she is; how are you, baby girl? Ready to rock this place one more time?" she asks, and when I look at her stunning face, I can see she is about to cry, getting emotional already. Shit!

"Don't you dare, Viv," I say sternly. "Don't you fucking cry, or I'm going to start, and then the make-up will be messed up," I wave my hands to fan my eyes from getting watery.

"I'm sorry, Bee!" she wails. "I'm trying, but it's bloody hard. I'm going to miss you!" She slumps down on the couch, dabbing at her perfectly made-up face with a tissue.

"I'm not going anywhere, we are still going to hang out, and you never know, I may have to request you as part of my new contract, wherever that may be." I take her hands and lift her, standing before me now.

"I love you, Vivian, and I'm still here. I promise," I tell her, and we hug it out.

"Good, because you and Will can't get rid of me that easily, you know," she looks in the mirror to fix her face. She has plans for Will I'm certain.

"Now. Let's get you ready. I've been saving the best for last," she walks over to the clothing rack and pulls out the most stunning dress I've ever seen. My eyes must be the size of saucers, because it's heavenly, ethereal. And I see why she saved it for my last performance.

"Viv..." I breathe.

"I know, Honey, I know," she nods in agreement. "It's a replica of the dress by costume designer Jacqueline Durran for Keira Knightley in the movie *Atonement*," she says so casually, like it's the same as the old T-shirt I sleep in most days. Like it's no big deal!

"It's a thirties-inspired delicate silk confection; the green is identical to the movie dress, it's like a bright gemstone, wouldn't you say? To match your eyes," and she holds it up next to my face, looking between my eyes and the dress. I'm speechless: it's so beautiful.

"But you can't wear underwear; this thing is so delicate, you will have to go commando tonight," she laughs. I don't care one bit: this dress is totally worth it. It's like a dress from a 1930s Parisian cocktail lounge, full-length flowing bias-cut green silk, backless, and as fragile as butterfly wings.

"I'll accept the risk to wear this masterpiece," my eyes caress the dress in awe. "Now, make me beautiful one last time, Master Da Vinci," I give her air kisses three times, as the French do.

Just over an hour later, and I'm ready. Leo has already popped his head in to give me the five-minute call; his eyes almost falling out of his head gave me the impression that Vivian's handiwork is on the money tonight.

I look at myself in the full-length mirror, my eyes a smoky green/grey, highlighting the green and amber perfectly, pale pink on my lips and cheeks gives me a youthful rosy glow.

No necklace or earrings tonight — the dress speaks for itself. My hair falls in soft waves, pinned back to one side with a delicate diamond comb, just enough for a little sparkle.

As we open the door to head outside, I'm stopped by the man waiting for me on the opposite wall. Leaning back so casually, his eyes sparkle and reflect the light coming from behind me. Those midnight blues.

"Vivian, give us a minute?" he asks, she gives Jarrod a nod, then looks back at me.

"Break a leg, baby girl, I'm so proud of you," and she sashays down the hallway into the packed cocktail bar.

Jarrod takes a second to look at me, from the full-length silk, draping over my body like water cascading down a waterfall, clinging to me in all the right places. He looks up as his eyes take in my face, and my hair, absorbing everything with heated admiration, devotion.

"God... you are so beautiful, Brooklyn," he tells me in a whisper, then leans in to kiss me, but he thinks twice, remembering I have my face painted like the Mona Lisa. I lean in, the barest of touches, and my lips feather across his.

"Thank you," I whisper into his lips. He takes my hands, he doesn't say anything, but when I look down to see what has his attention, I realise he is fastening a brilliant diamond bracelet on my left wrist. My eyes snap to his.

"It matches the diamond necklace; I bought them as a set," his eyes are saying more than his words.

I'm not only in shock at such a beautiful gift but also the realisation that he kept this for months. He didn't even know me when I wore the necklace, we officially met at his thirtieth birthday party. Yet he had already purchased the necklace and bracelet set for me.

My heart is racing like a thoroughbred at Royal Ascot. His gift is too much. He is too much.

"Jarrod…" I am lost for words.

"Angel, vous êtes incroyable," he murmurs. I think he called me incredible. I smile.

"Now go out there and show everyone how talented and extraordinary my girlfriend is…"

And I do.

Jarrod walks me to the microphone himself tonight, his hand finally letting me go once I stand on my mark. I look out into the crowd, a packed room, a sea of faces staring at me like I'm some kind of mythical creature.

"Good evening. My name is Brooklyn Grace Barrett, and this talented guy next to me is Leo Stewart. We'd love to entertain you one last time, is that all right?" I ask the patrons and loud applause rings out through the room. I nod to Leo to begin the first song. I take it all in, this performance, this room, these people.

Most are perfect strangers, but down the back, my family — the only family I've ever known — is here to support me. Will is not here in person, but I know his heart is in the room with me. Vivian will record some of the show and send it to him later. I know it will pain him to watch it, but I have faith that he will find his own peace and love one day. Whomever that is with, I know he will find his perfect match. His forever, like I have.

As we fly through tonight's set, part of me is content to complete another successful contract — a professional success, to be sure — but the other part, the one that found my heart's desire, my blue-eyed prince, is sorrowful to see the end. It's not like I won't be back, but it's the end of a chapter, and the beginning of a new one. It's a little nerve-wracking and exhilarating at the same time.

We make it to the last song of the night, and I want to get my last words out while I can still talk, the emotion starting to tickle the back of my throat.

"Thank you for being the best audience a girl could ask for," I tell them, and the crowd cheers as I continue. "My time here at The Wave has come to an end, and I want to extend my heartfelt gratitude to every single person who came to watch me perform; it meant so much," I say, my voice a little wobbly now.

"I want to thank my boys, Will and Leo, for their time and musical talents. I couldn't have asked for better," I look over to Leo, who gives me a wink, his cheeks going a little pink with the attention and whistles from the crowd.

"I want to thank my family," I say, looking down the back to the faces I love. "And to the amazing staff at the Houston Hotel — you made my stay an absolute dream come true," I look for that special person in particular. I find his eyes, just like I do every performance, and I watch him, while he watches me.

"This one is for you Jarrod," I blow him a kiss across the room. His eyes are a midnight sea under the stars. "If you know this one, sing along," I tell the crowd, and Leo starts strumming his acoustic guitar, the familiar chords resonating around the room, and the crowd breaks out in applause. We play 'Shallow' by Lady Gaga and Bradley Cooper.

Leo harmonises with me perfectly, and when the crowd starts singing with us, I smile: it's brilliant.

Almost two hundred people are crammed into this cocktail bar, singing with me to this emotional love song. My eyes can't hold back any longer, they release a couple of tears onto my rose-coloured cheeks.

When the song is over, Jarrod is there, taking my hand, leading me off the stage and into the hallway, away from the crowd of people. He knows just what I need. I need a minute to compose myself and take it all in.

"Brooklyn, you were flawless tonight. So breathtaking," he gently wipes my tears with a tissue.

I look up into his face, those eyes, and I have to tell him again, "I love you, Jarrod."

He takes a second to stare at me, a mental picture of this moment, as he does sometimes when we are together, "Angel, you have no idea how much I love you," and I think 'fuck the make-up', I kiss him like he is my next breath, the air I need to survive. This is what the song lyrics imply, crashing through the deep, more than saying I love him. I *show* him.

Jarrod breaks our connection, running his hand up my bare back. "Angel, you have people waiting to congratulate you. Let's have some drinks and we can continue this later." His smirk is telling me that he'd like to continue more than kissing.

I smile, as a thought pops into my mind. "Can you make time next week, to take a few days off?" I ask him, holding his hands in mine.

"I think so. I'd have to confer with Chris, but sure. Why?" he asks quizzically.

"Because you're going to take me to Paris, show me how the French do things," I state with a cheeky grin.

"Angel, I've been showing you how the French do things for months," and he leans in to peck me on the lips again, laughing now. I understood his dirty joke, but I was trying to be serious, so I hit him in the chest.

"Get your mind out of the gutter, Houston. I'm serious. I need a break. Paris, you and me…?" I wait for his response.

"My mind isn't in the gutter, it's in your *chatte*, your lovely warm *pot de miel*," he says, smiling, all white wolfy teeth on display.

I roll my eyes, but I can't help loving the look on his face, playing with me.

"I have no idea what that means, but I guess it's something smutty, by the look on your face," I say, laughing.

"In a nice way, it means kitty, pussy, honey pot, cun…" he tries to say, but I slam my hands over his mouth, his eyes are liquid fire.

"OK, let's save that for later, big guy; right now I need a drink."

Jarrod is still laughing as I take his hand and lead us to the VIP section, where a group of familiar faces is waiting to sandwich me into fierce hugs and smothering kisses. God, this has been one wild ride, I think, as I suck down a delicious cocktail.

The Wave turned out to be much more than I ever expected, and as I look over the people here with me, I know I've finally made it. No amount of fame or money could buy this type of happiness. These are my people, and I fucking love each and every one of them.

A week after the final performance at The Wave, I'm sitting inside a quaint café in Montmartre, Paris's 18th arrondissement, watching people go by, enjoying the winter sunshine while trying and failing to keep my eyes off the stunningly handsome human sitting opposite me. Jarrod has completely come out of his shell in the last few weeks; he is still so intense and direct, but less brooding, more relaxed, and happier.

We have taken a few days to ourselves. Paris is enthralling, and the lights at night around the city are especially magical. Jarrod has been taking me to some tourist spots like the Louvre Museum, where we got to see the real Mona Lisa in person, and introducing me to French cuisine — but I told him to leave out the Escargot when ordering because I'm not gagging on snails in front of a packed restaurant of people; totally disgusting.

We just spent the day at the Basilica of Sacré Coeur, walked the artisan markets and are now enjoying some hot chocolate and crêpes in a tiny little café. Locals and tourists meander by, no rush, like they have all the time in the world.

"Angel, I have something to tell you." Those blue eyes fix on me; I'll never get tired of him looking at me with his ocean eyes.

"What is it?" I ask, taking a sip of the best hot chocolate I've ever tasted in my life.

"I've spoken with my parents and Chris. I've been working for almost ten years running the hotel in London, and I need some time off, so I'm taking a couple of months sabbatical," he says, those eyes watching my reaction.

"That's great, Jarrod. I know how hard you work; taking time off sounds amazing. Any idea what you'd like to do?" I query, taking his hand across the table. He links his fingers with mine, giving my hand a little squeeze like he always does.

"Actually, yes… We are going to New York. The Houston Hotel needs a new musical act for eight weeks, and if you agree, I'd love to perform with you…" He takes a deep breath, like he's been holding it in for a while "How about it, Angel? You and me in New York, playing our songs together?" those eyes are sparkling at me from across the table, radiant and luminous.

I'm shocked. I have no idea how he arranged all this in such a short time. "Are you fucking with me?" I ask, because I'm flabbergasted at his offer, and the swear words come out when I freak out.

"No, Brooklyn, it's done. All you have to do is say 'Yes'," and he smiles with that beautiful perfect face.

I let it sink in for a few seconds, our eyes locked, speaking more than words or music ever could, and I answer him. I give him what he wants. All of me.

"Yes," I whisper, and the next thing I know, my dark and stormy prince is lifting me from my chair and kissing me, consuming me like I'm the best ice-cream, the best song, the best everything, in the middle of this little café in Paris.

The room erupts with clapping and cheers in French. "Toutes nos Félicitations"… "Amour"… we laugh. They probably think we just got engaged or something… And I think if he did ask me that, would my answer be the same? That's a question for another day.

Epilogue

Snow is falling outside our window on the twenty-ninth floor of the Houston Hotel New York City. Warm hands are gently making their way up my back and into my hair. I love waking up this way. The Jarrod way.

"What does this one mean?" he whispers into my neck. "It's a cross with two ends joined, a butterfly shape," he describes one of the tattoos on my back.

"That is Dagaz," I answer in a sleepy voice; I'm still exhausted from one of the best nights of my life. Jarrod and I played our first show here in New York to a packed crowd, including his amazingly lovely parents. It felt more like a dream: our music being shared in such an elegant venue. But more than that, New York and the Houston Hotel family have welcomed me with open arms. Our performance was incredible.

"Its magic symbolises good luck, the end of a journey, abundance, creativity, spiritual development," I tell him, and I think to myself how appropriate this one is. My life has been a journey: some really fucking hard times, yet now they have turned into something beautiful. Something magical.

I turn around to look at his face, the face that captivated me on the street all those months ago. Those eyes will hold me captive for eternity. I reach out to touch his face, his lips, when my eyes land on a foreign object currently sitting on the fourth finger of my left hand.

I suck in a breath. Holy shit! "Jarrod!" I practically scream, and sit up like the bed is on fire.

I'm staring at a humongous emerald with baguette diamonds, art deco vintage style, on my hand. I must have been asleep when he slipped it on.

"Don't panic, Angel." He lifts my chin, my eyes finally snapping to his face, and I'm not even sure I'm breathing right now, my chest is squeezing all the air from my lungs.

"It's just a promise. It's my commitment to you; and when you are ready, we can make it more," he runs his fingers over my face like I'm the most precious gemstone he's ever seen. "I want more with you, Brooklyn. Can you give me that… one day?"

I give him a different answer than the last time he asked me. That same question was asked at my front door many months ago. I wasn't sure then, but I am now.

"Yes, Jarrod, I will give you more."

I hope you enjoyed Bee and Jarrod's journey from The Wave. I loved writing their story more than anything. It's been a blast. Take care.
Tanya Rose.